THE THERAPY ROOM

OMJ RYAN

INKUBATOR
BOOKS

Published by Inkubator Books
www.inkubatorbooks.com

ISBN (eBook): 978-1-83756-614-3
ISBN (Paperback): 978-1-83756-615-0
ISBN (Hardback): 978-1-83756-616-7

PROLOGUE

As I take a couple of steps closer to the edge of the cliff, the warmth from the baby locked in my bare arms seems an odd contrast to the freezing water, which crashes against the jagged rocks below. Though it's a warm summer's day, the wind blowing hard against my cheeks is ice cold, and I can taste the salt on my lips. My bedraggled hair whips back and forth across my face, partially obscuring my view out to sea.

I can barely hear the little boy's agitated cries over the cacophony of noise that batters my senses. Just a few short days ago I cuddled him in my arms, imagining our future life together, whispering my heartfelt promises to never leave and always take care of him and his little brother – or sister – when they arrive in the very near future. But everything has changed since then. *Everything*. I feel numb. That world I envisaged filled with such joy has been torn down in front of my eyes, ripping out my broken heart and leaving me with nothing. There will be no brother or sister on the horizon, and there will be no happily-ever-after.

Standing on the edge of the abyss, my mind inevitably

wanders back to what might have been if things had worked out the way I had hoped. But sadly for us all, they didn't. He wriggles and kicks as he continues to cry, determined to escape my grip. But I'm not quite ready to say goodbye just yet. Not until *they* arrive. Because they need to see what they have done to me, and finally bear witness to the crippling pain they have caused which has ruined my life.

CHAPTER ONE

OLIVIA

God, my life is so tedious. And I mean everything in my life. Not just bits of it. Everything. Nothing exciting ever happens. *Ever*.

Take my job at Go Finance, for example. Here I am, sitting at my desk in my cramped little cubicle, staring at my computer with a raft of Excel sheets open on the screen. I'm supposed to be compiling a report on the total number of deposits placed in the last month that have a value of under £1,000. But the fact is, I have zero interest in this, or any other project I'm tasked to deliver day in, day out on behalf of the UK's largest online bank – their words, not mine.

So instead, with my boss on leave for a couple of days, I've spent most of the afternoon playing Wordscapes on my phone, where I'm typically struggling to find a seven-letter word. It's so damn irritating.

When I next look up at the top corner of my computer screen, I can see that it's almost five o'clock, which means I am just a few minutes away from getting through yet another shitty day at the world's most uninspiring workplace.

As soon as 16:59 becomes 17:00 on my screen, I log off, jump out of my chair and head for the exit. Many of my colleagues seem to enjoy the idle chatter as people file out of the open-plan office space, but I have no desire to talk to any of them. My philosophy is simple: if I wouldn't talk to you outside of work, why would I waste my breath in the office?

A few minutes later I make my way out the main doors of the building before walking briskly across the small car park. As usual, it appears full to the brim with vehicles belonging to those lucky enough to have paid for parking permits – in the main, the higher-ups of the Go Finance senior management team. Sadly, the rest of us who occupy jobs further down the chain enjoy no such luxury and are forced to fend for ourselves. And whilst I do own a car, I refuse to waste my meagre salary on extortionate city centre parking – unless it's absolutely necessary, like when it's chucking down. So on warm summer days like today, I choose to get the bus and then walk the rest of the way instead. It only takes about thirty minutes door to door from the bank's riverside offices to my home in the not so salubrious suburb of Fenham, just three miles west of Newcastle city centre.

As it's Monday, my housemates will inevitably be heading out to the local pub quiz just before 7 p.m. It's a regular event they insist on inviting me to every week – despite the fact I have never once said yes to them the entire twelve months I've lived at the house. They are simply not my kind of people. To avoid having to come up with more excuses each week for my continued absence, I find it easier to drop into my local coffee shop on the way home every Monday night. It's a habit I'd say I've learned to tolerate as opposed to enjoying. It's just after 5.30 p.m. when I take up my usual position, sitting on a high stool looking out the window, trying to guess what kind of lives are led by the people walking by.

As I've been carrying out this ritual for several months now, I recognise many of the faces as they walk by at the exact same time every week, often wearing the same clothes they wore seven days ago. Given the almost absent expressions on their faces as they shuffle by, I take some comfort in my assumption that none of them lead lives that are any more exciting than mine. I can't help but shake my head and wonder what the actual point is in many of us being here, taking up unnecessary time and space on this planet.

My phone buzzes into life on the narrow counter in front of me, and my heart sinks when I see the name on-screen. I consider letting it ring out, but she will only keep calling until I pick up. I sigh and hit the green answer icon. 'Hi, Nan,' I say without feeling.

'They're at it again, Olivia.' Nan's voice is shrill and laced with panic.

'Who's at it again?' I ask, but already know what the answer will be.

'The bad people have broken in. And they're trying to kill me, just like the last time.'

I exhale loudly through my nose. This is one of the now regular accusations that come from my dementia-consumed grandmother. 'They're not *bad* people, Nan. They're staff at the care home you live in.'

'Care home? What are you talking about, Olivia? I live in my bungalow with your grandfather, as you well know. And that's the other thing, he's gone missing again too.'

In fact, Grandad died ten years ago.

It's hard not to feel real sorrow at the deteriorating state of my nan's mind. Yet at the same time, these calls are becoming an almost daily occurrence and harder and harder for me to take, especially as I'm her only living relative. Well, at least the only living relative who actually gives a shit.

'You need to call the police,' she continues unabated, 'before it's too late.'

I close my eyes for a moment before responding, 'Let's not worry about the police, hey, Nan? Why don't I come round and see you instead?'

'Will you come straight away?'

'Yes.'

'You promise?'

'Yes.'

'OK. But hurry, won't you?'

'Of course. I'll be there within the hour,' I say as I wrap up the call and resign myself to yet *another* evening of trying to manage Nan's increasing and unfounded paranoia.

And that's when I see *her* striding towards the coffee shop. My heart almost stops as she pushes the door open and steps inside. Surely it can't be? My mouth dries in an instant, and my pulse quickens as I shift in my seat, attempting to look inconspicuous whilst unable to take my eyes off her. The woman joins the short queue. It certainly looks like *her,* albeit quite a bit older, which is to be expected after fifteen years. She's also dressed very differently to the last time I saw her. Her navy blue suit and tan leather satchel are in stark contrast to the casual clothes she used to wear when our lives came crashing together all those years ago. But, my God, it *really* does look like it's her.

For the next few minutes as she waits for her order, I do my best impression of someone who has no interest in what's going on around me whilst all the time never letting her out of my sight. But the more times I steal a glance, the more I'm convinced it *is* her.

A few minutes pass, and the barista hands over her drink. I slide off my stool and follow her out into the warm evening air. The street around me is alive with rush hour traffic, horns honking, engines humming and people shouting intermittently, but my entire focus is on her as I follow along at a safe distance.

Where is she going?

Thankfully I don't have to wait long for an answer as she turns through the open gate of an old Victorian villa twenty feet or so ahead and marches up the steps, disappearing inside the building.

As I reach the same red-brick building, I note the large sign fixed to thick poles in the front yard: The Alpha Institute.

I stand there staring at the old place.

Is it really her? I can barely comprehend the accidental reunion that might have just happened. If the woman really *is* who I think she is, then I've inadvertently bumped into Shelly Hunter. The woman who killed my little brother, Dan, fifteen years ago. And who, in doing so, got away with murder.

CHAPTER TWO

SHELLY

Hi. I'm Shelly, and at least once a day I fantasise about harming my husband and baby.

I've been replaying that sentence over and over in my mind all day in anticipation of being asked to share my innermost demons in what is only my second ever group therapy session this evening. I've had butterflies in my stomach since first thing this morning at the thought of opening up to total strangers, and once again I'm questioning why the hell I agreed to join Dr Galanis's weekly group at the Alpha Institute. But then again, the recent realisation that I'm somehow developing psychotic tendencies and losing my mind was motivation enough for me to try anything. *Anything.*

And so here I sit, alone in one of several chairs placed in a circle of the large ground-floor room of a rather shabby Victorian house, waiting for the other members of the group to join me. I had to hurry straight from work, so I'm still wearing my suit and feeling slightly overdressed for my surroundings. Somehow, I arrived early. I take a deep breath and exhale slowly, attempting to calm my pulse, which has been racing for most of today. I'm absolutely terrified that, as it's my second session, I might be asked to 'speak my truth' as Dr Galanis calls it.

If that *does* happen, then I'm genuinely at a loss as to where I would begin. Seriously, how do I admit to a room full of strangers that lately, I've been have recurring thoughts about covering my seven-month-old son, Alfie's head with a pillow when I put him to bed? Or that I regularly imagine plunging a knife into my husband Nick's chest when he's standing next to me in the kitchen? So much so that I've even bought flat-fronted knives in case I actually go through with it one of these days. At least that would give him a fighting chance of survival. I also find myself on car journeys contemplating how easy it would be to turn the steering wheel just a few inches to the right and drive headlong into traffic and wipe myself out.

I know Dr Galanis was adamant that anything is up for discussion in these sessions and that judgement is actively discouraged, but really? *I can't stop imagining hurting the people who matter the most to me – including myself.* I'm not sure anyone could hear that and not seriously consider me a nut job. The very idea of sharing those thoughts in this space makes my heart pound again, and I suddenly have no control over my right leg, which is bouncing frantically up and down like a spring.

When I first met with Dr Galanis for an introductory one-to-one session a couple of weeks ago, she suggested I was suffering with severe anxiety and OCD; something she believes is connected to the birth of Alfie and more than likely linked to postnatal depression, which I hadn't considered, but as soon as she said it, it made total sense, especially given how I've been feeling lately.

I'm beyond fed up of hearing people say that having a baby is the most joyful experience any human can have. For them, maybe, but not necessarily for me. Bringing Alfie into the world has turned my life upside down, and not always in a good way. It's hard to explain exactly what I mean, but ever since he arrived, my mind has not been my own.

For starters, the pain of sleep deprivation is very real because Alfie has never slept more than three hours at a time the entire seven months he's been with us. I'm like a walking zombie most days. Add to that the fact my hormones are still all over the shop. My mood swings from pure joy one moment as I find myself staring down at him snuggled in my arms, to overwhelming feelings of anger, resentment and abject despair as he wakes yet again in the middle of the night. I often find myself longing for my life to be as simple and easy as it was before he was born, and the guilt I feel for thinking that is like a living thing inside me – pulling at the threads of my sanity. I know it's wrong, but I genuinely can't help it. It's almost as if there are two people fighting for control of my mind: the first-time mother who adores her gorgeous boy. And the broken, terrified woman who genuinely fears the evil she might be capable of when darkness descends.

I mean, what on earth compels me to continually daydream about driving into traffic, or sticking a carving knife into Nick? My sweet, supportive husband, whose only crime is that, unlike me, he appears to be taking parenthood in his stride – seemingly unaffected by the lack of sleep and relentless routine of feeding, burping and nappy changing.

I close my eyes in an attempt to block out the terrifying images of crashing and stabbing that flood my mind. Dr Galanis calls them 'intrusive thoughts'.

A squeaking hinge from the door behind me brings me back into the moment, and a second later the rest of my fellow group members file into the room in almost deathly silence and take their seats. Interestingly, each of them chooses the same spot they did last week, just as I instinctively have.

In an attempt to stop my leg bouncing, I shift in my seat as I glance around and take in the small, stale-smelling room along with my four fellow members. The only sound now is the rhythmic ticking from the clock on the mantelpiece, which sits above the old, unused fireplace.

Dr Galanis made the introductions last week, and I'm surprised I can still remember their names this evening. Vikram, positioned to my left, is a young man who I'd guess is of Indian or Pakistani descent and likely in his twenties, but he dresses like someone twice his age. He catches my eye for a split second, seeming unsure of himself, before quickly averting his gaze and making me feel even more awkward than I already did.

The woman on my immediate right is called Polly, I remember, dressed smartly in a black trouser suit with a sharp, dark bob hanging just above the collar of her white shirt. As soon as she sits down, she begins examining her impeccable, brightly coloured nails. Her pained, almost sneering expression hasn't altered since last week, and without warning, she glances in my direction and catches me looking directly at her. I give her my best sympathetic smile and raise my eyebrows in acknowledgement of my gaze, but in the same way as Vikram did, she looks away, seemingly desperate to avoid eye contact as quickly as she found it.

I know I shouldn't make snap judgements about people – or judge people at all in this setting – but I've already decided I'm not a huge fan of Polly. I find her demeanour a little triggering, to be honest. I'm not sure what it is, but there's something about her that reminds me of my boss, Darryl, whose recent behaviour towards me is probably another contributing factor to my feelings of stress and overwhelm. I'm going to have to try to clearly distinguish between the two of them or risk Darryl's negative influence on my work life filtering into what is supposed to be a therapeutic space.

On the other side of Polly is Pascal, and even though he's seated, there's no hiding he is a tall man with long, slender legs crossed over at the knee. What's left of his thinning hair is salt and pepper in colour and matches the thick stubble covering his strong jaw. I have no knowledge of what he does for a living, as he remained silent for most of the session last week, but based on his wrinkled brogues, well-worn jeans and tweed sports jacket, I'd put money on him being a teacher of some kind. An educator who seems just as uncomfortable as the rest of the group in making eye contact with me when I cast my gaze in his direction.

The final member of the group is Claire, who sits opposite me. A small, wiry-framed woman with sallow skin that surrounds her dark recessed eyes. Her greying hair is tied into a tight bun, and her bony fingers are clenched into two fists, which she rests on her lap. Sitting in her purple fleece, khaki trousers and walking shoes, she has the look of a woman who prefers spending her free time outdoors. Claire hasn't attempted to acknowledge anyone since she sat down. Instead, she stares intently at the wall behind my head.

This whole set-up feels beyond ridiculous to me. We're supposed to be here to help each other, so why will no one engage with me? I can't help but feel like I've made a massive mistake choosing group therapy over one-to-one sessions, but Dr Galanis was adamant it would be better for me in the long run. That by listening and sharing with the other members, I would eventually learn to counsel myself through my fears, instead of relying on seeing a therapist for the next ten years or more, which was the last thing I wanted. Right now, I'm struggling to see how exactly I'm going to do any of that surrounded by such an unresponsive bunch. This evening's session hasn't officially started yet, and I already feel like running away and never coming back. But deep down I know that's not an option. For Alfie's and Nick's sakes and safety, as well as my own sanity, I need to at least try to give group a shot.

To try to stem my growing sense of anxiety, I turn my attention to the two remaining empty chairs that complete the circle around me. The one positioned to Vikram's left was taken by Dr Galanis last week. I wonder who the other one is for. Please God let it be someone who is willing to speak – or at the very least make eye contact with me so this incredibly uncomfortable experience is a tiny bit easier.

A moment later, as the clock on the mantelpiece chimes six, I hear the door hinge squeak behind me for a second time, and Dr Galanis – or Andrea as she prefers to be called in the sessions – strides into the room. She's tall and elegant with shoulder-length brown hair cut into a classic fringe, and she moves effortlessly across the room. She's dressed in a charcoal pencil skirt, matched with a crisp white blouse and black Mary Jane shoes.

'Good evening,' she says to us all as she moves to stand behind her chair. Her accent is unmistakably Greek, but her English is perfect. 'Some of you may have noticed an extra chair this evening.'

Glancing at my fellow members, I note that she now has full attention now. Well, *at least somebody does.*

'And that is because we have *another* new person joining the group,' she adds.

A palpable tension suddenly fills the air as this surprise update lands with my fellow group members. It makes me wonder if my own introduction last week caused a similar amount of unease. Based on what Dr Galanis told me at the outset, the group has been unchanged for some time, so I guess it probably would have. After all, in my own experience, very few people actually like change.

Dr Galanis smiles softly. 'I'd like you to meet Jess,' she says, before glancing back towards the door.

I swivel in my seat slightly as the young woman comes into view. She's petite with bright blonde hair. Very pretty with an elfin face, which is overwhelmed by her sad eyes and matched by her stooped posture. Looking at her now, I'm guessing she can't be any older than mid-to-late twenties.

Dr Galanis gestures for Jess to take the seat next to her, then looks at me. 'Like you did with Shelly in her first session last week, I know you'll all make Jess feel very welcome.'

Welcome? I feel like saying aloud. I'd hardly describe avoiding eye contact and saying almost nothing as making someone feel welcome.

As Jess sits down, she glances nervously around the room but sadly receives the same treatment I've been getting, a mixture of blank expressions and averted gazes, which gives me some strange comfort. At least I now know it's not just me they don't want to talk to. It gives me pause – maybe it's just because Jess and I are new that they're being quite cold with us and they may warm up eventually. If that's the case, then in the meantime it looks like it's up to me to make sure

Jess is made to feel more welcome than *I* have since joining. So I make a point of catching her eye and smiling. She offers the faintest of smiles in return, appearing awkward and unsure of herself, but at least she holds my gaze.

And as I continue to look at her, I feel a strange sensation that I can't quite explain. Almost as if there's some kind of connection between us. It's a feeling I'm really grateful for right now in this awkward environment, and much to my surprise, the fear that I've made a massive mistake joining the group doesn't feel quite as intense as it did before she sat down. I'm left wondering if, perhaps, Jess can somehow help me get something useful from group therapy after all – and if I can do the same for her, maybe.

And then, without warning, my attention is brought back to the stark reality of what I'm actually here to do. The moment I've been dreading finally arrives as Dr Galanis locks her eyes on me, flashes her perfect white teeth and says, 'So, Shelly, why don't you tell us what brings you to the group?'

CHAPTER THREE

OLIVIA

For the next ten minutes, I stand rooted to the spot on the pavement, just a few feet along from the path that leads into the Alpha Institute. From my position, I try to act as casual as possible as I watch several people make their way inside, one at a time and in total silence. Each of them appears lost in their thoughts as they pass through the open gate without even a cursory glance left or right. I wonder what on earth is happening inside that building?

Pulling out my phone, I type *Alpha Institute* into Google. The very first link on the screen identifies the building as a private clinic providing 'mental health and well-being support in today's frantic world'. It also proclaims Dr Galanis – a Greek national, so it seems – to be one of the UK's leading psychotherapists who specialises in group therapy.

So if the woman *is* Shelly, is that what she's doing inside that building? Taking part in a group therapy session? I feel compelled to find out, and it's as if I'm being driven by a motor when I instinctively head inside, rushing up the steps into the large, darkened hallway. Standing in the middle of the grand space, I find myself facing three doors, two of which are ajar, and a third, which is closed. Tentatively and without quite knowing why, I step towards the nearest open door to my left. A sign identifies it as *Therapy Room 1 – Dr Brown.* My heart beats in my ears as I push it open slightly and peer beyond.

The room is empty aside from two office-style armchairs positioned opposite each other, about four feet apart. The walls are painted a light shade of pink, adorned with pictures of seascapes in mismatched frames. The carpet on the floor has seen better days. With no idea what I might say if anyone finds me snooping around, I inspect the next room. It has a similar name plate on the door: *Therapy Room 2 – Dr Chakravorty.* It's pretty much identical to the first room, bar the colour of the walls, which are pastel blue.

Nearby voices catch my attention, and I stand motionless for a moment whilst I try to work out where they are coming from. I soon realise they're in the room next door. Moving back into the hall, I follow the low murmur to the third door marked *Group Therapy Room – Dr Galanis.* I step as close as I dare and lean in, trying my best to hear what's being said on the other side. From what I can make out, a woman is talking, her voice heavily accented – European, I think – and it appears she's making introductions of some kind. It's hard to decipher, but a moment later two words cut through the air and smack me hard in the face. 'Welcome, Shelly.'

I take in nothing more of what is being said as a sudden wave of nausea crashes over me, coupled with a tightness in my chest – the words ringing in my ears, '*Welcome, Shelly.*' I feel like the walls are closing in on me all at once, and my instinct is to get away. To escape while I can. Quite what I'm running from, I really can't say. But that's what I do. I run.

A minute later I'm rushing down the thick concrete steps with the only thought in my mind to escape, but then something makes me stop at the gate and pause. I turn back to face the building. I'm half expecting some form of reprimand from an angry member of staff or, worse still, a gung-ho security guard, but the reality is, nobody comes. As my adrenaline dissipates, I take a couple of tentative steps back into the yard and once again find myself staring at the large red-brick building. Something in my gut tells me I'm not quite finished here yet.

Casting my eyes around the grounds to ensure I'm still alone, I decide to make my way round to the rear of the building. But as I turn the final corner, I stop suddenly at the sight that greets me: Shelly sitting in full view through a large bay window. My heart rate skyrockets as I stare at the face of the woman who took my brother's life. I close my eyes and take a long silent breath as the image of Dan falling to his death fills my mind. Shaking my head, I do my best to banish the memory as quickly as it came, before opening my eyes again to see Shelly smiling and nodding her head. How can she sit there and smile, knowing what she did?

My mind fizzes. Could it be that after all these years, the enormity of her crime has ultimately got to her? That Shelly Hunter goes to group therapy to silence her guilty conscience? Is she finally ready to confess what really happened on that summer's day on the cliffs of Tynemouth Priory?

My desire to know what she's saying in that room is immediate and all consuming. I *must* find out if Shelly is confessing to what she did that day. But there's no way of knowing. Unless I can somehow become part of that group, but surely she'd recognise me as soon as I walked in, given the amount of time we spent on opposite sides of the courtroom after Dan's death. But then again, would she? After all, fifteen years ago I was twelve, and now I'm a grown woman. Realistically, why *would* she recognise me?

As I continue to stare at her, a feeling of total certainty washes over me, that by hook or by crook, I'm going to get inside that room. And finally – instead of the lies she spewed in court – I'm going to hear the truth about what drove Shelly Hunter to murder my baby brother.

CHAPTER FOUR

OLIVIA

No matter how many times I visit, I'll never get used to the smell of the care home. My nan has been living here for just under a year, and it never improves. A foul combination of industrial-strength disinfectant mixed with stale urine and the sharp stench of faeces. And it gets even worse at meal times when the smell of overcooked vegetables and cheap cuts of meat fills the corridors. I hate that my nan has to live here. I also hate that *my* inheritance is being used to pay for it.

As I walk into Nan's room at the far end of the ground-floor corridor, she's asleep. She looks so tiny slumped in a high-backed chair placed at the side of her bed, wearing a crumpled pink nightdress and her favourite purple dressing gown over the top. It's covered in stains around her chest. Remnants of her lunch, no doubt. Her white hair sticks out at all angles and looks like it's not been combed for days. The small flatscreen TV fixed to the wall opposite her bed is showing a news program of some sort.

I perch on the side of the bed nearest to her and gently touch her hand with mine. 'Nan,' I say softly.

She opens her eyes, and for a moment confusion is etched across her face, but then she realises it's me. 'Oh, hello, lovey.' She smiles. 'I must have nodded off.'

In that instant, she's back to being my nan. No dementia, no wild accusations or angry rants, just a grandmother looking at her granddaughter with genuine love and affection.

'Is everything OK?' I ask.

She straightens in the chair. 'Can you get me a drink of tea, Liv? I'm parched.'

'No bother,' I say, before stepping up and heading for the communal kitchen halfway down the corridor.

Nan likes her tea strong – almost builder's strength – so it's about five minutes later when I walk back into her room.

'Have you seen your granddad?' she asks as soon as she sees me, her voice tense.

My heart sinks as I place the mug of tea on the mobile table that sits in front of her chair. 'No, Nan, he's—'

'In the pub no doubt!' She cuts me off before I can explain. 'Always boozing, that one, while I'm stuck here cooking his dinner.'

'Nan, Granddad's dead,' I say as gently as I can before retaking my position on the edge of the bed.

If she hears me, it doesn't register as she continues unabated. 'And what about your dad? He was supposed to be home an hour ago.'

This is typical of the type of exchange I have to endure on a regular basis these days. It's heartbreaking and exhausting having the same conversations over and over.

'Dad doesn't live with you, Nan,' I explain for the umpteenth time.

'Don't be silly,' she protests. 'He was here this morning!'

I shake my head. 'No, Nan. Last time I heard from Dad, he was living in a hostel in Sandyford.'

'A hostel? Why would he be living in a hostel?'

'I told you. He's an addict. An alcoholic. Remember? The council evicted him from his flat for not paying his rent. So now he stays in the hostel.'

Nan looks at me blankly before responding, 'It's your mother's fault.'

'Oh, God. Not this again,' I mutter.

'If that slut had kept her legs closed, he'd never have wandered off.'

The fact that Nan is now convinced Mum slept around *has* to be down to the dementia because as far as I'm aware, she did nothing of the sort. The only memories I have are of her being a great mum. Until Dan died, that is. After that, she completely changed and fell apart, totally consumed by grief. I want to explain this to Nan. To remind her that Mum killed herself over eleven years ago. And it was Mum's suicide that led Dad to drink. But it's pointless. Even if I managed to jog her memory, she'll have forgotten everything I say by the time I leave. That's what normally happens, anyway. So instead, I decide to change the subject. 'I bumped into Shelly Hunter this evening.'

'Shelly Hunter?' She frowns. 'Doesn't she work behind the bar at the Hat and Feathers?'

I'm well aware Nan is unlikely to remember who Shelly is these days, even though she saw her at the trial quite a few times, but I'm desperate to share the events of my chance meeting with someone – anyone – and Nan is the only person I have left.

'No, Nan. That was *Shirley Hughes*.'

Nan nods, but I can tell her mind is already elsewhere.

'Shelly Hunter was the woman who took Dan from us.'

The room falls silent, and I wait for Nan to respond, but instead she turns her attention to the television, which is now showing one of the soaps. 'He's a dickhead, isn't he?' She points angrily at one of the characters on-screen. Being abusive is another symptom of dementia. 'And *she's* a silly bitch,' she adds as a female actor appears on-screen.

She's clearly not heard a word I've said, but I continue anyway. I need to get it out. 'I bumped into Shelly at the coffee shop near my house. You know, the one I took you to at Christmas.'

Nan's eyes remain fixed on the TV.

'I couldn't believe my eyes, Nan. She walked right in off the street. Bold as brass.'

Again, there's no response.

'So I followed her.'

The TV continues to play.

'It looks like she's getting therapy. Can you imagine that? A stone-cold killer talking about her feelings.'

Nan starts to blink slowly now, and her eyelids are looking very heavy.

'Shelly needs to pay for what she did, Nan...' My words tail off. I may as well be talking to myself as her head starts to loll.

I watch in silence for the next few seconds as her chin drops slowly to her chest. A moment later she's asleep, snoring gently in the chair once more.

I wait in silence for another five minutes before deciding

I've had enough of this place, and it's time to go. Stepping off the bed, I lean in and kiss her on the forehead. 'I'm going to make her pay, Nan,' I whisper. 'For what she did to Dan. For what she did to all of us.' I keep my eyes fixed on her as I straighten now. 'And I promise you this, by the time I'm finished with Shelly Hunter, she's gonna wish she never set eyes on that group.'

CHAPTER FIVE

OLIVIA

'I'm heading to the pub to meet the others. Do you want to join me?' asks Natasha as I walk through the front door of the crappy house I share with four other people.

Natasha – or Tash as she insists everyone calls her – is a junior doctor at the Royal Victoria Hospital in Newcastle city centre. She's a short, skinny woman with curly red hair, which always seems to be tied back in a ponytail. 'Jonty is convinced we're going to win this time. He's been swotting up on sport questions all week.' She has the unmistakable accent of a former boarding-school girl.

The Jonty she's referring to is one of the other medical-school cretins I'm forced to share this overpriced shithole with. I *was* living with my nan, but that changed when she had to sell the house to pay for the care home, which is how I ended up in this place. I certainly wouldn't choose to live here with this lot.

I give her my best fake smile. 'Sorry, *Natasha*.' I point-blank refuse to call anyone Tash. 'I've just had a rough visit with my nan, and I'm not really feeling up for company tonight.'

She tilts her head slightly to the side and nods slowly. 'That must be so hard for you, Liv,' she says with what sounds like forced sincerity.

I nod back. 'I think I'm just going to go to bed.'

'Well, I'm late, so I'd better get a move on, but if you change your mind, you know where we are.' She pulls on her jacket and heads for the door.

A moment later, I'm all alone. Peace at last.

After making myself a hot chócolate, I head up to my attic room at the top of the house and lock the door, just in case anyone comes home unexpectedly.

Sitting cross-legged on my bed, I open my laptop, ready to do some digging on Shelly Hunter.

I start with a quick search in Facebook, but none of the Shelly Hunters that appear are the Shelly I'm looking for. I do the same search in Instagram and TikTok but to no avail. And when the only results for Shelly Hunter I can find in Google are in newspaper articles from Dan's trial almost two decades ago, it makes me think that she either has zero digital footprint, or she must have got married and changed her surname since I last saw her. It's disappointing but not the end of the world. I have other things to be getting on with.

On the way home from seeing Nan, I came up with an idea of how I might be able to get into the group. The question is whether or not Dr Galanis will go for it, but I guess there's only one way to find out, so I type *the Alpha Institute* into the search bar.

As was the case when I searched on my phone earlier this evening, a bunch of links appear on-screen, all connected to what is described as ''Newcastle's premier mental health and well-being centre'. I click on the first one, which takes me directly to the Alpha Institute's website. Scanning through the various tabs, I find more detailed information explaining the benefits of group therapy, as well as what appears to be Dr Galanis's vast experience within the field. If her testimonials are to be believed, then she's a very smart woman, and for a moment I doubt whether my plan can work. But the truth is it's the only one I have, so if I want to get into that group, then it has to be worth giving it a go.

I click on the *Contact Us* tab at the top of the screen. A second later I'm redirected to a general enquiry form, and I quickly realise there are a couple of things that I need to sort out before I can fill it in – a fake name and an email to go with it.

The name is easy. I decide to stick with the fake one I pretended was mine whenever I got into trouble as a teenager. It always worked back then, and hopefully the familiarity of it will help me stay in character. Something the Hollywood actress – and my all-time hero – Samantha Morton says is so important when playing a role. I've always wanted to be an actor and even went to acting classes when I was a kid. But all that stopped after Dan died and my family pretty much fell apart. With so much pain and grief consuming our house, there was little time or energy for anything else. I glance up at the framed picture of Samantha on my wall, captured in her role as Claire in the movie *Enduring Love*. She was quietly brilliant in that film, and just looking at her, I feel totally inspired to reconnect with the actor within me and play my own part now as best I can.

The fake email is next on my list, and thanks to the modern world of non-existent identity checks, it takes just a few minutes to set up.

With everything in place, I fill out the basic information: name, email, mobile, etc. I then sit for a while as I work out how best to fill in the box asking me to share a little bit about my supposed issue. This is where my ability to live the life of my character will come into play once I'm in the group, and I figure it's best to give my story a vague semblance of truth, but the last thing I want to do is talk about Dan. As well as being far too upsetting, saying anything about Dan once I'm in front of Shelly will instantly alert her. So I make up a younger sister and use her premature death as the basis of my story. I also add in a few sentences about my dad's drinking and the fact my mum died when I was quite young, the truth of which I can lean into when I'm playing the part.

As I give it one final read-through before sending, I'm impressed by the tragic nature of my fake backstory, and I can't help grinning. 'Dr Galanis won't be able to resist,' I whisper as I press enter. A second later a message appears on-screen, confirming my enquiry has been sent and that someone from the institute will aim to be in touch within twenty-four hours.

'Here we fucking go,' I whisper as I shut my laptop and lie back on the bed, filled with a sense of nervous anticipation of what's to come. And for the first time in as long as I can remember, I feel like life could be about to get very interesting indeed.

CHAPTER SIX

SHELLY

Alfie had another bad night last night, which meant I did too. It was my turn to get up through the night, as Nick was due on an early train this morning for a midday meeting in London. I did eventually get back to sleep about 4 a.m. but was awake again just after six when Alfie started crying for his morning feed. By the time I staggered downstairs to sort his bottle, Nick had already left for the station, and the next couple of hours passed by in a blur as I attempted to get Alfie fed and dressed for nursery, as well as getting myself ready for work.

It's just after 7.30 now, and I need to be out of the house ASAP, or I'll be late again, but because I'm feeling so exhausted, my OCD is in overdrive this morning. I made the mistake of using the iron earlier, and no matter how many times I try to tell myself I've switched it off, I can't help but go back to check the plug over and over. I stare at the empty socket, now attempting to hardwire the image of the plug lying flat on the kitchen countertop into my brain, but I know as soon as I get to the front door, I'll be back to check again. That's what always happens when my head is fried like this.

Glancing at the clock on the kitchen wall, I know that if I'm to stand any chance of getting into the office on time, I need to leave the house in the next few minutes in order to drop Alfie at the nursery in the village by 8 o'clock so I can get on the road for 8.10.

After taking one last look at the plug of the iron resting on its side, I slip a little coat on Alfie, then place him in his car seat. I grab my bag and car keys and head for the front door, but as expected, as soon as I wrap my fingers around the handle, my mind starts to play tricks on me. Did I really see the plug was out of the wall? Or did I just imagine that? I glance back towards the kitchen, feeling an overwhelming urge to go back and check. But I know if I do that, I'll get stuck in a loop for God knows how long, checking and rechecking everything, and never get out of the house. Honestly, it's completely exhausting.

Mustering all the strength I can find, I push my paranoia to the back of my mind, then open the front door and head down the steps to the car.

With Alfie's car seat safely secured in the back seat, I jump in the front and switch on the ignition. But then, a second later, I switch it off again. Can I really be sure the iron is safe to leave as it is? I didn't check the hot plate on it. Could it still be hot enough to cause a fire? And while I checked the plug was out of the wall, I honestly can't remember whether I left it standing up or flat down. My head is suddenly filled with images of the iron smouldering away before the flames that follow engulf the kitchen. Damn it. I need to go back and check.

Leaving Alfie in his car seat, I run inside the house and,

to my great relief, find that the iron is indeed standing in a safe position next to the hob. 'Happy now?' I ask myself before rushing back out to the car, knowing that if I put my foot down, I can still probably just about make it into the office on time.

However, it seems Alfie is also determined to slow me down this morning, and as soon as I open the driver's door, I'm greeted by the sound of him crying and hit by the unmistakable stench of a dirty nappy. 'God. Not now, Alfie,' I growl. The right thing to do in this situation would be to take him back inside the house and change him, but I really don't have the bandwidth for this right now. So instead, I decide to leave it to the nursery staff to sort out. That's what I pay them for, after all. I'm sure one more shitty nappy won't make a difference.

Ten minutes later I race down the path to his nursery and virtually launch Alfie at one of the staff before racing back to the car, and it's not long before I'm speeding down the Coast Road towards the city. *I'm gonna make it, I'm gonna make it,* I tell myself, but my optimism is soon dashed, and my heart sinks when I see brake lights flashing in the sea of stationary cars in front of me, signalling a traffic jam up ahead. *Damn it.*

After sitting in the jam for close to thirty minutes, it's almost 9.30 by the time I reach my desk at Greystones Finance Solutions in the heart of the city. 'Bloody traffic,' I mumble to Jane, who sits opposite me, as I dump my bag on the desk.

Jane is one of the good guys. She's only a few years older than me, but I always think of her being closer to my mum's age. Mainly because she wears hand-knitted cardigans most days and keeps her glasses on a chain around her neck when she's not using them. 'Darryl's on the warpath,' she says, glancing towards the glass box at the end of the office.

'Of course he is,' I mumble as I take a seat. 'He's got fuck all else to do, has he?'

Me using foul language always elicits a chuckle from Jane, and this morning is no exception, but her face suddenly changes, and she stiffens in her chair now. 'Heads up, he's on his way.'

Just as I fire up my laptop, Darryl, the newly appointed head of the department, sidles up to my desk. 'Can we have ten in my office?'

I don't know why, but his Essex accent always sets my teeth on edge. It's not as if I have anything against people from Essex, it's just him that bothers me.

'Of course.' I force a thin smile as I stand up and follow him back to the glass box.

Walking behind him, I'm reminded how much I detest Darryl. There's something about the way he moves that irritates me. He has a habit of strolling around the office like he's God's gift to women when in actual fact his long limbs and gangly frame make him look awkward and gawkish. My negative view of him isn't helped by the fact he took my job when I was on maternity leave. It was only supposed to be a temporary thing while I took six months off, but things soon changed when I told the company that I wanted to work four days a week when I came back. Apparently you can't run an effective team doing a short week, so now Darryl is the permanent head of the department. Something he never tires of telling me.

'Do you want me to close the door?' I ask as we step inside the office. *My* old office, no less.

He nods. 'Yeah. It's a close-the-door kinda meeting.'

I have to stop myself from visibly flinching. What does that phrase even mean? I turn my back to him and mouth the word *wanker* as I shut the door behind me.

I sit down on the chair opposite his desk and wait for the torrent of management-speak that I know is imminent.

He links his fingers together as he leans forward across the desk, his brow furrowed. 'I'd like to share some robust feedback with you, Shelly, if I may.'

Robust feedback is an example of the latest management bullshit he's picked up on yet another training course he attended recently.

'Go on,' I say, barely able to hide my contempt for him.

'This is the third time in a month you've strolled in late—'

'I didn't *stroll* in, Darryl.' I can't help but cut him off. 'I virtually *ran* from the car park to get here as quickly as I could.'

He leans back in his chair now and folds his arms across his chest. 'So what's your excuse this morning?'

Now, if Darryl were a good boss – a nurturing and supportive leader who actually cared about his team – I could tell him the truth: I was late because I suffer with crippling OCD that keeps me a virtual prisoner in my own home most mornings. Not to mention the fact that I'm seriously struggling to balance being a new mum with being back at work. And that I could really do with his support and understanding as I try to figure out what my new world looks like. But sadly, Darryl wouldn't know how to support a chair with three legs, so instead I keep my reasons simple. 'There was an accident on the Coast Road. A lorry went into the back of a car near Jesmond Dene.'

His lips purse as he considers my answer. 'In that case, you should have called to let me know you were delayed.'

I can't help but recoil slightly. 'You're not my keeper, Darryl.'

He sits to attention in his chair now. 'No. But I am your boss.'

'In name only.' The words fall from my mouth before I can stop them.

A slight snarl forms on his top lip. 'I'm sure you're aware that the company is going through a period of rationalisation, Shelly.'

'Cost-cutting, you mean.' I'm really not doing myself any favours with how I'm reacting to him, but I simply can't help myself. He's such an arsehole.

His snarl intensifies as he continues unabated, 'And thanks to said rationalisation, everyone needs to be on top of their game to stay the course. Do you understand what I'm saying?'

I clench my toes in my shoes as I attempt to keep my disdain for him from showing on my face.

'I spoke to one of the project leads yesterday,' he adds. 'And they told me you were a day late sending through the reports on the HMRC system migration.'

'Do you mean Elliot?'

'Who it is isn't important right now.'

'Well, whoever you got your information from,' I snap back, 'did they also tell you that *my* documents were delayed because the hard data was delivered *late* to me the week before?'

Darryl sniffs in defiance. 'That's not really the issue here now, is it?'

'Isn't it? Well, then what is, Darryl?'

'Look, Shelly,' he says before clearing his throat. 'The bottom line is the HMRC account is up for tender in a couple of months. And as you well know, it's worth tens of millions in revenue to this firm over the next five years. So we can't afford any mistakes.'

'And there weren't any mistakes. Like I said, the data came to me late on Thursday afternoon, and I processed it as quickly as I could on the Monday morning.'

'That's right. I forgot. You don't work Fridays, do you?'

He knows damn well I don't work Fridays. He wouldn't be sitting in this office if I did.

As he glares across the desk at me, I have to fight the urge to tell him to go fuck himself as images of me slamming his head onto the desk repeatedly play over and over in my mind. 'Is there anything else?' I manage to muster finally.

'Actually, there is.' He reaches into the top drawer of his desk and pulls out an A4 document. 'Do you know what this is?'

I glance down at it, but struggle to read what's written, as the text is upside down and facing him. 'Should I?'

He taps his forefinger on the document. 'This is a blank PRP – which I'm sure you'll be aware stands for performance review plan.'

'I know what a PRP is,' I snap back. 'I used to run this department, remember?'

He glares at me now and ignores my comment. 'Based on your continued time-keeping issues, I should make you aware that if you're late one more time this month, then I'll have no choice but to put your name on this PRP.'

I can't help but shake my head. 'You want to put *me* on performance review? Someone with my experience?'

Darryl shrugs. 'Experience is one thing. Performance is another thing entirely.'

I hold his gaze in silence for a few seconds before responding, 'Well, I guess I'd better not be late again, then, had I?'

'That would be a start,' he says smugly.

'Is there anything else?' I ask.

'No.' He shakes his head. 'You can go.'

I'm up and out of the chair in a flash.

'But just remember, Shelly.' It seems he isn't actually finished. 'This business is changing, and everyone needs to be on top of their game to be part of its future.'

I nod without conviction before turning away and heading out of the office. As I walk back to my desk, the anger I feel in this moment threatens to completely overwhelm me, and I have to clench my fists and dig deep to keep the tears of frustration out of my eyes. On another day and in another life perhaps, I'd love to tell Darryl to stick his job up his arse, but the sad fact of the matter is, with Nick's business in a state of flux at the moment and a huge mortgage to pay every month, I really need the money.

CHAPTER SEVEN

OLIVIA

I never thought I'd find anything more boring than managing data like I do as part of my job at the bank. But that was before I was invited – more like forced, actually – to spend an entire day on a training course showing me how to operate the new data management systems that are being rolled out next month. They're not so different from the existing protocols, and if truth be told, I kinda figured out how to use them within an hour of the training starting at 10 a.m. Which means, for close to four hours now I've been killing time waiting for this mind-numbing torture to be over. And the worst part is, there's still another two hours of training still to come. Seriously, I swear this job is going to be the death of me – murdered by total boredom.

Finally, as the clock on the wall ticks over to 2 p.m., the rotund, sweaty man with the glistening bald head who's delivering the session at the front of the training room utters the words I've been longing to hear. 'Could everyone do with a short break?'

He doesn't need to ask me twice, and a split second later

I'm up and out of the chair as quickly as my legs will carry me.

'See you all back here at two fifteen,' he shouts after us.

I'm in no mood to respond and instead make my way out into the afternoon sunshine, which glistens on the river just a few feet in front of me. There's only one thing on my mind right now – the same thing that has consumed my thoughts for the last couple of days, Dr Galanis and group therapy. Their acknowledgement email claimed they would get back to me within twenty-four hours of my initial contact with them, but it's coming up for two days now since I shared my tragic backstory. What could be taking so long?

Dropping down onto a bench positioned near the water's edge, I pull out my phone and go straight to my email. The message that greets me stops me in my tracks, and my heart skips a beat when I read those four glorious words nestling at the top of my inbox. *Dr Galanis – Late Cancellation.* I have butterflies in my stomach as I click on the message and begin reading the note from Dr Galanis's secretary. It seems there's been a late cancellation, and they're wondering if I'd like to take the appointment. Perfect. Of course I would.

But as I read on, it appears there's a snag, because the appointment is at four o'clock this afternoon, and I'm due to be stuck in training until the end of the day. 'Goddamn it,' I mutter loudly, drawing a quizzical look from Katrina – one of my colleagues and fellow trainees – who's standing about twenty feet away with a vape in hand. Seeing her looking over at me now, her eyebrows raised, I'm reminded of how nosy Katrina is and how I could work that to my advantage with an impromptu acting performance. So after quickly replying to the message, accepting the appointment, I place my phone down, close my eyes and slowly, very deliberately, make a point of dropping my chin to my chest.

You see, in the aftermath of Dan's death, I quickly realised that crying gets you what you want, and I soon learnt how to cry on cue. A skill I still possess to this day. So sitting hunched over on the bench, I drop my face into my hands and allow my shoulders to heave slightly as I gently begin to sob, just loud enough to be heard by Katrina standing not too far away.

As I'd hoped, she's at my side in a flash. And that's because, like I say Katrina is super nosy and a total busybody. She's one of those people in life who *loves* nothing more than knowing everyone else's business, so a crying colleague sitting all alone outside is like mana from the gods to her.

'Are you OK?' she says gently as she sits down next to me on the bench.

I lift my face from my hands and flash a weak smile.

Katrina is a tiny woman with close-cropped dark hair and quite a pronounced nose, which only seems to amplify her nosiness. 'Do you want to talk about it?' she asks, and I'm reminded of a shark circling chum in the water.

'It's my nan.' I make sure my voice breaks as I answer. 'She's in a home with dementia and just called telling me someone is trying to kill her.'

Katrina tilts her head to the side as she places her hand on my back. 'Oh, you poor thing.'

'She was crying, saying she needed me to protect her from the bad people, and I don't know what to do.'

'You should go to her.'

I sniff my tears away and wipe my nose with the back of

my hand. 'I don't think Sunny would be very happy if I missed the training.'

Sunny is the team leader of the data management department and has also been stuck in the training session all day with me.

'Don't be silly. He'll understand.'

I force more tears out. 'I don't think he will. The new system is very important.'

Katrina straightens. 'But not as important as your nan.' She stands now. 'You leave Sunny to me,' she adds, and a split second later I watch as she marches back towards the main entrance. Seriously. You gotta *love* a busybody.

A few minutes pass before I see Sunny step out the revolving door and start making his way across to where I'm sitting.

His brow is creased with concern as he reaches my position and drops down next to me on the bench. 'Katrina told me about your nan. That sounds really tough.'

I nod softly as a tear streaks down my cheek.

'You get yourself off,' he says.

I pretend to swallow a lump in my throat. 'But what about the training?'

He smiles. 'Don't worry about that. I can fill in any blanks for you when it goes live if needed.'

'Are you sure?'

'Absolutely. Family comes first,' he says firmly.

'Thank you so much.' I lean across and hug him, which he clearly wasn't expecting as he stiffens within my grip. 'Sorry,' I say, pulling away. 'I probably shouldn't have done that. It's just my nan means everything to me.'

His smile returns as he holds my gaze for longer than necessary, and it occurs to me that Sunny might now have a new favourite in the team. Something that could come in very handy in future.

'Go on,' he says. 'You go see your nan. And if you need to take any time off tomorrow, just let me know.'

'Thank you. I really appreciate you doing this for me.'

'Not a problem at all.'

We stand up together, and Sunny checks his watch. 'I'd better be getting back. It won't look good if the boss is the last one in, will it?'

I watch for a moment as he wanders back towards the main entrance, and congratulate myself on my sterling performance. But that was just the warm-up act, I remind myself, because if I'm going to get into that group right under Shelly Hunter's nose, my best is yet to come.

CHAPTER EIGHT

OLIVIA

The inside of Dr Galanis's room is very similar to the rooms next door that I peeked into on my first foray inside the building. The framed pictures on the walls in here, however, depict Greek mythology as well as a large image of the Acropolis, photographed lit up at night.

'So why don't you tell me a little bit about yourself?' Dr Galanis's accent is strong, but every word is delivered in perfect English. She sounds how she looks: confident and assured.

By contrast, I'm quite nervous now sitting in the armchair opposite her, which I guess is to be expected as I find my feet in my new role. 'Where would you like me to start?'

Her face softens. 'Wherever you like.'

I take a deep breath. It helps steady my nerves, but I also think it helps me appear quite vulnerable, which is a key component in my plan to get the doctor on board. 'So much has happened in my life, I'm not sure what's the most important bit to tell you first.'

Dr Galanis glances down at the notepad on her knee for a second and then returns her gaze to me. 'Tell me about the death of your sister.'

The directness of the request takes me by surprise, and for a moment the backstory I've created slips clean out of my mind. 'Erm.' My mouth is open, but no words are coming out.

'Take your time.' Her voice is soft and reassuring now.

'Marie passed away when I was twelve years old,' I begin, suddenly remembering my freshly created fake past.

Dr Galanis nods slowly but remains silent.

I'm not sure whether I should wait for her to reply but carry on regardless. 'She was having flu-like symptoms all the time and was constantly tired. The doctors thought nothing of it to begin with, but then she started having heavy nose-bleeds. That was when they ran some tests and found it...' I let my words trail off for effect.

She still doesn't respond.

I drop my chin to my chest. I've seen Samantha Morton do it loads of times in different movies, and it seems to get the right reaction from whomever she's talking to. 'Leukaemia. She died six months later. I was at her bedside when she passed.'

When I lift my head again, Dr Galanis's face hasn't changed one bit. It's like the woman is made of stone.

'What do you feel when you remember the day she died?' she asks finally.

For some reason I'm immediately struck by the memory of watching Dan fall onto the rocks, and my stomach tightens. 'Pain,' I manage to mumble, because that's what I'm feeling now as I remember my brother's death. Immense pain all over my body. Without even trying, I'm crying now, tears streaming down my face.

Dr Galanis leans over with a box of tissues. I take one and wipe my nose as I try to compose myself. I'm actually quite shocked at how good my acting is. I'm so deep into my character, I'm pretty sure I'd believe me if I were sitting in the opposite chair.

'Please take your time. It must have been very traumatic watching your sister die,' she says. 'It's bound to have had a profound impact on you.'

It's my turn to nod silently as I take another tissue and dab at my eyes.

The session continues, and over the next forty minutes Dr Galanis asks more questions about my fake life. We talk more about life after Marie's tragic death, talk briefly about my mother's suicide, and then move on to my father's addiction issues. Just top-line stuff because time is flying by, and it's clear she's trying to garner as much information as possible before the session comes to an end.

With five minutes left, the questions suddenly stop as the doctor scribbles in her notepad for a time before laying her pen down and allowing the room to fall silent for a moment. 'Based on what you've shared with me this afternoon, I think you are likely suffering with PTSD – post-traumatic stress disorder – brought on by witnessing the death of your sister first-hand. I also think you show signs of CPTSD, which is complex post-traumatic stress disorder.'

She's been taken in by my sterling performance, and I fight not to smile as I ask her to clarify the difference between the two conditions.

'PTSD usually relates to one significant traumatic event such as Marie's premature passing. CPTSD is more often brought on by a series of smaller, yet still significant traumatic events over time. In your case, being told your mother had committed suicide, as well as witnessing your father's growing dependence on alcohol, and everything that goes with living with a parent with an addiction.'

I nod again and try to look like I'm struggling to process what she's just told me.

Dr Galanis continues, 'I certainly think you'd benefit from a series of one-to-one therapy sessions.'

No. No. That's not what I want at all. I want to be in the group with Shelly.

'I have several slots that are available,' she adds. 'And I'd recommend you try to come on the same day and at the same time each week. Makes it easier to remember and gives you a certain amount of structure, which can be very helpful when dealing with trauma.'

I'm thinking on my feet now. 'I don't really get on with one-to-one therapy,' I blurt out. 'I had it after Mum died and didn't get much from it.'

'Oh.' She raises an eyebrow, then checks a printed sheet sitting on her notepad. 'According to the notes from the contact form you filled in, you've never had therapy.'

Shit. I forgot I'd said that. 'Erm, I meant I hadn't had group therapy. I thought because you specialise in that area, that's what the question was about.'

Her eyes narrow. 'You want to do group work?'

'Yes. Exactly. That's why I'm here.'

'People don't normally jump straight into group. It's quite an intense environment, and ideally, I'd prefer clients to have some experience of the therapeutic process on a one-to-one basis first.'

I can feel my chance of getting in front of Shelly slipping

away. 'Like I say, I've had therapy. Lots of it. About five years back.'

'And where did you have that?'

I'm trying my best to hide the fact I'm starting to unravel. 'Newcastle,' I blurt.

She smiles. 'Which clinic?'

Shit! How the hell do I answer that? 'The name's on the tip of my tongue,' I say, 'but it's been a while.' I crumple my forehead and pretend to be thinking.

'Was it Greenacres, by any chance?' she asks. 'They do a lot of work with bereaved kids and young adults.'

'Yes!' I nod vigorously. 'That's it. Greenacres.'

'And how long were you with them?'

I blow out my lips, attempting to buy myself more time. 'Erm... two... years, I guess.'

Dr Galanis stares at me in silence for what feels like an eternity. 'If you did two years with Greenacres, then you should be pretty well versed in the therapeutic process. If that's the case, I'd be happy to give you a spot in one of my groups. And as luck would have it, I have two spots available. One in the Monday night meeting and one in the Wednesday. Both start at 6 p.m. Which—'

'Monday!' I can't help but cut her off.

'You really are keen to get into group, aren't you?' she says with a smile.

She really has no idea just how keen.

'In that case, my secretary will email you the client agreement and terms and conditions over tomorrow. Is this email the best for you? Jessica2511@gmail.com?'

'That's the one.'

'And once you start in the group, do you prefer to be called Jessica or Jess?'

'Jess,' I reply firmly. 'Please call me Jess.'

CHAPTER NINE

SHELLY

Monday Night Group, Session Two

'Can you explain a little bit more about how you imagine harming Alfie in these intrusive thoughts you're experiencing?' asks Dr Galanis. This is clearly for the benefit of the group because she and I have already discussed this issue at length in our initial one-to-one.

I exhale sharply before answering. I'm ashamed enough as it is simply admitting that I have the thoughts in the first place, and I feel like everyone in the room has to be judging me right now. 'Sometimes I think about how easy it would be to put a pillow over his face,' I say eventually.

Dr Galanis does what she seems to do best – she nods in silence.

I can feel all eyes on me now, and despite an overwhelming desire to get up and run out of the room, I force myself to continue. 'And other times I imagine him falling back in the bath, and doing nothing to help him, so the water covers his mouth and nose.' I drop my gaze to the floor for a second. The self-loathing I feel is unbearable.

The room around me falls silent for a few seconds, and I'm left wondering if I've really just said all that out loud. My fellow group members must think I'm a terrible human being – and an even worse mother.

'Have you ever felt like you were actually going to do any of those things?' Polly asks, which takes me by surprise. For whatever reason, I never imagined she'd be the first one to respond to my confession.

I lock eyes with her and shake my head. 'God no. And I really don't *want* to do any of them either. It's as if my mind conjures up the absolute *worst* thing I could possibly do in certain situations and plays them on a loop in my head. I think it's more the fact I have the power to act them out that's so unnerving, rather than wanting to carry them out.'

Polly goes back to being silent again. It appears she has nothing more to offer on the matter.

'Have you told your doctor about any of this?' Claire cuts in now. Her fists are no longer clenched, and instead she's folded her arms across her chest in a way that can only be described as somewhat defensive.

I move my attention to her now. 'No. I haven't.'

'Well, I really think you should,' she says curtly.

'I'm sorry.' I flinch. 'Why would I do that?'

'Because they need to assess whether you're a danger to your son.'

Her response almost knocks me off my chair, and my mouth falls open for a moment. '*Excuse me?*' I say, regaining my composure. 'I'm not a danger to Alfie. And who are *you* to tell me that I am?'

'I'm a doctor, if you must know.'

I'm struggling to keep my simmering anger in check now. 'And your job gives you the right to suggest I'm a danger to my son, does it?'

Claire opens her mouth to speak, but Dr Galanis jumps in before she can reply.

'You've been very vocal about your feelings around children's safeguarding in previous sessions, Claire. Is there a potential that your views on that subject could be limiting your ability to really *hear* what Shelly is sharing with the group, which is actually very brave of her given it's her first time telling us how she's feeling.'

Claire glares back at Dr Galanis for a second, and her eyes appear as though they're dancing in her head.

'You don't look like you appreciate my feedback, Claire,' adds Dr Galanis flatly. 'Have I annoyed you?'

Claire scowls like a petulant teenager. 'I was just offering my professional opinion as a doctor. Clearly, I need to keep it to myself from now on.'

'Nobody is asking you to do that,' replies Dr Galanis, and for the next couple of minutes the pair of them go back and forth with each other as they try to reach an agreement on the value of sharing how one truly feels versus projecting one's feelings or frustrations onto another. In all honesty, I can hear the exchange taking place, but I take very little of it in, as my entire focus is on the resentment I now feel towards Claire, who has made me feel like a total freak and a danger to my own son. The complete opposite of what I was expecting in a supposed judgement-free space. I suddenly feel incredibly exposed and even more vulnerable than when the session started.

Eventually the room goes quiet again, and Dr Galanis turns back to me. 'Please continue, Shelly.'

I shake my head vehemently. 'I think I've said enough for one day. If you don't mind, I'll let someone else have a turn.'

This provokes another silent nod from Dr Galanis, which appears to be her trademark reaction and is already starting to irritate me. Just like this group. The way I'm feeling right now, I have a good mind to tell them all to stick their opinions and get up and leave. But that would only cause a scene, and I have zero energy for any more drama in my life right now. I feel totally drained. So I say nothing and resign myself to simply listening passively for what's left of the session.

With me sitting back, it's Polly who decides to fill the space – keen to talk about her 'cheating bastard of an ex-husband', as she calls him.

For the remaining thirty minutes, I pretend to listen to what she has to say about her ex's new, much younger girlfriend and her 'ridiculous fake breasts' – amongst other things that have upset Polly this week – but the reality is that her words are just background noise to me now. All I can think about is emailing Dr Galanis as soon as I get home to tell her I'm done with therapy. I really thought group might help with my problems, and I was totally up for giving it a go to see if it could work, but the reality is I feel more stressed and anxious now than I did before I joined. Mercifully Polly holds the space for the remainder of the session.

Dr Galanis finally utters the words I've been longing to hear. 'We'll have to wrap up there.' My relief is palpable.

Whilst the rest of the group slowly set about gathering their things and making their way out, I'm already halfway out the door with my bag in hand. A few minutes later I step out into the early evening sunshine and move quickly down the steps, along the path and out onto the road, where I make my way to my car. I'm still fuming as I replay the conversation with Claire over in my mind. 'How dare she?' I mutter. 'Who does she think she is, making me feel like a total bloody psycho?'

As I return to my Range Rover Evoque, I activate the automatic boot release before angrily flinging my workbag in, then closing it again.

'I thought she was bang out of order in there,' says a small voice from over my shoulder.

I spin round to find Jess standing there. Up close, she looks even more vulnerable than when I first saw her in the session, like a strong wind might blow her away. 'I hope you don't mind me saying so, but I found what you said really heart-warming,' she adds.

Her words catch me off guard, and I raise my eyebrows. 'Er... OK.'

'I've never felt as nervous as I did tonight coming into that group. And I really wasn't sure it was for me. Talking to total strangers. But hearing you speak so bravely about what you're going through – especially as you're new to the group like I am – that made me think maybe these sessions can help me too.'

I daren't tell her I have absolutely no intention of coming back. 'Well, I really hope they do,' is the best I can muster in the circumstances.

'Yeah.' Her voice cracks, and she looks like she could burst into tears any second. 'Because I can't carry on like this.'

There's something about Jess that pulls on my maternal instincts. She looks so small and damaged. 'Are you OK?'

'I'm fine,' she says, but it's obvious she's not as a tear streaks down her cheek.

I really don't know her at all, so I'm surprised at how distressing it is to see her so upset. I'm not sure why, but I feel a really strong connection to her, like it's important for me to help her in some way if I can. I check my watch; it's just after 7.30 p.m. 'Look, my mum's babysitting, and my husband's out for the night, so I'm in no rush to get home. Do you fancy a quick drink?'

Jess appears shocked at my question. 'A drink. With *me*?'

I smile. 'I don't see anyone else standing here, do you?'

Her face softens, and her eyes light up.

'You up for that?'

'Yes,' she says, her voice lighter now.

'Great. The Red Lion is just up the road and has a fab beer garden. We can sit in the sun and have a glass of fizz. How does that sound?'

'Perfect,' says Jess. 'I'd really like that.'

CHAPTER TEN

OLIVIA

I can't believe how well things have worked out tonight. I must admit I was so nervous when I was first introduced to the group and almost wet my pants when Shelly first looked at me when I sat down. I was convinced she must have recognised me, but evidently not. Otherwise I wouldn't be sitting here on a bench in the beer garden of the Red Lion as she carries the drinks outside. I knew I could do a good job of playing the character of Jess, but I've surprised myself at how well she's been received by everyone Jess has come into contact with so far.

'It was Diet Coke you wanted with your vodka, wasn't it?' Shelly asks as she places the drinks on the table.

'Yes. Thank you,' I say, using Jess's slightly uncertain tone.

Shelly takes a seat opposite me. 'God, I need this,' she says before taking a mouthful of her Prosecco.

Over to the right of where we're sitting is a large crown green bowling green, which, from what I've read online, has been attached to the pub since it first opened in the early twentieth century. The signs on the walls around us remind drinkers that only members are allowed on the green, but that new members are welcome to join at any time. Right now there are two games in play, and the different groups involved appear to be taking it very seriously indeed.

Shelly has obviously noticed me watching them as I take a sip of my vodka. 'You ever tried that?' she asks.

I turn to look at her. 'Bowls?'

'Yeah.'

'Once or twice, when I was a kid. My nan used to play with my granddad when he was still alive.' This is actually true and adds colour to Jess's history without compromising Olivia, so I'm happy to share it with her. 'She was pretty good at it, actually. Had her own set of woods and everything.'

Shelly's brow wrinkles. 'Woods?'

I nod in the direction of the games being played, where a man is getting ready to take aim. 'The bowling balls are called woods.'

'Oh, wow.' She raises her eyebrows. 'You learn something new every day.'

I offer a faint smile before changing the subject back to something far more pressing. 'That must have been difficult in there,' I say. 'The way Claire went for you tonight.'

She shakes her head wearily. 'I certainly wasn't expecting that kind of response, that's for sure. Especially as it's supposed to be a no-judgement zone, or whatever the hell Dr Galanis calls it.'

I take another sip from my drink now. 'No. It did feel very unfair to me.'

'Totally. And she had no right saying I was a potential

danger to Alfie. I was talking about my warped imagination, not my reality.'

'At least Dr Galanis stepped in and pulled her on it,' I add.

Shelly grins. 'Yeah. Claire didn't like that, did she?'

I chuckle. 'No. She looked like a scalded cat.'

She takes another sip, then rests her glass on the table. 'And how are you feeling? You seemed really upset back at the car.'

'I'm better now.' I give her my best broken smile in an attempt to project Jess's immense vulnerability. 'Thanks to you.'

'I didn't do anything.'

'No, but you did. You went out of your way to make me feel better.'

She waves me away. 'Don't be silly. I love a drink in the sun. And drinking is much more fun when you're with a friendly face.'

I nod without conviction. 'That's not something I'm blessed with.'

Shelly's brow wrinkles, and she seems surprised by my comments.

It's time for me to share some more of Jess's backstory. 'After my mum died, I lost all my confidence and didn't really want to go out. After a while, the few friends I did have started asking me out less and less, and then before I knew it, they stopped asking me at all.'

'That must have been tough on you.'

'I did think about trying to get back in touch, but then when my nan got sick and it fell to me to look after her, I never really had much time for socialising anyway. So I gave up bothering. I just go to work during the day and visit Nan in the home most evenings these days.'

Shelly offers me a sympathetic smile. 'That's a lot of responsibility for someone your age. This is the time you should be out having fun, not acting as a carer.'

'I know.' I shrug. 'But what other choice have I got? I'm Nan's only living relative. Well, apart from my dad, but he's a drunk, so we never see him anymore.'

'God. You haven't had it easy, have you?'

'I try not to think about it too much. I guess it's just the way things are.'

Shelly falls silent for a time as she takes another drink, and then clearly decides she wants to change the subject. 'So what is it that you do?' she asks.

'I work in finance.'

'Really?' Her eyes widen. 'Me too.'

'Well, I say finance, I'm a data analyst for an online bank, so it's more finance admin.' I take another mouthful of my vodka. 'What about you? I bet your job is a lot more interesting than mine and much better paid, judging by your car.'

She snorts. 'Interesting is one way to describe it.'

'How so?'

It's her turn to shrug now. 'I used to enjoy it, but when I went back after maternity, I ended up essentially getting demoted. Replaced by a complete prick who hasn't got a clue what he's doing.'

'Is that legal?' I ask. 'Being demoted, I mean. Don't you have rights when you're on maternity?'

'Yeah, you'd think so, and I did challenge it, but the HR team insisted it was all above board based on the fact I only wanted to work four days a week, and they felt the team-leader role needed to be available Monday to Friday.'

'You should fight that,' I say with conviction. 'Speak to a lawyer.'

'I thought about it,' she says. 'But in the end I realised I haven't got the energy for the drama and upheaval it would bring. So I decided to put up and shut up. And sadly, the reality is Nick and I have a big house in Tynemouth with an even bigger mortgage. We really need the money at the moment.'

'Couldn't you get another job somewhere else?'

'Not on the same salary.' She sighs. 'Not many firms are willing to take on people at my level four days a week, either. I'm only able to do it at Greystones because I got pregnant while I was working there. I'm sure given half the chance, they'd get shot of me if they could do it legally.'

'Do you really think so?'

'Absolutely.' She drains her glass. 'Darryl, my boss, is utter dogshit. And because I used to do his job, *he* knows that *I* know how rubbish he really is. If he saw even the slightest chance to get me out, he'd jump at it. And that's why he's desperate to put me on a PRP.'

'What's a PRP?' I ask.

'Sorry. Bullshit bingo again. It stands for performance review plan. It's basically his way of setting me targets I can't hit and then using them against me to suggest I'm not doing my job – and ultimately creating a legal argument to fire me.'

'That's sounds terrible.'

'It is and totally unfair.' Shelly folds her arms against her chest. 'Because aside from my lateness, I'm actually pretty good at my job.'

'So is being late enough of a reason to fire someone?'

'If it happens regularly enough, then yeah. It can be. And it's one of the reasons I started in group, as it happens.

To try to get my OCD under control and reduce the number of times I'm late.'

'And how does your OCD make you late?'

She lets out another sigh. 'It takes me ages to get out of the house in the morning, checking my straighteners, the iron, the gas. Is the door locked? It's a nightmare, and if I don't manage it properly, I can get stuck in the loop of checking and rechecking for up to half an hour sometimes.'

'That sounds awful,' I chip in.

'It is, believe me. And I know that if I can't find a way to get past it, then it'll give Darryl all the ammo he needs to get me out.'

My mind is fizzing with possibilities now. If Shelly *were* to lose her job, then how will she pay the large mortgage she was just talking about? She could essentially lose her house. A thought that gives me a tingle of excitement.

'And I guess that's why I should really try to persevere with the group. Even though I was adamant I was going to quit when I walked out of there tonight.'

'You weren't really going to quit, were you?' The surprise in my voice is real.

'I was. I bared my soul in front of them all, and Claire made me feel like shit on her shoe.'

It's my turn to wave her away this time. 'Fuck her.'

Shelly recoils and laughs. 'Wow. That sounds funny coming out of your mouth.'

I carry on. 'You can't let her stop you getting help, just cos *she's* a miserable bitch.'

Shelly's laughing harder now. 'You're feistier than you look, aren't you?'

'When it matters I am.' I pause for effect. 'You looked out for me tonight. And now I'm looking out for you. You have as much right as anyone to be in the group. Especially if it's going to help keep that arsehole Darryl off your back.'

Shelly says nothing for a long moment, her mouth turned up at the edges. Then she nods. 'You know, you're absolutely right. I am going back to group next week. And I *am* going to be beat this sodding OCD.'

'That's the spirit,' I say.

She bangs her fist lightly on the table for effect. 'Like you say, *fuck* Claire and *fuck* Darryl. They're not going to tear me down.'

I flash her a wide grin. No. *They're* not. Because in time, that pleasure is going to be all *mine.*

CHAPTER ELEVEN

SHELLY

In an effort to catch up on my overrunning projects and stave off any further disciplinary action from Darryl and the threat of his PRP, I stayed back and worked late tonight. Not that I actually got that much done. I've not been in a great place today after last night's group. I've struggled all day to get Claire's words out of my head – wondering if she actually has a point. Should I be speaking to my doctor about my intrusive thoughts? Plus, on top of that, I've been questioning if being so gung-ho about going back to group when talking to Jess last night was the right thing to do. After all, she's not exactly in a great place mentally herself. If I do ultimately feel group isn't for me and decide to walk away, I'm worried I'd now feel responsible to her in some way.

By the time I head for home, it's just after 9 p.m., and the sun is threatening to set over the sea as I drive through Tynemouth village. Orange and pink hues fill the evening sky, and it's a view that usually raises my spirits, but tonight it does little to improve my mood.

As I walk through the front door, the delicious aromas of

garlic and ginger fill the air, and I realise I've not eaten since breakfast. With so much going through my mind, I completely forgot.

Nick is standing next to the stove with his back to the door when I wander into the large open-plan kitchen, his broad shoulders and muscular back straining against his white work shirt.

'Something smells good,' I say, laying my laptop bag down on the island in the middle of the room.

'Thai fish curry.' He turns and smiles at me, and even though the shadows around his soft brown eyes betray the fact he's tired, he still looks handsome – the salt-and-pepper stubble covering his chiselled jaw matching the colour of his thick wavy hair. 'It's out of a packet, but it's the best I could do this late in the day. I've only just got Alfie to sleep.'

I move next to him and kiss him on the cheek. 'He's late going down, isn't he?'

'Yeah. He wouldn't settle for some reason. Maybe he was missing his mummy.'

'Maybe,' I mutter. 'How long will dinner be?'

'Not long. Once the rice is done, we'll be all set. Probably about ten minutes. There's wine in the fridge, if you want some.'

'That would be nice,' I say. 'I'll just go and look in on Alfie first.'

Leaving Nick to finish dinner, I head upstairs. The door to Alfie's room is slightly ajar when I reach the landing, the warm glow of his night light emitting from within. Stepping inside, I can hear him breathing in the cot positioned against the wall opposite. Moving next to his bed, my heart swells as his little body comes into view, lying on his back in a baby sleeping bag – his arms up next to his head, which is tilted to the side, his eyes locked shut. God, I love my gorgeous boy *so* much it hurts.

I know I risk waking him, but I can't resist leaning over and scooping him up in my arms, causing him to grumble slightly as I lift him out. Holding him now, I'm struck by how clean and scrumptious he smells and can't help but feel warmed by his chunky little body, which is as cosy as a hot-water bottle against my chest. Staring down at his perfect face as he snores gently, I marvel at the love I feel for this special little man who has brought so much love into our lives – as well as so much uncertainty. And there, without warning, the intrusive thoughts ambush me again. Suddenly I cannot help myself but imagine how easy it would be to simply let go of him and watch his tiny body fall to the floor. It's a horrific image, and I hate myself for even thinking it. But I simply don't know how to stop these fantasies from hijacking my mind.

I need to protect him and get him out of my arms right now. So as quickly as I can, and without waking him, I place him back in his bed, exhaling sharply as I do. My relief at getting him away from any potential danger is palpable, and my loathing at myself is off the scale. When are these thoughts going to leave me alone?

Watching him sleep for a moment, I wish to God there was an easy way to make them go away. Forever.

A tear escapes and runs down my cheek. 'Mummy loves you,' I whisper as I swat it away before turning and leaving the room as quickly as possible.

Back downstairs, I march into the kitchen and straight to the fridge, pulling out the ice-cold bottle of Chardonnay, which Nick has already opened. Grabbing a glass from the rack next to the fridge, I pour myself a generous measure and gulp down two large mouthfuls before exhaling like a thirsty kid on a hot day.

Nick turns to look at me, a lopsided grin on his face. 'Sounds like somebody needed that.'

I take another mouthful as I lean back against the countertop. 'It's been a tough day.'

He nods. 'I know the feeling,' he says, before turning back to the pot, which is bubbling on the stove.

'Sorry. How did your meeting go?' I've been so lost in my own problems, I totally forgot he was meeting with the bank today.

It's Nick's turn to take a mouthful of wine before placing the glass back on the counter. 'It wasn't great.'

My heart sinks. Nick's property development business has been having cashflow issues for quite a while now after one of his investors went belly-up last year.

'They said they can extend the overdraft to twenty K, but that's it.'

'And how much do you need?'

'Thirty was what I was hoping for. That would see us through the next four months until we break ground on the Rothbury development. Once that happens, we can start securing buyers and refinance on the back of that. Twenty leaves us short.'

'So what are you going to do?'

He sighs as he moves to drain the rice over the sink, steam rising into the air. 'Right now, I honestly don't know. My head's done in, so I think I just wanna eat, drink and go to bed. Have a fresh look at it in the morning.'

'Sounds like a plan,' I say as I rub the nape of his broad neck with my hand. It's then that my eye is drawn to the large knife resting on the chopping block next to the sink. In that moment, I imagine grabbing it and thrusting it up into Nick's side, slicing through his flesh and lodging it between his ribs. I shudder and shake my head as I attempt to banish it. But it lingers in my mind's eye and won't leave me be. Leaning over and with the lightest grip possible, I pick up the knife by the handle and gently place it into the deep Belfast sink, out of the way.

Nick has seen me handle a knife this way several times before in the last few months and knows exactly what's going on with me. 'You having those intrusive thoughts again?'

'Yeah,' I say softly.

'You know they're *just* thoughts, don't you?' He puts the cooked rice down on the side and places his thick hands on my shoulders. 'From what I've read online, they're quite common in people suffering with stress and anxiety. There's no way you'd actually act on them.'

At six feet three, he towers over my five-foot-two frame, and as I look up into his eyes, I suddenly feel so helpless. 'But what if I do?'

'You won't. I know you, Shelly. It's not in your nature.'

I wish I could believe him, I really do. But the truth is, the thoughts are getting more frequent and more vivid as each day passes. I'm genuinely starting to worry that it's only a matter of time before I *could* act them out.

Nick plants a long lingering kiss on my forehead before turning back to plate up the food.

I return to the fridge and top up both our glasses.

'You want to eat at the table or in front of the TV?' he asks.

'TV, please. I'm looking forward to getting comfy.'

'Sounds like a plan,' he replies as he passes me a steaming plate of Thai fish curry and jasmine rice.

'Whatever happens, we'll be OK, won't we?' I say as I pass over his wine.

'Yeah.' He raises his glass in the air. 'For better, for worse, hey, darling?'

I nod sombrely, a sudden sense of foreboding gnawing at my gut. 'For better, for worse,' I mumble back.

CHAPTER TWELVE

OLIVIA

It didn't take long to track down where Shelly works at Greystones Finance Solutions on the edge of the city centre. A quick Google search gave me the address, and when I spotted her Range Rover in the car park, I knew I'd found the right place, which gave me a real sense of satisfaction. Less pleasing, however, was the fact that unlike the majority of her colleagues who left at 5.30, Shelly must have decided to work late tonight. And that meant I was stuck in my own car, watching and waiting for her to leave until just after 9 p.m., when she finally walked out the main entrance of the building and across the car park.

I decided to give visiting Nan a miss tonight, so I had the time to spare, and a couple of minutes later, I slipped my little Honda into traffic behind her 4x4 as she set off back to her expensive house by the sea.

The village of Tynemouth is one of *the* places to live in Newcastle because of its position overlooking some of the best beaches in the country. Not to mention the raft of boho restaurants, cafés and bars and surf clubs that make up the area, so I was expecting her to have a pretty decent house – especially as she'd made a comment last night about the size of her mortgage. But nothing could have prepared me for the enormous three-storey town house that greeted me as she pulled up outside on the main road that runs through the centre of the village. If I hadn't seen her walking up the front steps and in through the large double-height door, I'd never have believed she could call such a place home. But she evidently does, and it's quite incredible.

With the sun setting now, I get out of the car and take it all in. I'm wearing a hoodie with the hood pulled up to hide my face as I stand in the shadows of the large trees, just in front of the old red-brick buildings of the exclusive boys school that sits opposite her house.

How can she afford this kind of place on her salary? I know she works as a senior business analyst, which I'm sure pays well, but from what she's told me about the job, surely not enough to cover a mortgage on a place like this. It has to be worth close to a million. Maybe it's the husband, Nick, who earns the big bucks, I wonder. Either that or she comes from money. Either way, a three-storey mansion just a few minutes' walk from the beach is a far cry from the shitty shared house in the arse end of Fenham that I get to call home. The unfairness of it all strikes deep at the heart of me. How can Shelly Hunter get away with murdering my brother, destroying my family in the process, and then go on to live a life of privilege like this?

I can feel my fists clenching down by my sides as the anger and resentment bubbles inside me. This isn't right. Not one little bit.

A light goes on in the ground-floor room at the front of the house, and because the blinds are open and the windows run from floor to ceiling, I can see someone moving around inside. Instinctively I step out of the trees and move across the street to get a closer look. It's Shelly, carrying a plate of food in one hand and a large wine glass in the other. After placing the drink down on a coffee table in front of her, she picks up a remote and flops down onto the oversized couch. She seems to be talking to someone out of my view. A second later the room around her is illuminated as the massive flatscreen TV bursts into life on the wall opposite. The inside of the house is just as impressive as the outside, and one thing is for certain, if she lived where I do, she wouldn't be leaving the blinds open for the world to see. Not a chance. Because if she did, the local crooks and lowlifes would strip the place in a heartbeat.

A second later I see whom she's been talking to as a tall, muscular man in a white shirt and dark suit pants wanders into the room, carrying his own food and wine. This must be Nick. Wow, not only is he loaded, he's also incredibly good-looking.

My jaw tightens, and my stomach turns watching them both smiling and laughing as they tuck into their food. This cannot be happening. How can our lives have turned out so differently? After what she did to me, how does Shelly Hunter have so much, and I have so little?

With the rage growing inside me, I'm consumed by a red-hot desire to wreak my revenge, right here, right now. I spy a chunk of broken brick on the path in front of me. My first instinct is to pick it up and launch it through the window. With a bit of luck it will hit Shelly along with shards of broken glass, but I soon dismiss the idea. I would draw too much attention to myself, and I could end up getting caught on CCTV or a doorbell camera. Whatever I do needs to be done quietly and out of sight. I have to remain in the shadows and exact my revenge carefully and quietly. And now I know where she lives, I can come back whenever I want to, to do just that.

Unable to stomach any more of Shelly's perfect life, I turn away to head back to the car. And that's when my eyes are drawn back to Shelly's Range Rover parked a little further up the street, gleaming under the street lights. The sun has set, and as an idea flashes into my mind, a wide grin spreads across my face. I know exactly what I can do tonight – just to balance the books a little and take the edge off my growing sense of injustice.

Marching back to my car, I open the boot and lift up the compartment that contains the spare wheel. After a bit of rummaging around, I find what I'm looking for: a large, heavy-duty screwdriver left by the previous owner. Picking it up, I hold it in my hand for a second to inspect the length of the shaft. It must be close to a foot long and flat at one end. 'This'll do nicely,' I whisper, before closing the boot and heading back to where I came from.

CHAPTER THIRTEEN

SHELLY

'Some bastard has vandalised my car!' I bellow into my mobile.

'You're kidding,' Nick replies on the other end. 'What's happened?'

A flock of seagulls caw as they fly over me, standing in the road, shaking my head in disbelief as I stare at the damage to my virtually brand-new Range Rover. 'They've slashed the driver's tyre and scratched the paintwork all down one side.'

'No way. Which side? I didn't notice anything when I left the house.'

'It's the side facing the road.'

'Ah, shit. That explains it. I drove off the other way this morning when I left, so no wonder I didn't spot it.'

'I can't sodding believe this,' I growl. 'It's going to cost thousands to fix this lot.'

'Well, we'll just have to put it through the insurance.'

'Which means my premiums will go through the roof!' My shouting draws bemused looks from a couple of commuters walking past on their way to the Metro station, which is located about a hundred yards behind me.

'Try not to worry about that now, babe. We can sort all that out when I get home.' Nick's doing what he always does, trying his best to calm me down, but it's not working this morning.

'I'm going to be *so* bloody late. Darryl will go off his nut.'

'Sod Darryl. He can't blame you because some arsehole smashed up your car.'

'He can and he *will*. He's just itching to get rid of me. I'm telling you now, he'll absolutely make this my fault.'

'Where's Alfie, by the way?' Nick cuts across my rant.

'In his car seat in the hall. He *was* in the car, but I had to put him back in the house when I walked round to the driver's side and spotted the damage.'

'You've left him in the house on his own? Is he OK?' Nick's voice betrays genuine concern for our son's welfare. It's something I've not heard from him before, which only ramps up my already soaring stress levels. 'He's fine. He's asleep, but unless I can get him to the nursery in the next forty-five minutes, he'll miss the morning session, and Mum can't have him today.'

'Well, we need to get you sorted as quickly as possible,' he cuts back in. 'I can't remember. Do you know if your car has a spare?'

My temples feel like they're locked in a vice, and my patience is rapidly running out. 'I don't know,' I bark. 'I'm not a bloody mechanic.'

'Calm down. I'm only trying to help.'

'I know. I know.' I nod and raise my left hand in defence as I take a breath. 'I'm sorry. If I do have one, where would it be?'

'In the boot most likely. Under a pull-up panel. There should be a fabric loop you hook your fingers through.'

I activate the automatic boot release and move to the rear of the car. After a quick scan inside, I spot the panel he's talking about and pull it open. Inside is what can best be described as a miniature wheel. Jet black and clearly unused. 'I've found one, but I'm not sure the dealership has put the right one in. It's absolutely tiny.'

'It sounds like it's a space saver. It's designed to get you to a garage so they can put a proper tyre on for you.'

I glare down at it and have absolutely no clue what to do with it. I'm feeling so overwhelmed and frustrated I just want to scream.

'Have you ever changed a tyre?' Nick asks.

'No,' I say flatly.

'Right. OK. In that case, I'll have to call the AA and see if they can come and do it.'

'And how long will that take?'

'I dunno. Depends if they've got a recovery vehicle in the area. I'll give them a ring and see. Let me try them, and I'll call you straight back.'

He rings off, and I'm left on my own with just the tiny wheel for company. Leaning closer, I can see what looks to be some form of illustrated instruction guide wedged between the floor of the boot and the base of the tyre. I pull it out, but my heart sinks as I realise it's a concertinaed information pack containing instructions in what looks like every language under the sun. 'Oh, for fuck's sake,' I growl as I open it up in search of the English translation.

A minute later as I read the tiny print, I find myself getting more and more agitated and overwhelmed as I attempt to make sense of them, but with no luck. Frustratingly, when I'm stressed like this, I find it almost impossible to process even the slightest amount of written information. 'Bollocks!' I launch the booklet back into the boot before I turn away and link my fingers behind my head as I try to stop myself from completely melting down.

Just then my phone starts vibrating in my coat pocket.

I pull it out. It's Nick. 'I've spoken to them, and it'll be at least an hour before they can get to you.'

'You're joking.' My frustration and overwhelm skyrocket exponentially now. 'If I wait around that long, I'll be out of a job! And what the hell am I supposed to do with Alfie?'

'I'm sorry, babe,' Nick replies. 'I don't know what else to tell you. That's the best they could do. You could always get a taxi.'

I hear his suggestion, but in the moment I'm struggling to process what he's saying. Just when I feel like my stress and anxiety can't get any higher, the sound of Alfie crying cuts through the morning air. 'You've got to be kidding. That's all I need.'

'What's up?' says Nick.

'He's woken up, and he's upset.' I rush back up the steps and into the house, where I'm struck by the sheer volume of Alfie's crying.

'So do you want me to book the AA or not?' Nick asks.

I can see from the clock in the hall that I now have less than thirty minutes to get Alfie to the nursery before they lock the gates. 'No. There's no point,' I shout over the noise as I crouch down and tuck his pacifier into his wailing mouth. 'I'll just have to do it myself.'

'Really?' Nick's tone is incredulous. 'Why don't you just get a taxi?'

'Because it'll cost a fortune into the city, and there's no

guarantees I'll even be able to get one round here at such short notice.' Alfie's crying increases in volume, and I genuinely feel like my head could explode any moment. 'Look, I've got to go,' I mumble before ending the call without waiting for him to reply. A second later I follow Nick's suggestion and dial our local taxi firm, but unsurprisingly, it's engaged. I hang up and try again but frustratingly get the same result. Next I jump on the Uber app, but it needs my password, and it's been so long since I used one of their cars I have no idea what it might be. I try a couple of the usual suspects, but the login page remains unchanged, defiantly telling me that each attempt I make is incorrect. 'Damn it!'

With the clock ticking and my blood pressure rising rapidly, I turn back to the car and make a decision. I either fix it myself – or I may as well hand Darryl my head on a plate.

CHAPTER FOURTEEN

OLIVIA

Monday Night Group

'And what difference did it make to your anxiety, being able to change the tyre by yourself?' asks Dr Galanis from her position in the chair, surrounded by my fellow group members.

Shelly's eyes light up. 'It was quite incredible, really.' She looks annoyingly pleased with herself. 'I couldn't believe I did it, to be honest. Especially as it felt like I was just seconds away from a complete meltdown.'

Polly sits forward in her chair slightly. 'So how did you stop yourself from going under at that point?'

'I dunno.' Shelly shrugs. 'I mean, in that moment when I was crouching in the hall, trying to get Alfie to stop crying, I seriously thought I was close to losing my mind under the pressure of it all. I remember thinking, *This is it. This is where I finally lose it.*'

Glancing around the room, each of the group members is nodding along like lapdogs.

'And then, out of nowhere' – Shelly is in full flow now – 'I had the idea to check on YouTube for a tutorial. Nick's always banging on about the fact you can find any instructions you might need on there. So I did a quick search, and there it was. The exact make and model and the same mini tyre. I just did what the video told me to do, and I had it sorted in about fifteen minutes flat.' She chuckles. 'No pun intended.'

Polly flashes a rare smile. 'Well, good for you.'

Shelly grins back inanely, looking like a village simpleton. 'It was surprisingly easy.'

What about the paint job? Did you fix that? I feel like barking across the room.

'And did you manage to get Alfie to nursery on time?' Polly asks.

'By the skin of my teeth. They were closing the gate as I ran up the drive, but thankfully they let me in.'

'I bet that was a relief,' adds Polly, evidently keen to be Shelly's new best friend.

'It was. But nothing compared to the fact I managed to get into the office *before* Darryl. Apparently his train was delayed by a broken-down train near Durham.'

'Well, I hope you called him out for being late.' It's Pascal's turn to cut in now.

'Chance would be a fine thing,' says Shelly. 'He walked straight past me and into his office. Never said a word to anyone all day.'

'Clearly scared what you might say,' adds Pascal.

'Yeah. He knows I wouldn't let him get away with it.

Especially as he's always talking about the senior guys setting a good example to the rest of the team.'

I'm trying hard to keep the boiling resentment I feel in the pit of my stomach from reaching my face. My demolition job on Shelly's car was supposed to be an act of retribution that would make *me* feel better and seriously piss *her* off. Instead, the exact opposite has happened. Somehow in all this, my actions have empowered her and given her a boost of confidence, which makes me so I angry I want to leap out of the chair, lift it in the air and smash it down on the heads of each and every one in this room, one by one. I feel like steam is ready to explode from my ears any second.

'Well, I'm pleased you managed to regain some control, Shelly. Both at home and at work,' says Dr Galanis in her uber-annoying Greek English. 'It's really encouraging to see you making this level of progress so quickly.'

Oh, piss off with your progress, I want to say. *She* didn't make progress. *I* gifted it to her. But instead of saying anything, I bite my lip and stare at the floor, which seemingly doesn't go unnoticed.

'Are you OK, Jess?'

I look up to see Dr Galanis's staring at me. 'You've been very quiet so far this evening.'

'I'm just quite tired,' I lie. 'My nan's been having more issues in the home and calling me at all hours.'

'Would you like to share how that's making you feel?'

I shake my head. 'Not tonight. I don't feel like I have any energy left. Is that OK?'

'Of course,' replies Dr Galanis. 'You take whatever time you need.'

'Thank you,' I say, smiling weakly.

As the good doctor turns her attention back to the group,

I glance across at Shelly, who's staring back at me. She winks surreptitiously and then smiles.

It takes all my strength to stay in character as Jess and flash a smile back when all Olivia wants to do is scream with frustration. But I do what needs to be done. Shelly may have won the first battle, but I intend to win the war. *Whatever it takes.*

CHAPTER FIFTEEN

OLIVIA

Despite my best efforts this morning, I've not been able to shake the image of Shelly sitting smugly and looking so pleased with herself in last night's session. As if she'd made some kind of serious breakthrough when all she actually did was change a bloody tyre. And what makes it worse is the fact that *my* actions were entirely responsible for her new sense of self. It's been driving me mad, and I simply haven't been able to think of anything else since I arrived at my desk. Which means once again I've done absolutely no work so far today. Not that anyone seems to care.

My boss, Sunny, rarely says a word to me – or anyone else in the team for that matter – unless absolutely necessary. Instead, he seems quite content to sit at his computer and get on with his own work. He's very much a modern manager in that sense, promoted because he's good at his job, but with no real idea how to actually manage people. And because *his* boss is made from the same mould, not very much managing goes on in our department at all. Still, I'm not complaining, their combined lack of awareness makes life a lot easier for me.

After another hour slips by without my mood improving, I decide it's time for a change of scenery and head out for what the recent @everyone email described as a 'Fresh air break'. Basically, it's the company's way of compensating the non-smokers, who, until recently, felt disadvantaged compared to their fellow colleagues who were allowed to take cigarette and vape breaks all day long. It's another attempt by the top brass to get into the Top 100 employers list so they can add yet another badge to their already bulging email banners. Personally I think it's a load of woke nonsense, but I figure if the option is there, I may as well take it.

Heading out into the late morning sunshine, the slight breeze blowing off the River Tyne just fifty yards away feels crisp against my cheeks as I take in the scene around me. Glancing to my right, it's impossible to miss the imposing Tyne Bridge in the distance. It's green arches synonymous with the city. Closer to me, I can see lots of people making their way over the newer but equally striking Millennium Bridge, crossing between the towering Baltic Flour Mill art gallery on the Gateshead side of the river and the bars and restaurants that litter the Newcastle side of the divide. Some are walking, some cycling and others are running. Rather them than me.

To my left I spot a few faces from my office: Chantelle, a short, peroxide-blonde girl who dresses for work every day like she's heading to a nightclub. And Vicky, a muscular, tattooed lesbian dressed from head to toe in black and who regularly boasts to anyone who'll listen about how many women she beds each week. She's standing next to my boss,

Sunny. The three of them are huddled round Vicky's phone and seem totally engrossed in whatever it is they're looking at on the tiny screen. Because of my engrained disdain of small talk, my natural instinct is to turn away and pretend I haven't seen them, but before I can move a muscle, Chantelle glances up and looks directly at me.

'Hey, Olivia. You've gotta see this.'

I sigh silently, because I really don't.

Sunny beckons me over now, and as much as I'd rather stick pins in my eyes than spend my break hanging out with these guys, I know it's in my own interests to keep Sunny sweet. So after producing my best fake smile, I wander over and feign interest. 'What's up?'

Vicky is laughing as she turns the phone to face me. 'Have you seen this?'

I take a step forward to get a closer look and feel my eyes narrow as I watch the video play out on-screen. A young woman is performing oral sex on a man who apparently is holding the camera it was filmed on.

'Do you recognise her?' asks Chantelle.

'Should I?'

Chantelle giggles. 'Yeah, man. It's Ellie Pointing.'

I'm still none the wiser, and my bemusement obviously shows on my face because Vicky jumps in to explain, 'The kids' TV presenter.'

I literally have no clue whom she's talking about.

'Her career is totally over,' says Charlie.

'Oh, yeah,' Vicky adds. 'She's screwed. Quite literally.'

All three laugh out loud at their apparent hilarity. I still couldn't care less.

'You never know, though,' says Sunny. 'It could actually *help* her career.'

Charlie's face wrinkles. 'How do you work that out?'

'Well, sex tapes can be good for business, can't they? I mean, look at Kim Kardashian and Paris Hilton. Filming their most intimate moments didn't do either of their careers any harm, did it?'

'True,' Vicky replies. 'But they weren't kids' TV presenters, were they? There's a big difference when your whole brand is about being squeaky clean and family friendly.'

'Yeah.' Chantelle chuckles. 'When you put it like that, she really is screwed.'

They all laugh again, and I force myself to join them, but all the time I'm thinking of how I can get away. I have zero time for inane chatter like this.

'Unless it's a deep fake,' says Sunny.

'No way.' Vicky shakes her head. 'That's real.'

'*You* want it to be real!' Chantelle adds with a cackle.

Vicky produces a wicked grin. 'I must admit, I wouldn't say no.'

'You never do.' Chantelle continues the inane banter.

'Seriously, though.' Sunny points at the phone. 'I think it could be fake. Just look at her chin. Something's not quite right with it.'

I'm just about to make my excuses when Vicky turns her attention to me. 'Come on, Olivia. Settle the argument, will you? Is this real or fake?' She passes me the phone.

I honestly couldn't give a flying one, but it's easier to play along than it is to try to make my excuses. So I glance down at the screen and watch intently as the video plays again.

Sunny moves closer and points to the girl's chin onscreen. 'Look. There's a slight distortion around her face there. As if it's been superimposed on someone else's head.'

I look up at him. 'You can actually do that?'

'Oh yeah. With AI it's really easy. And you don't even need video of the person you're faking it with. You just take a still photo and feed it into the program, and it does the rest.'

'You seem to know a lot about it,' jokes Chantelle.

'Er, my mate told me about it.' Sunny pretends to look awkward before laughing along.

My eyes are back on the screen. If this is fake, it's absolutely incredible how realistic it looks. 'It must cost a fortune to do it though,' I say.

Sunny shakes his head. 'Not at all. You can get apps like FaceFitz and MorphMaker on your phone.'

'Really?' My surprise is genuine now.

'Yeah,' he says. 'I had a mate who used FaceFitz to get his own back on his ex who cheated on him. Made a fake sex tape and uploaded it on one of the porn sites so forever more any of her future boyfriends will think she used to be a porn star.'

'That's brutal,' says Chantelle.

'It really was.'

I continue to stare down at the video – my mind is buzzing with ideas now of how I can use this new technology to my advantage. 'What did you say the names of the apps were?'

'FaceFitz and MorphMaker,' replies Sunny.

'You gonna make a video and get even with your ex?' Chantelle says with a giggle.

'Yeah.' I smile now. 'Something like that.'

CHAPTER SIXTEEN

OLIVIA

With the door to my room locked, I sit down on my bed and open the laptop. I already know which of the two AI apps I'm going to use, as I checked them both out on the bus ride home from work tonight. FaceFitz is my preferred option for two reasons: the interface looks a little more user friendly, and it's also available as a desktop version. Having had a play with it already, it's clear that the entry-level, free-of-charge version is too basic for what I need, so I've opted into the free seven-day trial of the professional version. In reality I'll use it to create what I need tonight and then cancel the subscription. So it's essentially costing me nothing.

I spend the next half an hour scrolling through YouTube, watching various tutorials on how to get the most out of the app. I'm reasonably tech savvy, but I must admit that when I started the process this evening, I felt a little intimidated by the whole AI thing. Now, however, having watched the tutorials, I'm quietly confident I can pull this off.

Feeling as ready as I'll ever be, I log on to Facebook using the fake account I set up for Jess when I first created her character, and go in search of Shelly's profile, which sits under her married name of Shelly Walker. Thankfully she has minimal privacy settings activated, and I can scan through her pictures without having to be accepted as one of her friends. Judging by the lack of up-to-date posts in the last twelve months, I'm guessing Shelly is currently not a big social media user. Still, there are a few shots from the last couple of years that match what she looks like now and will do the trick.

I take the necessary screen grabs, which I drop into the FaceFitz program along with the video I've already selected online and imported earlier. I link the images with the video and choose the highest quality threshold available, which is 1080HP. It's not quite 4K quality, but it'll do the job I need it to. With everything in place, I hit the render command on-screen and set the deep-fake process in place. A pop-up window appears a second later, complete with a spinning circle and text that states the final video will be ready in approximately ten minutes.

With nothing else to do while I wait, I decide to click back onto Shelly's profile. So far, aside from our initial conversation in the pub, she's not shared that much about herself or her life outside of the group, and I'm curious to know more about her.

I click on the Albums folder, which leads me to a page full of thumbnail images with various titles. I'm immediately drawn to the folder named 'Wedding Pics'. Opening it up, I scroll through what appears to be hundreds of photos of Shelly in a classically cut ivory wedding dress. She's pictured either standing next to Nick, who's wearing a blue suit and olive tie combo in the more formal shots, or dancing with him in what look to be photos from other people's smartphones.

The pair of them beam out of each shot like a couple of Cheshire cats, and their 'Kodak Moment' expressions make me nauseous.

As I continue to click through, the gnawing feeling of anger begins to bite at my gut once more. Especially when I click on the last photo in the stack, a professional wedding shot that shows them standing together in the sunshine, looking longingly into each other's eyes. The ruins of the Tynemouth Priory sit proudly in the background. 'How dare you?' I mumble, unable to take my eyes off the picture. Of all the places to pose for wedding photographs, knowing full well what she did at that very location fifteen years ago.

My jaw clenches as I click into another folder. This one is called 'Finding Myself' and appears to consist of older photos that are quite low quality. Scrolling through the images, I get an insight into what appears to be Shelly's tour of the southern hemisphere from quite a few years ago. And when I check the dates on the succession of photos that feature Shelly in locations such as Bangkok, Singapore, Sydney, Australia and Queenstown in New Zealand – I feel sick to my stomach. She was there around the time of the Millennium. Just a few months after she walked free from court for Dan's murder.

While *my* life and *my* family were literally falling apart, Shelly Hunter, a stone-cold killer, was backpacking around the southern hemisphere, getting pissed and lazing around on picture-postcard beaches. The absolute nerve of the woman!

Staring at her face now smiling out from the screen – all suntan and teeth – it takes all my strength not to smash my fist into the laptop screen. But then I'm reminded, why attack the virtual version of Shelly when I can go after the real thing for myself?

At that moment, a loud ping indicates the AI deep-fake rendering is complete, and I can hardly wait to see the results. Clicking out of Facebook and back into FaceFitz, I open the file aptly titled 'Fuck Shelly' and press play.

As the video rolls out on the screen in front of me, I can hardly believe what I'm looking at. It is quite literally the most incredible thing I have ever seen in my entire life, and I cannot help but grin from ear to ear. 'Oh, Shelly,' I whisper, 'you are sooo screwed.'

CHAPTER SEVENTEEN

SHELLY

Two Days Later

I wish I could be this organised every morning. I have Alfie in his car seat ready for nursery, I've tied my hair back in a ponytail so there are no straighteners to worry about, and my breakfast consisted of natural yoghurt and rolled oats, so there are no gas hobs to think about either. For the first time in as long as I can remember, I'm ready for work with plenty of time to spare.

After locking up the house, I secure Alfie into the back seat and a moment later get behind the wheel of my courtesy car, which I'm using while mine gets a respray. It's not as nice as my car, but it'll do the job while my Evoque is in the shop.

Just as I'm about to start the engine, my phone buzzes into life in my handbag on the passenger seat next to me. Pulling it out, I can see it's my boss, Darryl. What the hell does he want? I wonder. Well, whatever it is, it can wait until I get to the office, so I hit decline and send it to voicemail.

I fire up the ignition and check my mirrors as I'm ready to pull away from the kerb, but once again my phone begins to buzz, and it's Darryl's name that appears on-screen for a second time. Checking the clock, I can see it's just after 8 a.m. For him to continue to call out of hours means he clearly wants to speak to me. What about, I have no clue.

Reluctantly I hit the green answer icon and activate the speaker function. 'Darryl.'

'Oh, er, hi, Shelly.' He sounds unusually unsure of himself, and his accent seems less affected than usual. 'Erm. Look, I need to speak to you urgently this morning.'

I can feel my forehead wrinkling. 'What about?'

'I'm afraid I can't say on the phone. It has to be in person.'

My adrenaline spikes, and I feel suddenly nauseous. 'Do I need to bring a cardboard box?' I say with forced levity.

He ignores my question. 'I'll be at the Hilton Hotel next to the Tyne Bridge at nine.'

I can feel my panic rising now, and my mouth is so dry my tongue clicks loudly against my palate when I finally talk again. 'Is this a dear John meeting?'

Again he deflects my question. 'Come straight here. I'll see you in the bar area just past reception at nine.' He rings off before I can respond.

Holy shit. I think I'm about to be fired.

With my head spinning at a hundred miles an hour, I pull up Nick's number and press dial. It rings out to voicemail. So I try again, and the same thing happens. 'Bloody hell, Nick. Where are you?'

I try one more time, but again it goes to voicemail. Shit. Shit. Shit.

Behind me in the back seat, Alfie begins to grumble and mumble. The last thing I can cope with right now is a wailing baby. So doing my best to keep it together, I pull the car out into the traffic and race to the nursery.

After handing him over to the nursery assistant, I rush back to the car and head for the city centre. As usual, traffic is horrific, and I find myself sitting stationary for the best part of twenty minutes where the coast road intersects with Jesmond Dene – which is the absolute last thing I need and only adds to my feelings of total helplessness. I repeatedly try to get through to Nick's phone, but wherever he is and whatever he's doing, he stubbornly refuses to answer my call.

This has to be a dear John meeting, I say to myself over and over. I mean, why else would Darryl want to see me off-site? And at the same time, what in the hell kind of reason are they going to use as an excuse to fire me? I've not done anything wrong since I was late, and as yet he's not even put me on performance review.

Traffic begins to move again, slowly at first, but before long I'm racing along towards the central motorway that cuts through the middle of the city, and arrive at the Hilton with five minutes to spare.

I leave the car in the underground carpark and then make my way up the stairs and out into the large, double-height main lobby. The relaxing music and sunlight flooding into the massive glass atrium feel incredibly at odds with my mood as I wander past the reception desk towards the bar area. That's when I spot Darryl sitting at an isolated table in the far corner of the room, staring at his phone. My heart sinks when I see his companion, the senior HR assistant, Sapna.

I'm screwed.

I'm just a few feet away from them when Darryl looks up from his screen and sees me walking towards them. The look on his face all but confirms my suspicions. Sapna's is the same.

He stands but doesn't shake my hand. Instead he gestures to one of two chairs on the opposite side of the table. 'Please. Take a seat.'

As I sit down, my stomach is turning hoops, and I feel sick to my stomach.

'Thanks for coming,' says Darryl, the side of his neck suddenly flush. He's clearly nervous, which only adds to my own growing sense of dread. He glances down at his notepad before continuing, 'I'll get straight to the point if I may?'

I can almost hear my heart beating in my ears now.

Darryl clears his throat. 'We, erm, received an email in the last few days, the content of which was quite troubling.'

I say nothing. My gaze fixed on him.

'In fact, considering our client base, the content was of very great concern to us.'

'And what has that got to do with me?' The words catch in my throat.

'The content relates to you,' Darryl mumbles without looking at me.

I can feel my eyes narrow as I try to make sense of what he's saying, before turning my attention to Sapna in the hope she might offer me a straight answer. 'What's he talking about?'

Her expression is grave. 'The content in question came from an explicit site in America.'

I flinch. 'What on earth are you talking about? What kind of explicit site?'

'We were sent a pornographic video,' she says flatly.

'Well, it didn't come from me, if that's what you're insinuating.'

Sapna shifts in her seat. 'No, Shelly. You misunderstand. We're not saying you sent the video. We're saying you're *in* the video.'

I hear the words, but I cannot process what they mean, as everything seems to be happening in slow motion. 'There must be some mistake,' I mutter.

'I'm afraid there isn't,' she fires back. 'It's definitely you in the video.'

My mind races now to the one time I let an old boyfriend film us having sex when I was travelling round Australia. But that was years ago, back when Nokia phones were all the rage, and he promised he'd deleted it. And even if he didn't, why post it after all this time?

They're both silent now.

'Show me the video,' I find myself saying.

'I don't think that's a good idea,' says Sapna. 'Not here, at least.'

I glare at her now. 'If it's me in the video, as you say, I have a right to see it. To defend myself against it.'

'Why don't I send it to you?' suggests Sapna in a patronising tone.

'Show it to me now.'

She sighs heavily. 'If you insist.' Turning her laptop to face me, she presses play. 'I've muted it, for obvious reasons.'

I watch as the video bursts into life, and my eyes widen in an instant. I cannot believe what I'm seeing. Me – or at least someone who looks exactly like me – being penetrated on-screen by two men in what looks to be a hotel room. 'That's not me,' I manage to mumble.

I spot Darryl giving a knowing look to Sapna.

I shake my head vigorously. 'I'm telling you. That's not me. I've never had a threesome in my life!'

A woman passing nearby offers me a furtive look, but I ignore her.

'It has to be a fake,' I protest. 'They happen all the time. I mean, it happened to the kids' TV presenter just last week. What was her name?'

'Ellie Pointing,' says Darryl.

'That's her. She's been in all the papers, claiming she's been the victim of a faked video. The same thing has obviously happened to me.'

Sapna presses pause and closes her laptop. 'Look, Shelly. We understand your position here, but even if it was faked, that video is out there in the world for anyone to find. And we cannot have one of our senior business analysts involved in explicit content that's freely available for any of our clients to see.'

'So, what? You're firing me?'

'No,' says Sapna. 'We're giving you the opportunity to step down quietly and walk away with your reputation intact.'

I sit back in the chair, shaking my head. 'I don't fucking believe this.'

Sapna reaches into her bag and pulls out a large envelope. 'In return for your cooperation, we're offering enhanced terms of three weeks' salary for every year you've been with the company, plus your three months' notice, as well as any outstanding holiday owing to you.'

I shift awkwardly in my seat. 'And what if I won't cooperate?'

'Well, in that case,' says Sapna, 'you'll be suspended without pay pending an investigation and likely be dismissed for bringing the company into disrepute.'

I let out an involuntary laugh. 'This is a stitch-up.'

Darryl still refuses to look at me, his eyes fixed on Sapna.

'It's a good deal,' she says as she places the envelope on the table.

I don't look at it and instead turn my attention to Darryl. 'You're behind this, aren't you?'

He does a double take. 'You what?'

I lean closer and point my finger at him. 'You've been itching to get rid of me since I came back from maternity. Because I know just how shit you *really* are.'

His mouth opens now, and he looks like a landed fish.

I continue unabated. 'Hiding in your office all day, playing at being the boss when in reality, everyone else around you is carrying your lazy arse.'

'I beg your pardon!' He finally finds his voice.

'Well, you've gone too far this time. And I'm not going to stand for it. Do you hear me?' I reach across the table and grab the envelope before standing. 'You haven't heard the last of this!' I say, then turn away and storm off.

CHAPTER EIGHTEEN

SHELLY

The next few hours pass by in a blur, and I eventually find myself at home just before lunchtime, waiting for Nick to arrive. I finally managed to get hold of him an hour ago when his phone was back in range. Turns out he'd been out in the wilds of the Northumberland countryside, looking at a potential development site all morning with pretty much zero phone signal where he was. As soon as he came back within range and heard what had happened at the Hilton, he said he was coming home immediately.

Sitting alone on a high stool at the kitchen island, I stare into space. I feel totally numb, and I can't quite believe what's just happened to me. I've just been fired for being involved in a sex tape that I never made.

The sound of Nick's key in the door breaks my train of thought, and as soon as I see him walking into the hallway to my right, every emotion that has been building up inside me floods to the surface, and I burst into tears.

Nick is on me in an instant, wrapping his thick arms

around me and pulling me into a tight embrace. In that moment, I cannot help myself but sob like a baby.

When my tears have finally subsided, he releases his grip, and I sit back on the stool as he slides onto the seat next to me. He passes me a box of tissues, and for the next few minutes as I recall the events of the meeting with Darryl and Sapna in full detail, he nods quietly as he takes it all in. When I'm finished bringing him up to speed, he cocks his head slightly to one side as if searching for the right words. 'So... what exactly were you supposedly doing on the tape?'

I close my eyes for a moment as the video flashes into my mind. 'I can't bring myself to say it out loud.'

Nick looks deep into my eyes now. 'It's OK. You can tell me.'

I swallow hard before answering. 'It was someone who looked like me having sex with two men.'

'What kind of sex?'

'Does it matter?' I snap back.

He doesn't bite and instead offers a soft smile. 'If I'm going to help you deal with this, I need to know what we're up against.'

I shudder at the thought of the content on that video. 'There was one man behind the woman, who was on all fours on the bed, having sex from behind while she was giving the guy at the front a blow job.'

He raises his eyebrows. 'Wow.'

'Yeah. Exactly. "Wow" indeed.'

'So did they give you a copy of the tape?'

'God no.' I shake my head vigorously.

'What about the site it came from? Did they tell you which one it was?'

'No. And why would I want to know?'

'I dunno.' He shrugs his shoulders. 'It just feels weird to think that something like that is out there in the ether, yet you don't have access to it.'

I take a moment to consider what he's saying, and it dawns on me that he actually has a point.

'I mean, after all, it's so personal to you—'

'But it's not!' I can't help but cut him off. 'It's not personal to me at all. It has absolutely *nothing* to do with me. It's a fake.'

He raises his palms in defence. 'I know that, babe. But sadly these days, perception is often people's reality. If someone thinks something is real, then to all intents and purposes, it is to them. You only have to look at the state of social media to see that that thought process has become the norm.'

'Oh. God.' A wave of nausea crashes over me, and my stomach churns. 'Please don't say that. People won't honestly believe that it's me on that video, will they?'

'They might.' His brow furrows. 'I really think you need to get a copy of that tape.'

'How? I mean, what will Sapna think if I email and ask for one?'

'Does it matter at this stage?'

'It does to me, Nick.' I can feel tears of frustration aren't far away.

'I'm sorry,' he says softly. 'I didn't mean to upset you.'

I bite my lip as I try to process the conversation I'm having with my husband. It certainly wasn't one I would ever have expected to have.

'You can just say you need to show it to the police. I mean, that would be the obvious next step.'

I flinch on the stool. 'I'm not talking to the police about it. No way.'

'Really? Why not? You're the victim of a crime, after all.'

'Maybe I am, but I still can't go to the police, Nick. I'd be so ashamed.'

'But like you say, it's not *you* on the tape, is it? It's a fake. And if we're going to get it taken down, then we'll need the police's help to do that.'

The nausea I feel is growing by the second. 'I just can't believe this is happening to me,' I mumble as a tear runs down my cheek.

'I know, babe. And I can only imagine how hard this must be. But I really do think you need to get a copy of that video.'

I avert my gaze and stare across the room in silence as I consider my options, but deep down I know he's right. 'OK,' I say, nodding.

'I can speak to Sapna if it'd be better,' he says.

'No.' I wipe my nose with a tissue. 'The request should come from me.'

'Are you sure?'

'Yes. I'll speak to Sapna myself. But I'll do it tomorrow.' I suddenly feel very tired as I slide off the stool. 'I couldn't face doing it now.'

He smiles faintly. 'Hopefully things will all look better in the morning.'

'Hopefully,' I say without conviction. 'Because right now, I can't imagine things could get any worse.'

CHAPTER NINETEEN

OLIVIA

Monday Night Group

I've lost count of the number of times I started to type a message to Shelly into my phone since I sent that video, but managed to stop myself at the last minute. I so badly want to know what happened, but at the same time I don't really have a plausible excuse to contact her. And the last thing I want to do is raise any suspicions about my involvement, so instead I've kept my powder dry for tonight's group session. I'm so excited to witness the fallout I can hardly contain myself, which is a bit of a challenge considering Jess is supposed to be a forlorn, severely damaged and emotionally vulnerable individual. It takes all my energy as I step into the grounds of the Alpha Institute to force myself into character, looking troubled and sad.

Shelly is nowhere to be seen in the waiting room, and for a moment my heart sinks as I consider the possibility she might have followed through on her threat to quit group and won't be coming tonight. But my fears are short-lived when I follow the rest of the group members into Therapy Room 3 and find her sitting in her usual spot, staring at the floor in silence.

As I take my seat, I try to catch her eye, but she doesn't see me as her thousand-yard stare continues.

It takes a few minutes for everyone to get organised and take their seats before Dr Galanis opens the meeting. 'Would anybody like to share anything with the group?'

My eyes are locked on Shelly, her subdued, timid posture adding to my sense of anticipation. The room remains silent, and I can almost feel myself edging forwards, willing her to tell us all what's been going on.

Shelly lets out a silent breath. I spot it, but I doubt anybody else does. And then she lifts her head. 'I can't quite believe what's happened to me this week,' she mumbles softly.

Bingo!

Dr Galanis turns her full attention to Shelly now. 'Would you like to tell us about it?'

Shelly nods before clearing her throat. 'I was called to a meeting on Thursday with my boss that came as a total surprise. I knew something bad was coming... but I had no idea just how bad it was actually going to be.'

The only thing that would make this moment more perfect would be if I had a large bag of popcorn and a comfy recliner. Still, I'm happy to make do with the small armchair under my butt as I sit back and enjoy the show as she spends the next twenty minutes telling us all just how successful my plan has been. I mean, I knew when I sent the video it would cause problems, but I could never have expected them to fire her on the spot. It's incredible. And what's even better is the fact that, by the sounds of it, they really didn't believe her when she tried to suggest it was faked. I congratulate myself; not only am I smashing it in my role as Jess, I've also discovered I have a serious talent for using AI. Honestly, I couldn't be happier right now.

But then, the story takes an unexpected turn when Claire cuts in. 'So I take it you've reported it to the police?'

My eyes dart between the two women as my pulse quickens.

'Yes,' says Shelly. 'I really didn't want to, but Nick thought it was the right thing to do.'

'And what did they say?' I ask, trying to keep the rising tension I suddenly feel out of my voice.

'I actually spoke to a friend of mine, George, who's a detective inspector in CID,' she says. 'He and I are both trustees on the board of the Autumn Hearts charity. I couldn't face the indignity of having a patrol car pull up outside the house, and George was thankfully very discreet. I was really worried that he was going to judge me, but he couldn't have been sweeter or more understanding.'

'Is he going to try to find the person who sent it?' Claire cuts back in again.

Shelly nods. 'Yes. He's talking to Sapna in HR to get the email address the video was sent from. Hopefully one of his digital forensic guys will be able to trace the IP address and the location of the computer that it came from.'

I can feel my panic rising now, and I slide the backs of my hands under my buttocks on the chair to try to steady myself.

'Does he think he can find them?' says Claire.

'He'll certainly give it a go.'

It's Vikram's turn to show an interest now. 'And can he get the video taken down from the porn site?'

Shelly blows her cheeks. 'He said he'd try, but he couldn't make any promises. It's US based, and they fall under different laws to us. It's much harder to censor content in the States.'

'It certainly sounds very stressful for you, Shelly,' adds Dr Galanis.

Shelly shakes her head. 'Honestly, it's been horrendous. Absolutely horrendous.'

Dr Galanis offers one of her trademark slow-motion nods as my mind races. If the police are now looking for me I need to get home and delete all traces of the email account I sent the video from. I may even have to get rid of my laptop altogether.

'There is one good thing to come out of all this though,' Shelly continues. 'I'm going to use some of my payoff to help finance Nick's business. He's been struggling to get all the money he needed from the bank and was about ten thousand short. So I'm going to give it to him.'

'Well, that's some consolation, I suppose,' offers Polly.

'Yeah.' Shelly sticks her chin out defiantly. 'Darryl and his cronies can do something worthwhile for once.'

Dr Galanis's mouth curls into a faint smile. 'It's good to see you taking the positives from such a difficult situation, Shelly. I can imagine how hard this must have been for you.'

'I am trying to. In fact, I'm also thinking about using some of the money to take a few months off. To try to get myself back on track. Reset a little and focus more of my energy on stuff that matters, like supporting the charity where I can. I've been a trustee for a few years now but never had time to really get involved in the day-to-day, which is something I've always wanted to do. Thanks to the payoff, I can do that now. I have some big ideas I think can really make a difference to the elderly people we support. That really means a lot to me.'

Pascal, who has said nothing up until this point, offers his opinion now. 'I was just going to suggest that you take a break from work given how much stress you've been under lately. And it sounds like getting more involved in the charity will do you good.'

'I really think it will, you know. Now I've spoken to George and he believed me when I said the video was faked, I'm actually starting to feel quite relieved to be out of Greystones, if I'm honest. I don't think I realised how much I'd started to hate going to work every day, having to put up with an incompetent idiot like Darryl. Plus I don't have to put Alfie into childcare every day, so I can spend some quality time with him.'

'And if you're not actively stressed all the time,' adds Dr Galanis, 'you might find you can manage your intrusive thoughts and OCD better as well.'

'That's what I'm hoping.' Shelly's voice cracks slightly, and she appears close to tears now as she flashes a defiant smile. 'If that could be the upshot of all this mess, then I could almost accept it.'

Dr Galanis pulls a box of tissues from the small ornamental table to her right and holds it close enough for Shelly to grab one.

'I'm just trying to see the positives where I can,' she says as she dabs her eyes.

'Well, you certainly look like a weight's been lifted off your shoulders since you first joined the group,' says Pascal.

Shelly lets out a sigh of relief. 'I definitely feel lighter, that's for sure.'

If I could get away with smacking Shelly in the mouth right now, I would because of the rage I feel inside. This woman is like a bloody cockroach. No matter what I throw at her, she keeps bouncing back. It was bad enough that by vandalising her car I somehow gave her the boost of confidence she'd been missing for so long. Now she's using the money she's getting from being fired thanks to my sex tape to take time out to work on herself – when she should be reeling from the fact her boss thinks she's a porn star! It's unreal. Totally unbelievable. But I'm not finished yet. Not by a long shot. I got into this group with one intention and one intention only – to destroy Shelly Hunter. And no matter what it takes, and how long I have to stay the course, I am going to do just that. By hook or by crook, I am going to ruin her life, just like she ruined mine.

CHAPTER TWENTY

OLIVIA

Despite the fact the TV was playing at a super-high volume in Nan's room, she was asleep again when I arrived for this evening's visit. One of the nurses caught up with me in the corridor before I got to her room, and warned me that might be the case. Seems she's been put on some new medication to try to help stabilise her moods, and one of the side effects is drowsiness and lethargy. The nurse I spoke to suggested it might be best to let Nan sleep whenever she needs to at the moment as her body adjusts to the new meds. That's fine by me. If I'm able to fulfil my moral duty to her without being subjected to her wild accusations about the staff or my grandad, then I'm happy to sit quietly in the armchair at the side of her bed during tonight's visiting hours.

And if truth be told, it gives me a chance to do a bit of research into Autumn Hearts, the charity that Shelly is a trustee for. I've not been able to stop thinking about what she said in last night's session, and realised that if that's where she's going to be spending more of her time now she's been fired, then maybe that's one of the places I may be able to get at her.

On any normal day I would have had a good rummage around online while I was in the office, but thanks to Shelly's revelations last night that the police are potentially investigating the source of the video, I was forced to call in sick this morning and spent most of the day trying to remove all traces of the video from my computer, as well as any digital connections between me and Sapna, the HR manager at Shelly's work. The fake email account I set up has been shut down and deleted, and I even did a factory reset on my laptop after watching a TikTok video that suggested it was an easy way to mask my digital footprint. How true it is, I don't know, but I figured it wouldn't hurt to do it.

So with Nan virtually comatose in the bed next to me, and feeling confident I've done pretty much all I can to distance myself from the sex tape, I jump onto Google and see what I can find out about the Autumn Hearts charity.

The website appears third in the stack of search results. I click onto it and find myself looking at images of elderly people pictured smiling and having fun as they take part in a variety of activities like coffee mornings, sing-alongs, trips out to the seaside and bingo. Reading through the *About Us* section, I can see that the charity exists to support elderly people living in the north-east of England. Reducing loneliness and promoting well-being in the elderly is promised further down the page alongside an open invitation for volunteers to join the team and help deliver the projects. 'Er. No thanks,' I say firmly. I have enough to do supporting Nan as it is.

Next I click on the *Meet The Team* tab, and as I scroll down past the sea of headshots and the unknown do-gooders,

I eventually come to a picture of Shelly, who is listed as a trustee and finance director. I can feel a snarl form on my top lip as I stare at her smug face leering out from the screen. Seeing her hiding in plain sight, pretending to be a pillar of the community when in actual fact she's a killer and a fraud, makes me so angry I could scream. But that's not going to help. Right now I need to stay in control, stay focused, and keep my eye on the prize: destroying her.

Even though it pains me to do it, I take a few minutes to read through her profile, which explains she's been involved with the charity since it started up five years ago, and her main role is to manage the finances and distribution of the funds raised. 'Bully for you,' I mumble as I move on to the next person listed, George Edwards.

A quick glance at his profile tells me he's a serving senior officer in the Northumbria Police, and I'm guessing he's likely the friend Shelly turned to to try to trace the origins of her sex tape. He looks to be in his fifties and has the blotchy red skin of a man who likely enjoys a drink, which wouldn't surprise me given his job. I remember when Dan died that the top cop leading the investigation stank of whisky no matter what time of day it was. Since then I've often wondered if that was one of the reasons why he did such a bad job, which allowed Shelly to walk free.

I stare at George's headshot for a little while longer before my attention is drawn back to the TV as the local news program starts up. It always seems to be playing during my visits, but then I do tend to come at the same time each day. I recognise the man in the news pictured walking into Newcastle Crown Court this morning, which is located just a few hundred yards along the Quayside from my work. I don't know him personally, but I do know he was once my local member of parliament for Fenham.

According to the news anchor, his name is Kevin Galbraith, and he's just been sentenced to eighteen months in prison for embezzling public funds and fiddling his expenses to the tune of twenty thousand pounds over a four-year period. The news anchor continues, sharing the fact that when the judge was sentencing him, she'd stated that if the law had allowed it, she would have given him a much longer sentence. As it was, eighteen months was the maximum she could hand down, but she was at least consoled by the fact Galbraith's career was over, and the damage to his reputation would be a life sentence on its own.

As the image switches to the prison transport van leaving the court just over an hour ago, carrying Galbraith to his new home at HMP Frankland in Durham, a spark of inspiration hits me. I think I might have just come up with an idea that will finish off Shelly Hunter once and for all.

CHAPTER TWENTY-ONE

OLIVIA

Monday Night Group

I've spent the last week carefully crafting my plan, and tonight it's time to start putting it into action. I've rehearsed my story back to front, and I'm feeling very confident that I have the acting chops to pull off a stellar performance as Jess. I've decided it's the appropriate time for Jess to speak her truth and share her tragic past for the first time. All with the sole intention of getting deeper inside Shelly's head in order to suck her into my web. If I play my part as I believe I can, Shelly will feel compelled to want to reach out to me outside of the session again. And if she does that, then I can really go to work on her.

As I walk up the street towards the Alpha Institute just before 6 p.m., it's time to get into character. I ended up watching Samantha Morton in one of my favourites, *The Burning Girls*, last night and picked up some very useful traits from her character, Jack, when she's upset. I've spent a lot of time in the toilet at work today, copying them and practising in the mirror. By the time I left the office, I think I pretty much had it down pat.

Taking long, deep breaths, now I imagine Jess's pain at seeing her sister die at a young age and her father's subsequent slide into addiction. It's an odd sensation, as I can almost feel her pain as if it were my own. God, I'm really good at this acting stuff.

Five minutes later, sitting in what has become my usual seat and surrounded by my fellow group members, I follow Samantha's lead as I bow my head slightly with my eyes closed, ready for my most important performance yet. The room is silent.

As soon as the session is officially opened by Dr Galanis, I lift my head and open my eyes. 'I'd like to share tonight, if I can.' I blink rapidly and sniff loudly in an attempt to appear as if this is really hard for me – but still something that I really need to do.

My delivery appears to have landed just right, as a collection of sympathetic faces look back at me.

'Please go ahead,' says Dr Galanis.

I exhale sharply and smile weakly as I pretend to be looking for the right words.

Dr Galanis shifts in her seat. 'The first time can be quite tough, Jess. So take your time. We're all with you.'

I nod and allow my bottom lip to tremble before I begin. 'My sister, Marie, died when I was twelve.' My voice cracks for real now, reminding me that I'm fully in character. 'Leukaemia.'

You can hear a pin drop in the almost total silence that surrounds me. The only sound I can hear is the usual rhythmic ticking of the carriage clock sitting on the mantel at the other side of the room.

'She was seven when she died, and despite the age difference, we were best mates.' I can feel my chest tightening, and it's as if I've tuned into Jess's pain for real, even though I'm acting. I take another breath to help steady my now racing pulse. 'Even though we knew it was coming, when she did finally pass away, it was a real shock, and I felt like my whole world had been turned upside down.'

Glancing around, I see heads nodding in unison, and it's obvious they are hanging on my every word. The power I feel is immense, and I find myself struggling to keep a satisfied grin from hijacking my face.

'It sounds like a lot to deal with it at such a young age,' says Dr Galanis.

'It was. Especially because I felt that somehow it was my fault that Marie died.'

Polly shakes her head at me now. 'How could you think that? You didn't give her the leukaemia.'

I look over at her. 'No. But I didn't take it away either.'

'What do you mean by that?' asks the doctor.

I channel my inner Samantha Morton, blinking rapidly as I look down for a moment and then look up with tears in my eyes. 'Marie's only real chance of survival was to find a matching bone marrow donor, and the doctors were hopeful that as her older sister, I could be that match.' I pause for effect. 'But I wasn't. If I had been, then maybe she'd still be here.' Hot tears escape and run down my cheeks. Again, I'm almost floored by the fact I can actually feel Jess's pain. This is turning out to be an epic performance.

'What you experienced there is known as survivor's

guilt,' says Dr Galanis as she passes me the box of tissues. 'It's very common in children who have lost a sibling.'

I wipe my nose and nod silently before allowing my eyes to land on Shelly, who appears to be biting her bottom lip as she stares back at me with sadness in her eyes.

The doctor continues, 'The surviving child cannot understand why they lived, and their brother or sister didn't. They feel like it should have been them who died. Often their parents' abject grief at losing their sibling will add to their belief that the wrong child survived and that the parents would have preferred it if it was them who died instead.'

Despite the fact this is all an act, I find myself nodding along at her explanation, and for a moment I wonder if she's talking to *Jess* about Marie's death or *Olivia* about Dan's murder. Because right now, everything she's saying reminds me of how I felt when Dan died.

'But you must know, Jess,' says Dr Galanis, 'your parents would have felt exactly the same and suffered an equal amount of grief if it had been you who had died instead of Marie.'

'Well, why did Mum kill herself if that was the case?' The words are out of my mouth before I can self-edit. 'Why wasn't I important enough for her to stay alive?'

The questions are real this time, and I suddenly feel quite exposed and strangely vulnerable.

Dr Galanis's slow nod-and-blink combo returns in all its annoying glory, and I find myself grinding my teeth as I stare back at her.

'Grief can be all consuming, Jess. And for some parents who lose a child – as may have been the case with your mother – they simply cannot live with the tremendous pain that follows. It doesn't make it any easier for those who are left behind, but it can at least go some way to explaining why they ultimately make the decision to take their own life.'

I suddenly feel overwhelmed as my heart pounds in my chest, coupled with the urge to scream at the doctor. Who the hell is she to tell me what it's like to have a parent kill themselves?

It quickly becomes clear that I mustn't be doing a very good job of hiding my rage.

'You look like my explanation has upset you, Jess,' says Dr Galanis.

It has, I want to shout back, along with, *You haven't got a bloody clue, you silly cow*. But that will only prolong this conversation. And that is the last thing I want right now. So instead, I shake my head. 'I'm not angry.'

'I think you are,' she pushes. 'And I think exploring that anger could be of real benefit to your healing process.'

A big part of me wants to challenge her ridiculous notion, but thankfully I have the presence of mind to recognise that this is a trap I can't allow myself to fall into. I didn't come here tonight to explore Olivia's feelings. I'm here to share Jess's story. And now I need to somehow figure out a way to get that plan back on track.

The room falls silent again as everyone waits for my response. 'I think I've shared enough for one session,' I say in a deliberately broken voice. 'Somebody else can have the space.'

'Are you sure?' says Dr Galanis.

'Yes.'

She offers a supportive smile now. 'Well, well done, Jess, for being so candid so early with the group. We all know it's not easy.'

Gripping the tissue tightly in my right hand, I drop my gaze to the floor as I try to make sense of the emotions surging around my body. I feel a mixture of anger and resentment as well as sadness for what might have been if Dan had lived. They're the type of feelings that I learned to block out many, many years ago after Mum died, but clearly my deep dive into Jess's character has had a powerful effect on my nervous system, and my body has now confused Jess's pain with my own.

By the time I look up again, Pascal has taken on the baton and is telling the room about something that happened to him at work in the last week. I'm not really paying attention, to be honest, and as I glance up at the clock, I can see we only have thirty minutes left before the session finishes. That means I can get to work on the next phase of my plan.

I pull myself together set about doing my best to look dejected and damaged and wait for a chance to catch Shelly's eye. Something I'm sure won't be that difficult to do, because by the looks of it, she's as bored with Pascal's ramblings as I am.

A few minutes later, Shelly shifts her weight in her seat and, as she does, glances in my direction. I offer my best pained expression as if seeking her support. She gently winks and smiles back. I move my hand to scratch my nose, but at the last second make a surreptitious drinking motion.

She spots my suggestion and replies with the faintest of nods in return.

Allowing my shoulders to visibly soften, I smile softly – she's just walked straight into my trap.

CHAPTER TWENTY-TWO

SHELLY

I'm so pleased Jess suggested going for a drink. As much as it's been nice to be at home with Alfie over the last week or so, I'm looking forward to some proper adult conversation that doesn't involve feeds, naps or nappies. We both enjoyed sitting in the sunshine of the beer garden at the Red Lion the first time we had a drink together. As it's another warm summer evening, we decided it was as good a place as any to catch up again this evening.

So while Jess headed inside to get drinks, I made my way out back to secure us a table in the sun. Despite the fact it's a Monday evening, it's still quite busy, but thankfully there are a couple of long benches free. I opt for the one furthest from the back doors to the pub based on the direction of the sun, figuring it'll get the sunshine for at least another hour, if not longer. As was the case last time, three or four people are playing crown green bowling nearby. As I take a seat, I can hear the gentle sound of the woods knocking into each other, and I'm struck by how comforting it feels to be here in this space – a very British beer garden.

Jess appears a few minutes later and, after placing the drinks on the table, drops down onto the bench opposite me. She slides my drink across. 'One gin and Slimline, and one vodka and Diet Coke for me.'

'Cheers,' I say as I clink my glass against hers before taking a long drink of my gin.

'Cheers,' she says back, then takes a sip of her vodka.

The ice-cold drink tastes delicious, and within seconds I feel a wave of relaxation wash over me. 'God, I needed that.'

'Me too after all that in there,' Jess replies.

I place my glass down on the table. 'How was that for you?'

'Harder than I imagined it would be, actually.'

'Yeah. It's not easy saying that stuff out loud, is it?'

She shakes her head. 'No. Not at all.'

'Would it help to talk about it? Or would you prefer we chat about something else?'

'Definitely something else,' she replies. 'If that's OK with you?'

'Of course it is.' I take another mouthful. 'So what do you have in mind?'

'I dunno.' Jess shrugs. 'How about your week? What have you been up to now you're a lady of leisure?'

I blow my cheeks. 'Not a lot, really. I guess I'm just getting to grips with the new routine, really. I've been so used to running around like a lunatic in the mornings to try to leave the house on time with Alfie that it's hard to know what to do now I'm not working any more. I feel a bit lost as to what to do each day.'

'Are you missing it?' Jess asks. 'The job, I mean?'

I shake my head. 'No. I don't think so.'

She takes another sip from her drink. 'You don't sound so sure.'

I take a moment to consider my answer. 'I definitely don't miss Darryl and the politics. Or the constant worrying about being late or missing deadlines and that kind of stuff. But I guess it's the routine that I'm struggling to live without.'

'How do you mean?'

'Well, when you have to be somewhere for a certain time each day and are expected to deliver projects on specific dates, it's easy to focus your mind and keep you on track. And I find that very helpful. Whereas as a full-time mum – aside from a few days in the office at Autumn Hearts – I don't really need to be anywhere or do anything unless I have a doctor's appointment or a trip to the hairdresser's planned in, etc. So my days are pretty much my own at the moment.'

'Sounds like bliss to me,' says Jess.

'You'd think so, wouldn't you, but I'm actually finding it quite hard. I've literally had to force myself to get all the life admin sorted that needed doing.'

She raises an eyebrow. 'Life admin?'

'You know, logins and passwords for online accounts and all that stuff. Because I was at Greystones for so long, I stupidly used my work email for nearly all my accounts, so I've had to get all those changed over.'

'Sounds like a right pain in the backside.'

'It was,' I say.

'But you got it sorted?'

I find myself cringing now, and it obviously shows on my face.

'What is it?'

'Well, it is sorted, but I think I might have switched one

problem with another because I used my Autumn Hearts email account to replace my old work one.'

'And why's that a problem?'

'I don't know. I guess I'm just worried it might not be considered appropriate for a trustee to use the charity email as a login for my Netflix account.'

Jess giggles. 'Depends on what you're watching, I suppose.'

I laugh too. 'I should have set up a Gmail account, but if truth be told, I just couldn't be bothered.'

'Well, I'm sure no harm will come from it.'

'I know. I think I'm just being a bit paranoid after everything that's happened.'

We both fall silent, and the hum of chatter from the other patrons fills the air around us for a minute or so before Jess speaks again, her expression serious now. 'And how is Alfie? How are you finding being at home with him all the time?'

'Yeah, it's fine.'

Her eyes narrow. '*Just* fine?'

I sigh. 'Look, don't get me wrong, I love my boy more than anything in the world...'

'But?'

'But looking after him all day every day is exhausting. I mean, it's relentless, and I feel like no sooner have I fed him or changed him than I'm doing it again.'

'Can you put him in nursery a couple of days? You know, to give you a break?'

'We could, but childcare is so expensive. Especially with me not working.'

Jess takes another drink. 'Doesn't the government give you money for that these days?'

'Not for another couple of months, but even then it's only thirty hours a week at his age, so the onus is still on me to look after him, unless I decide to get another job, that is.'

'Is that something you're thinking about?'

'Not at the minute. With the whole sex-tape thing still being investigated, I'd be constantly worried someone would see it before it can be taken down. I couldn't face going through all that again.'

'What's the latest with that?' says Jess.

'Still waiting to hear back from my friend George.'

'So they've not had any luck tracking down the person who sent the video to your bosses?'

'If they have, they haven't told me. George did say it would be a long shot.'

'I'm sorry. That must be really tough.'

I tap my finger against the stem of my glass. 'Nothing I can do about it, is there?'

'So did you get a copy of the tape? Like Nick suggested?'

'Uh-huh,' I reply, trying to keep the grin from my face.

Jess raises her eyebrows again. 'Why do you look strangely happy about that?'

I feel myself blushing, and I can't help but giggle. 'Look, don't judge me, Jess, but when Nick and I watched it, well, it, er...'

'What?' Jess giggles too.

I glance left and right so as not to be overheard by any of the people sitting on the tables around us before leaning closer so she can hear me whisper. 'Well, it ended up making things a bit more spicy in the bedroom.'

Jess recoils playfully. 'No!'

'Yes!'

'But how? You were so upset when you first saw it.'

'I know. Tell me about it.' I'm nodding now. 'That's the weird thing. Once I'd come round to the idea that leaving Greystones was actually something I wanted – and that the payoff money was going to help keep Nick's business afloat – it really lost its power over me.'

'And Nick, was he all right watching it?'

I lower my voice again. 'Well, he knew it wasn't real, so it's not as if he was actually watching *me* doing those things with two other men, was it? It was just a fake video at the end of the day.'

'So how's it spiced things up?'

'Well.' Again I glance left and right to check no one is listening. 'A few nights after we'd been sent the link, we decided to check out a few different adult sites. To see if it had been uploaded to any others aside from the one that was sent to Sapna.'

'And had it?'

'No. Not that we could find, anyway. But we had to scroll through *a lot* of videos to be sure. We ended up watching loads of random people having sex for the best part of four hours. And then that night in bed, well, let's just say one thing led to another.'

Jess leans in closer now and giggles. 'Ha. You're kidding.'

'I'm not.'

'You dirty dog.'

'I know,' I mouth almost silently.

'Every cloud.'

I drain my glass. 'Yeah, I guess so. I've never known Nick to be so adventurous.'

'You lucky thing,' says Jess.

'It's fair to say I got *lucky* that night,' I joke, before realising Jess's demeanour has suddenly changed, and now she looks sad. 'Are you OK?'

She smiles, but there's no conviction in it. 'Yeah. I'm fine.'

'You sure?'

She runs her finger down the side of her glass. 'I guess listening to you talking about Nick makes me realise how lonely I've been feeling recently. And how that's unlikely to change any time soon. Not with Nan needing all my attention every day.'

'That has to be hard for you.'

She shrugs. 'Nothing else I can do, is there. My life is work, Nan, work, Nan – and then once a week, group. That's it. I have nothing else at all. How sad is that at my age?'

'Well, it's funny you say that.' I fold my arms across my chest. 'What if I could help you do something about that?'

Jess flinches, a look of suspicion on her face. 'What do you mean?'

'Have you ever thought about volunteering?'

Her brow wrinkles. 'Volunteering for what?'

'Autumn Hearts.'

'As in your charity?'

'Exactly that.'

Her frown remains. 'How is working for a charity going to help me find a man?'

I can't help but chuckle. 'I'm not saying it will, but it might give you something else in life to think about besides your nan and work.'

'I'm not sure I'm cut out for charity work. I mean, I hate the smell of the shops when you go in. Stale clothes and all that.' She seems to catch herself. 'No offence.'

I laugh out loud now. 'None taken.'

'God, that sounded awful. I'm so sorry.'

'Don't be.' I wave her away. 'Actually, it's refreshing to hear that kind of honesty, and it's one of the reasons I think you'd be a great fit for Autumn Hearts. Since I've been spending more time there over the last few weeks, I've realised how old-fashioned the place is. I could do with someone like you to help me modernise the whole set-up.'

'But what can *I* bring to the table? I work for an online bank.'

'Which will come in very handy when we move the organisation onto a new digital fundraising system. You could help with that, couldn't you?'

She takes a moment to reply. 'I guess so, yeah.'

'I could really do with your help, Jess.' I reach across and place my hand on her wrist. 'Whaddaya say? Will you come and help me sort these old biddies out and bring Autumn Hearts into the twenty-first century?'

She stares back in silence.

'Come on. It'll be fun, and it'll give you something else to do outside of work aside from visiting your nan.'

Her eyes narrow as she tilts her head slightly.

'You know you want to,' I say with a smile.

She matches me now as she nods. 'Go on then. I'm already looking after one old biddie. What's a few more?'

'Excellent!' I grab both her hands in mine now. 'I'm so pleased. You're just what the place needs.'

'I'm not sure I'll make much of a difference,' she says. 'But I'll give it a go.'

'You'll be brilliant. I know you will.' I let go of her hands and straighten now. 'I think this calls for a celebration. Fancy a glass of fizz?'

Her eyes light up. 'Why the hell not?'

I clap my hands together. 'Excellent! You won't regret it. I promise you.'

I jump up off the bench, and as I head inside in search of a couple of glasses of Prosecco, I feel a wave of positive energy washing over me. After years of being diminished and dragged down by the way of things at Greystones, I feel like I'm finally finding some purpose in life. Not only am I helping to eradicate loneliness in the elderly with my Autumn Hearts charity, which means such a great deal to me, I also have a strong feeling that I can help Jess navigate some of her challenges too. That young girl reminds me so much of me when everything went so badly wrong all those years back and I almost went under. I know I'm lucky to still be here, and I'm determined to make sure the same thing doesn't happen to her. It's no accident that we joined group at the same time, I'm convinced of it. The connection I felt in our first meeting was very real. We came into each other's lives for a reason. I can feel it in my bones.

CHAPTER TWENTY-THREE

OLIVIA

'It's great that your work were so relaxed about you taking some time off at such short notice,' says Shelly, taking a lick of her ice cream as we stroll along the seafront in Tynemouth. It's another blisteringly hot summer's day. 'I really wasn't expecting you to be able to get started so quickly.'

I lick my own chocolate-chip cone. 'Yeah. They're really good like that.' I'm lying, of course. The truth is I called Sunny on Tuesday to tell him I *thought* I had Covid – because nobody bothers to test anymore, do they? – and he told me to stay away for the week, just to be safe. Especially as Carla, one of the girls on the team, has Crohn's disease and effectively no immune system. So thanks to the self-imposed isolation, I've been able to get started at the charity. Today is my third day in a row working in the office, which is located above the Autumn Hearts charity shop in the centre of Tynemouth village.

'Shall we sit down for a few minutes?' asks Shelly as we approach a bench that overlooks the sea.

'Yeah. That would be nice.'

We drop down onto it in unison and stare out at the clear blue skies and almost millpond sea ahead of us.

'I love this view,' says Shelly. 'When the sun is shining, there's nowhere else like it on the planet.'

'And what about when it's raining?' I tease.

Shelly chuckles. 'Now that's a *very* different kettle of fish.'

'I can imagine.' I go back to munching on my ice cream.

'The last place you'd want to sit on a cold winter's day is here facing the might of a North Sea wind. It's brutal.'

Seagulls caw as they circle overhead. The beach, which sits about thirty feet below us, is packed with families enjoying the sunshine. The sound of kids screaming and laughing drifts through the warm air, and for a moment I almost feel content.

'How have you found your first few days in the office?' she asks.

'I've enjoyed it,' I lie. The truth is I'm just about tolerating the old ladies who lurk around the shop all day every day, pretending to work but actually doing very little. And as I expected, the whole place reeks of staleness. Even the office where I've been spending most of my time each week smells musty.

Shelly continues, 'Edna and Nancy love you.'

She's talking about the old dears who volunteer in the shop. I pretend to smile as I spin my ice cream round on my tongue.

'Which is no mean feat,' she adds.

'Maybe it's because of Nan and the amount of time I've spent with her over the years. I understand how to talk to older people.' Which is in fact true.

'Well, whatever it is, it's impressive. They don't normally take to newbies all that quickly, but they seem to have accepted you as one of their own already.'

'I guess there has to be some kind of upshot from growing up without a mum,' I say wistfully.

Shelly frowns as she turns her attention to me. 'I can't imagine how hard it must have been for you, Jess.'

I shrug. 'You get used to it, I suppose. No choice, really. Nothing I could do or say was ever going to bring her back.'

'I'm so sorry, Jess.'

I hold her gaze for a few seconds before replying flatly, 'Me too.'

We both fall silent now, and it feels like the perfect time to enact the next phase of my plan. 'Let's lighten the mood, shall we?' I pull my phone from my pocket. 'Have you seen that animal quiz doing the rounds on Facebook?'

'Animal quiz?' Shelly looks confused.

'Yeah. You answer a few questions, and it tells you what animal you're supposed to be. I did it last night with my housemates, and it turns out I'm a hedgehog. A spiky exterior covering a soft underbelly or something like that. Would you like to have a go?'

Shelly glances at her watch. 'We've got another fifteen minutes left of our lunch break. If we can do it in that time, then why not?'

'It literally takes five minutes,' I reassure her.

'In that case, fire away.'

'Right. Here goes.' I hold my phone in both hands, ready to type the answers. She thinks I'm typing into a ready-made quiz sitting online, but the truth is these answers are going straight into the notes app on my phone. 'So, what was the name of your first pet?'

'Whiskey,' she replies. 'Our little West Highland terrier.'

'Whiskey,' I recite as I type. 'Next question. What was the first street you lived on?'

'Lightridge Road.'

I smile as I note it down.

'Your favourite colour?'

'Pink,' she says without hesitation. 'Always pink.'

'What was your first car?'

'A clapped-out VW Golf,' she replies. 'I bloody loved that old banger, too.'

'Your birthday, including the year you were born.'

'Twenty-third of July, 1985.'

And so it continues for the next few minutes as I garner as much personal information as I can without arousing any suspicion. Finally, with everything noted down in my phone, I pretend to ask the algorithm for the results. What I'm actually doing, in fact, is clicking into my photos in search of the fake results page I created last night using my now go-to resource – AI. With the false result filling the screen, I reveal her animal. 'Shelly is a rhino,' I say, narrating from the image. 'Tough, fiercely loyal and not to be messed with. Shelly has protective instincts and will stop at nothing to defend her family from all foes. She has elegance and strength in equal measure, but can charge into things without thinking sometimes.'

'Sounds about right,' she cuts in.

'Shelly presents to the world that she has thick skin, but underneath she is far more vulnerable than people could possibly imagine.'

She raises her eyebrows at that last bit. 'Has Dr Galanis written that?' she says with a wry grin.

'Sounds like it, doesn't it?' I chuckle. 'Told you it was good, didn't I?'

Shelly smiles. 'Nick will love that when I tell him. He's always telling me I'm like a bull in a china shop. Well, now I can correct him. I'm not a bull, I'm a rhino!'

I laugh even though I don't think it's the slightest bit funny.

'Come on,' she says, checking the time again. 'We'd better be getting back before Edna and Nancy send out a search party for us.'

Back at the office, I spend the bulk of the afternoon transferring charity donor information from several ledgers into an Excel spreadsheet as part of my attempts to digitise the Autumn Hearts database. It's the latest of a long list of tasks so far this week, which conveniently has also included updating banking logins from quite low-strength security to far stronger IDs and passwords. I couldn't actually believe my luck when Shelly asked me to organise it all for her yesterday afternoon. It was literally half the information I needed to be able to action the next part of my plan. And now, thanks to our little lunchtime quiz, I have almost everything else I need. Almost everything. There are still a couple more things I require.

Thankfully I don't have to wait long for the first remaining thing on my list because when Shelly announces she's heading to the toilet, she steps away from her desk and leaves her purse behind. As soon as I hear the door lock next door, I'm out of my chair with my phone in hand. Luckily, her bank card is exactly where I hoped it would be, nestled in the first pocket located on the inside of her purse. Whipping it out, I take a photo of the front, then the back before putting it back where I found it. I also spy her photo ID driving license in another pocket and figure it won't hurt to have a copy of that too. So again, I take a picture of the front and back before returning everything to where I found it.

At that moment, I hear the toilet flush through the paper-thin walls.

Making my way back to my desk, I grab my empty mug, and as soon as Shelly walks back into the office, I spin round. 'Fancy a cuppa?'

'Yeah,' she says enthusiastically. 'That would be lovely. See if you can find some biscuits too, will you?'

'Sure,' I reply before heading out of the room.

The kitchen is located downstairs, out of sight and behind the shop. After filling the kettle and switching it on to boil, I make my way into the empty shop, where Edna and Nancy are standing with their backs to me sorting through bags of donations, which sit just in front of the counter. 'Would either of you like a cuppa?' I say.

Having spoken to them a few times over the week so far, it's evident that their hearing is perhaps not what it once was. So when they both make no effort to acknowledge I'm even standing behind them, I seize my chance to swipe the spare door keys, which are hanging on a hook next to the till.

Heading back towards the kitchen, I make my way to the back door, where I take a few moments to figure out which of the three keys unlocks it. It sticks when I first try it, and it would appear that the back door has not been used regularly for some time. This actually works in my favour because if it's not been opened much, I assume that nobody will miss the key while I'm borrowing it. Removing it from the key ring, I slip it into my pocket before returning the rest of the keys to their storage hook, unnoticed by Nancy and Edna, still busy sorting through their bags of donated clothes. With that all sorted, I head back to the kitchen to make two mugs of tea.

A few minutes later, with a packet of biscuits secured under my arm, I carry the two drinks back upstairs to the office. 'Do you mind if I nip out in a bit?' I ask Shelly as I place her steaming tea down in front of her. 'I have a couple of errands to run.'

'Of course not.' Shelly stops what she's doing and takes a tentative sip of her hot drink. 'You do what you need to do, Jess. You're a volunteer, after all, so your time is your own, and at the end of the day, you're the boss of you, not me.'

'I get that.' I take a careful drink of my own tea now. 'But, you know, I'm here to do a job, and I want to make sure I do it properly.' The irony of this comment is not lost on me given the kind of job I'm planning on doing on Shelly.

'You really are a breath of fresh air,' she says, cradling the mug in both hands as she relaxes in her chair. 'You've already made such a difference to the place in just a few days.'

I pretend to feel embarrassed. 'I've not really done that much.'

'Nonsense. We're halfway to getting this place digitised thanks to you.'

'Not quite,' I say. 'But thanks all the same.'

'So you take as long as you need for your errands.' She sits forward now. 'In fact, why don't you get off early? It's almost four, and we'll be closing up at five.'

'Are you sure? Because I won't be back in again now until next week.'

'Of course.' She shoos me away. 'Get yourself out of here. Do what you need to do.'

'Well, in that case, I'll just nip downstairs and tidy the

kitchen before I go. I noticed a few things needed washing in the sink.'

'Leave the kitchen,' she says. 'I can sort it. Honestly. You've done more than enough for one week.'

I smile, and this time my happiness is genuine. Because if Shelly thinks I've made an impact with what I've done so far, wait until she sees what's coming next.

CHAPTER TWENTY-FOUR

OLIVIA

After leaving the office, I quickly head to the cobbler's on the high street and get a copy of the back-door key cut. It only takes a few minutes, and when I'm done, I pay a visit to the mini-market a few doors down and load up on supplies. I have a feeling it could be a long night, and I want to make sure I don't go hungry. At the same time, I cannot have anything that leaves a smell behind, as I don't want anyone to be alerted to my presence. Ten minutes later and with a bag full of tortilla chips, chocolate, iced coffee and some cans of Diet Coke, I make my way back to my car, where I wait for the Autumn Hearts shop to shut up for the evening and everyone to leave.

As the time approaches 6 p.m. on the car's dashboard, I figure Shelly will be safely at home by now, and Edna and Nancy will be long gone. I jump out, and with my bag of treats in one hand and my laptop in a backpack on my back, I make the short five-minute walk back to the office.

Because I already recced the backyard gate earlier in the week, I know it doesn't have a lock. It seems that security in a charity shop is not a major priority. I also know that because the bulk of the surrounding buildings are commercial units and shops, it's unlikely that anyone will spot me as I make my way through the rear entrance. However, just to be on the safe side, I slip on a baseball cap, pulling down the peak so it covers my eyes and nose. And for added protection, I keep my head down as I make my final approach to the gate.

Once inside the yard, I move quickly towards the back door and, using my freshly cut key, open it up without an issue before I step inside and close it behind me.

First things first. I walk through into the shop and ensure I reattach the original back door key to the bunch hanging on the hook. With that sorted, I make my way upstairs to the office, which thankfully – and as expected – is now empty. It takes a few minutes to log back into the systems, and while the PC I've been using all week fires up, I take out my laptop and snacks, which I place on the desk, ready for the evening ahead.

I always prefer to work with music playing, and last night I created a playlist especially for tonight. A bunch of songs from the late nineties and noughties that remind me of the fun times I had as a kid with Mum, Dad and Dan – long before Shelly effectively put an end to my family. The music helps me focus on the task in hand as well as keeping me motivated to get the job done properly. Because if I do it right, then there's absolutely zero chance that even Shelly could turn what I have planned into anything positive.

With the music playing nice and loud and my laptop open and ready on the desk next to me, I log in to the Autumn Hearts systems using the generic admin details that I updated earlier this week. Next, I open the banking app and, using Shelly's login and password, access the charity accounts, which look very healthy indeed with over eighty thousand pounds in cash sitting in the business account. I pause for a second as I stare at the figures on-screen. I've never seen that kind of money in real life, and I wonder what I would spend it on if it was mine. A new car would be nice, and a trip to Los Angeles and Hollywood would be high on the agenda too. I'd love that. Celeb spotting and trying to catch glimpses of the world's biggest movie stars would be right up my street.

Turning my attention back to the task in hand, I pull out my phone before opening my laptop and firing up the software that I bought a few days ago called HackCrafter. It's AI driven and helps anyone wishing to identify someone else's security logins. It really is amazing what you can buy on the internet these days.

Following the prompts on-screen, I key in the answers to the questions I asked Shelly earlier this afternoon. With that done, I add in all her names as listed on her driving licence, along with her date of birth and, finally, Nick's and Alfie's birthdays, which I managed to work out from various posts on her Facebook page. Then with one click of the mouse, I set the software running.

As expected, the estimated completion time appears on-screen and suggests the task will take approximately sixty minutes. With nothing else to do for the time being, I turn up the music, sit back, relax and get stuck into my tortilla chips and iced coffee.

Just under an hour later, a loud sonic ding signifies that the top twenty combinations of passwords are ready for me to review. Ordinarily, I'd only get three chances to try to identify the passwords correctly before the system kicks me out, but by opening the banking website *inside* Hack-

Crafter's specially built browser, it somehow manages to disable that function, and I can try any of the suggested passwords as many times as I like without it triggering the security protection.

I have butterflies in my stomach as I jump back onto Shelly's bank account and begin matching the options using her Autumn Hearts email as the login. When the first five attempts fail, I can feel my anxiety growing, and I wonder if this is actually going to work. Is this software any good, or have I been sold a dud? When the next two options draw a blank too, my frustration threatens to boil over. And then, just as I'm beginning to lose hope, I type in the next password on the list. Suddenly the screen changes, and I can't quite believe it. I'm in.

With my heart racing, I take a few moments to orientate myself with the various accounts listed on Shelly's profile; there's a current account, a savings one too and what can only be described as a bloody enormous mortgage account. Jesus. How on earth can she afford to pay £3,500 for her house every month? Not for the first time, the gulf in our living arrangements smacks me in the mouth, and I can feel the anger threatening to explode out of me.

But I don't have time for my anger right now. That can keep. Because now I've been granted access to her accounts, it's time to plant my ticking time bomb.

CHAPTER TWENTY-FIVE

SHELLY

For the first time since that horrific conversation with Darryl and Sapna about the sex tape, I actually feel good. Happy. Relaxed, even. Helping out more at the charity has been good for my soul after years of working for people I didn't respect, delivering projects that had lost all meaning. Seeing Jess doing such sterling work at Autumn Hearts – watching on as she herself finds her way again – has provided me with a level of satisfaction I haven't felt in years. And despite the sometimes awful events of the past few weeks, I surprisingly feel a strange sense of gratitude for everything that's happened. It's like someone blew up my life, and now I'm being forced to put it back together again, but in a way that feels so much better for me – and my family for that matter.

Nick and I are getting on better than we have done in a long time. The additional capital I was able to inject into his business has taken a huge weight off his shoulders, and as I confessed to Jess on Monday night, our sex life has improved no end.

And the best thing of all to come from all this is that I'm

having fewer and fewer of the intrusive thoughts with each day that passes. Meaning bathing Alfie has become a pleasure again, and I can put him to bed without worrying. Not to mention the fact I now feel comfortable cooking a meal for me and Nick without fearing I'll thrust a knife into his back. And that's what I'm doing right now, making a beef casserole, which I'll serve with Nick's favourite for dinner – my mum's recipe for creamy mashed potatoes.

Alfie, having had his dinner already, is sitting in his bouncer in front of the TV, giggling away at the latest episode of *Peppa Pig*. I'm convinced he cannot understand a word of what's being said, but he squeals with delight every time Daddy Pig makes an appearance on-screen. It makes my heart swell, and I smile like a Cheshire cat every time he does. I seriously couldn't love that little boy any more than I do right now. He really is the love of my life.

Focusing back on the cooking, I pour two-thirds of a bottle of red wine into the casserole mix, keeping enough back for me to enjoy a glass myself while I tackle the potatoes. Taking a mouthful of the smooth Spanish rioja, I savour the rich flavours on my palate and allow myself to relax as the alcohol gets to work. A happy boy, a delicious meal on the way and the feeling of contentment I get whenever I take the time to glance around my beautiful kitchen. To really appreciate the stunning home Nick and I have made for ourselves. If bliss does exist, it's in moments like this that allow me to really believe in it.

About an hour later as the time approaches 7 p.m., with the casserole cooking in the oven, and the potatoes boiling on the stove, I take a seat on one of the high stools at the kitchen island. Aside from the sounds of Peppa and her friends emanating from the TV, along with Alfie's delighted giggles floating in from the living room, the whole house is silent. And for the first time in a very long time, I feel comfortable in my own skin, sitting here in my beautiful house. I'm starting to get back to my old self and breaking free from the anxiety that has plagued me for so much of my life. I can really feel it.

A few minutes of peaceful contemplation pass before the tranquillity is broken by the shrill ring of our antique doorbell – one of the original Victorian features we kept when we renovated the place.

Sliding off the stool, I head out of the kitchen and across the long parquet-covered hallway towards the front door, where I can see a figure standing beyond the mottled glass. By the looks of their tall and wide frame, it's a man.

Opening the door, I'm surprised to see George Edwards standing on the stoop with his back to me, gazing out across the street.

'Well, this is a pleasant surprise,' I say cheerfully.

He swivels to face me, and my heart sinks when I see his grave expression. 'Can I come in,' he says flatly. 'I need to talk to you.'

'Sure,' I manage to mumble as I struggle to swallow the lump in my throat, and my adrenaline spikes.

A moment later he follows me into the kitchen, which suddenly doesn't feel like such a tranquil place anymore, and I turn to face him as I reach the island. 'Can I get you a drink? A tea or coffee? Something stronger?'

He shakes his head, his thick brow furrowed.

'What is it, George?' I can barely contain the fear in my voice. 'Is it about the sex tape?'

'No.' His tone is unusually clipped for him. He's normally such a jolly fellow.

'So what is it?'

He clears his throat, and his eyes dart around the space. 'I received an anonymous call at the station today, Shelly.'

I feel my own brow furrow. 'Really? What about?'

'Financial impropriety within the charity,' he replies flatly.

I recoil. 'You've got to be kidding? From who?'

'Like I say, it was anonymous.'

'And what exactly did they say?'

His eyes lock on mine now. 'That a significant amount of funds have been stolen from the Autumn Hearts fundraising account.'

'What?' I let out an involuntary giggle. 'That's ridiculous. I look after all the finances personally, and all the money was accounted for when I logged off last night.'

He nods now. 'I don't doubt that, but as a trustee, you can understand I still need to check and make sure everything is OK. Just to be sure.'

'Well, if it's that important, we can always go into the office tomorrow and look over the accounts together.'

He stares at me intently. 'Don't you have remote access?'

'Yeah, I do.'

'So you could check it now?'

'*Right* now?'

'If you could. Yes.'

'But it's Friday night, George. Nick will be home soon. Can this not really wait until tomorrow?'

'I'm afraid not, no.'

I blow my cheeks in frustration before heading upstairs to the office to retrieve my laptop, returning to the kitchen a few minutes later.

George remains silent as he stands to my right for the few minutes it takes me to log on.

As soon as the laptop fires up, I load the web browser before logging on to the Autumn Hearts online bank.

'How much was in there at the last count?' he asks.

'Eighty thousand give or take a few pounds,' I reply as I work my way through the security questions on-screen.

A few seconds later with the final check passed, the accounts home screen loads. 'See—' I cut myself short as I stare at the number in front of me. 'I don't understand,' I mutter.

George leans in closer to get a better look at the figure on-screen. 'That looks like seventy-five thousand to me,' he says.

My mouth is open, but for a moment I cannot speak. 'There must be some mistake,' I say finally.

'Can we see all the transactions?' he asks.

I'm already one step ahead of him, and the full list of incomings and outgoings appears on-screen, and I instantly feel sick to my stomach when my eyes land on the last outgoing payment in the stack: £5,000. 'But that doesn't make sense...'

George taps the screen. 'Can you see where it went?'

My mouth is now bone-dry, and I can feel my neck flushing as anxiety floods my body. I manage to steady my shaking hand to click on the transaction and take a few seconds to review the sort code and account number listed as the receiving bank account for the payment. And that's when I feel as if the floor is falling away from under me. 'No. No. That can't be.' I can barely get the words out. 'There has to be a glitch in the system.'

'Do you recognise the account, Shelly?'

I nod but can't bring myself to say the words out loud.

'Who does it belong to?'

My heart is beating so loudly in my ears I feel like my head will explode.

'Where did that money go, Shelly?' he asks firmly.

I swallow the lump in my throat before turning to face him. 'According to this, it was transferred into *my* current account.'

George nods. 'That was what the tip-off said had happened.'

I shake my head vigorously. 'You can't believe I did this, George?'

He glares at me with brooding eyes that give him the air of a gravely disappointed parent. 'How else do you explain it, Shelly?'

'It has to be a glitch.'

'How? How do you explain the fact the money was transferred from the charity account that you manage to your own personal account? How could a glitch like that possibly happen?'

'Maybe it's a mistake with the bank themselves, and they moved money between the two accounts without realising. I've made the odd transfer between them when I needed to pay myself back for purchasing something on behalf of Autumn Hearts. So the link is already in place.'

He exhales sharply. 'Is that even possible?'

'Of course.' I'm nodding vigorously now. 'Banks move money around by mistake all the time. Especially now every transaction is digitised.'

His face softens a touch.

'I didn't do this, George. You have to believe me.'

He nods.

'What are you going to do now?'

George pauses before answering, 'I'm going to have to log it at work and launch an official investigation into it.'

I do a double take. 'As in a *police* investigation?'

'Yes.'

'Surely that's not necessary?'

'I have no choice, Shelly. I'm a serving officer with Northumbria Police. And I'm also on the board of trustees for Autumn Hearts. I have to do everything, and I mean *everything*, by the book.'

I cannot believe what I'm hearing.

'And to that end, I'm also going to have to ask you to stay away from anything to do with the charity until this matter is resolved.'

'Come on, George. You don't have to do that.'

'I'm afraid I do. Which means you're suspended from all Autumn Hearts duties, effective immediately.' He wipes his mouth with his thick hand. 'I'm sorry, Shelly. I don't have a choice.'

CHAPTER TWENTY-SIX

OLIVIA

I can think of more interesting ways to spend my Saturday afternoon than sitting in my nan's stifling hot room in the care home. Especially as she's having another episode where she still thinks Grandad is alive and well and expecting his dinner on the table this evening. I've been deflecting her questions about where he is since I arrived a couple of hours ago, and I'm seriously worn out by her incessant chirping now. The only respite comes when she nods off every now and again. Thankfully that just happened about five minutes ago.

I feel a bit guilty saying this because I do love her, but I find visiting Nan really tiresome these days. When she's not confused and mixing up the past with the present, she's either asleep or shuffling to and from the en suite bathroom because she's on water tablets that make her constantly need to pee. And whilst all that's going on, I'm forced to sit in the armchair next to her bed, going stir-crazy in this oppressive heat. I've tried watching the TV, but as it's terrestrial, there's absolutely nothing on worth watching.

So in an effort to amuse myself, I turn my attention to my phone and the message I've been attempting to write since I got here, in between Nan's confused outbursts and toilet breaks. I'm desperate to know what happened to Shelly after I tipped off her mate in the police, George Edwards. When we spoke on the phone yesterday morning, he said he'd look into my claim, but I have no idea whether he was taking me seriously. I'd hope he was, considering I made it very clear that Shelly had stolen five grand from the charity. But you never know with coppers. Recent history would suggest they have a habit of protecting their own, and if that *is* the case, I'll be forced to take it higher until someone investigates. Anonymously, of course.

Whether he has or hasn't spoken to her, not knowing either way is killing me. I did consider calling Shelly just to say hi and then move the conversation round to what's been happening since we last spoke, but given the fact I only saw her on Thursday afternoon, that might arouse suspicion.

So I've come up with another idea.

Thanks to my fake Covid self-diagnosis last week, I still have a couple of days remaining of my enforced sick leave. So my plan is to message Shelly and see if she could do with any help in the office on Monday. It's a natural question to ask – and text keeps it casual – and will hopefully open up a line of conversation, at which point I can gently probe to see what's going on with her. Plus, given I have access to the systems, me asking to work again should hopefully distance me from the stolen money. Because if she somehow thought I had been involved in any way, why would I be returning to the scene of the crime?

I keep the message short and sweet.

Hey Shelly. Happy Saturday. I hope you don't mind me messaging on a weekend, but I have a few more days holiday to take. Do you need a hand in the office on Monday? Take care. Jess xxx

I read it aloud one more time before pressing send.

An audible whoosh indicates it's left my phone, and a moment later, a green tick appears on-screen to let me know it's landed at the other end. Almost instantly three grey moving dots appear on-screen below my message. I can't take my eyes off my phone, knowing that someone – hopefully Shelly – has read it and is now responding. This is so exciting.

The grey dots continue to dance for a few seconds longer and then disappear completely for a moment. I'm gutted. She's gone.

But then a moment later the dots return. Is she typing? I wonder.

I don't have long to wait for my answer, as my phone pings, and a message lands.

I can hardly contain myself as I read her short reply.

Can't talk right now, but don't come in Monday. I'm not well, and I won't be in to work next week. I'll explain more when I see you. S.

I feel a surge of excitement as I type my response.

OK. No worries. Hope you're feeling better soon. Jess. Xxx

I press send and wait a few moments as the grey dots

once again do their little dance on the screen below my message. A few seconds later they disappear without a reply.

With my eyes still locked on my phone, I wonder if her sudden sickness could actually be genuine – or is it just a front for the fact she's been caught snaffling five thousand pounds of charity funds into her personal account. Given the fact she looked in A1 condition when we parted ways on Thursday evening, my money's on the latter.

Magic.

CHAPTER TWENTY-SEVEN

SHELLY

Monday Morning

My anxiety levels have been sky-high since George dropped his bombshell on Friday night, and my state of mind was not helped by a visit from two of his colleagues from the Northumbria Police on Saturday morning. What must the neighbours have thought seeing a patrol car parked up outside the house for over an hour on a weekend?

During that hour, whilst being perfectly pleasant, the lead officer, PC Siddiqui, explained that my role as finance controller for Autumn Hearts was under investigation and that they would hear in due course whether or not the Crown Prosecution Service thought there was a case to answer for fraudulent use of charity funds. The CPS and fraud? I genuinely can't believe it. How can this be happening to me?

As I struggle to keep the dark thoughts that fill my mind

from overwhelming me, I attempt to make Nick some breakfast while he's getting ready for work.

He appears from behind me five minutes later as I'm plating up his scrambled eggs and toast. He places his hand on my arm and kisses me on the top of my head. 'How are you feeling this morning?'

'Numb,' I say as I take a few steps to the left and place the empty frying pan in the sink. 'I still can't believe this is happening.'

'Like you say, it's gotta be some kind of glitch,' he replies as he pours himself a filter coffee from the machine.

I hand him his plate of eggs. 'But I don't understand how a glitch like that could have happened. It doesn't make any sense at all.'

Nick grabs a fork before taking a seat on one of the stools at the kitchen island. 'I'm sure once the police speak to the bank this morning, they'll be able to figure it all out and set things straight.'

'But what if the bank doesn't set them straight? What if they suggest I really did steal that money?'

He shakes his head as he spoons in some eggs. 'They won't, Shell. There's no way that's a likely scenario in anyone's world.'

'Well, it must be. Because someone called George to tip him off, didn't they?'

His brow furrows as he stares back at me.

'I mean, who would want to do that? And how would they know about the money in the first place?'

He blows his lips. 'I honestly don't know.'

I pour myself a coffee and stare down into the dark liquid sitting in the mug on the countertop. 'I've got a horrible feeling in my guts about all this, Nick.'

'You'll be fine, babe.' Nick's tone is less than convincing. 'George will see it's all been a big mistake.'

I remain silent and watch as Nick demolishes the remainder of his breakfast. I wish I could believe he's right.

Ten minutes later, Nick is ready to hit the road.

'I've made you some lunch.' I pass him the tuna sandwich I prepared just after 5 a.m. when I gave up trying to sleep and came downstairs.

'You didn't have to do that,' he says, smiling softly down at me.

'You've got a long drive ahead of you up to Berwick.'

'I can cancel, you know. Stay here if you need me around to help with Alfie.'

'No.' I pat him on the chest. 'This guy could be the investor you've been looking for to get the business back on track. You can't risk messing him around.'

'I can if it means you're not sitting here alone all day, worrying.'

I shake my head. 'I'll be fine. I can always take Alfie round to my mum's.'

'As long as you're sure.'

'I am.'

'OK.' Nick slips his sandwich into his open briefcase before closing it and grabbing it in his right hand. 'I'll be back about seven, but I'll have my mobile on and should be in range all day if you need me.'

'I'll be fine,' I say, even though I'm really not sure I will be.

He kisses me on the top of my head again, then turns and heads for the door, and as I watch him close it behind him, an overwhelming sense of unease – a kind I've never felt before – washes over me.

For the next couple of hours with Alfie playing on his activity mat, I attempt to keep myself busy by making the beds and tidying the house. And whilst the jobs get done, my mind refuses to think of anything but the missing money. How could this have happened? I just cannot understand what's going on.

By midday I've had enough of cleaning, and as Alfie looks ready for his lunch, I head back to the kitchen. I know *I* should eat because I've hardly managed a thing since Friday, but the constant state of nausea I feel continues to make it impossible. Instead, I force down a protein shake as best I can. It's about as much as I can face right now.

Fifteen minutes later, I place Alfie in his high chair next to the dinner table in readiness to feed him his pureed chicken casserole and cauliflower cheese from a jar I got in the supermarket. It looks disgusting, but he seems to like it. Just as I'm placing the first spoonful of the thick mixture into his mouth, my phone begins to ring at full volume on the kitchen bench a few feet away. It's so loud and so unexpected, I jump with fright as my adrenaline spikes yet again. I'm living on the edge of my nerves just now.

I take a deep breath to steady my heart rate as I step up from the dining chair and retrieve my phone. I can see from the name on-screen that it's Jess calling. I'm tempted to send it to voicemail, but at the last second I decide to answer it. Maybe a friendly voice could be a welcome distraction right now.

'Hi, Jess.'

'Shelly?' She sounds surprised. 'I wasn't expecting you to answer. I was just going to leave a voicemail. How are you?'

'Not great.'

'You said on your message you weren't well. Is everything OK?'

'Yeah. I'm fine. I just won't be in work this week.' I hate lying, but I haven't got it in me to tell her the truth.

'Well, would you like me to fill in for you while you're off? Like I said on Saturday, I have some time still to take. I could cover you tomorrow and Wednesday if that would help?'

'Er. No. It's fine.' I really don't want anyone in the office when I'm not there just now.

'Are you sure? I really don't mind.'

'No. Honestly. There's no need.'

At that moment the doorbell rings unexpectedly and startles me. 'God,' I mutter in fright.

'What's happened?' asks Jess, sounding genuinely concerned.

'Sorry. It's just someone ringing the bell. Gave me a shock.' I glance at the mottled glass of the front door and can see two people standing on the other side. Who the hell is that now?

'Do you want me to stay on the phone while you answer it?'

'No. No. It's fine. Look, I'd better go.'

'Call me if you need anything,' says Jess just before I hang up.

Leaving Alfie in his high chair, I walk slowly down the hall. As I do, whoever is outside rings the doorbell again. Twice this time before banging on the glass impatiently.

'Northumbria Police.' It's a man's voice. 'Open up.'

Those words stop me in my tracks. Not again.

Whoever it is bends down and opens the letter box. 'Mrs

Walker, can you come to the door, please? It's the police. We need to talk to you.'

I swallow the lump in my throat and clench my fists. It feels like my heart could explode any second as I grip the handle and open the large double-height door. 'Yes?' I can hardly get the words out.

A tall, well-built man with wavy dark hair, wearing a white polo shirt and black jeans, is standing on the top step. He's flanked by a petite, blonde woman with a round face in a blue shirt and grey sweater vest, who appears half his size.

The man grabs the ID lanyard hanging around his neck and holds it up so I can see it. 'I'm DC Sherratt, and this is DC Allinson. Can we come in?'

I can feel myself nodding on autopilot as I allow the door to open wide.

Just then, Alfie, who's obviously wondering why his lunch has been paused, starts to cry in the kitchen. I rush back along the hall and retake my seat in front of him. 'It's OK. Mummy's here.'

DC Sherratt appears a moment later, with his partner a few steps behind.

'If this is about the missing money, I'm sorry, but I've got nothing else to tell you.'

DC Sherratt clears his throat. 'Mrs Walker, the time is now 1306 hours, and I am arresting you for fraud by abuse of position, under the Fraud Act, Section 4—'

'You're what?' As I spin round to face him, it's like everything is happening in slow motion. I feel like I've just been hit over the head with a hammer.

DC Sherratt continues, '—you do not have to say anything, but it may harm your defence if you do not mention something, when questioned, that you later rely on in court. Anything you do say may be given in evidence.'

I'm up on my feet, and my mouth is open, but I cannot find the words.

DC Allinson steps forward. 'Is there someone who can look after the baby?'

'What?' I'm struggling to process what's happening. 'I can't leave him.'

'I'm afraid he can't come with you,' says DC Allinson. 'If you don't have anyone, we can speak to social services, who will assign him foster carers on a temporary basis.'

I'm under arrest, and Alfie is going to be taken into foster care. This cannot be happening. 'I'll call my mum,' I manage to mumble in my punch-drunk state. 'How long will this take?'

'That's up to the CPS,' says DC Sherratt. 'But by law you can be held in the custody suite for up to twenty-four hours in the first instance. Longer if necessary.'

CHAPTER TWENTY-EIGHT

SHELLY

The next couple of hours passed by in a blur because as soon as my mum arrived to look after Alfie, I was handcuffed and placed in the back of the unmarked police car before being driven to the police HQ in the centre of Newcastle. Since I arrived an hour ago, I've had a mugshot taken along with my fingerprints. And now I'm standing on the opposite side of a raised desk in the middle of what has been explained to me is the custody suite, answering questions from Sergeant Jones, who is the custody manager for today. He's a round man with an equally round and red face under close-cropped black hair.

'So would you like to speak to a solicitor?' he asks, now he's finished explaining the reasons for my detention, which were exactly the same as those given for my arrest by DC Sherratt at home.

'Yes,' I say, still unable to comprehend where I am and what's going on.

'OK, love.' Jones has a warm and caring tone matched

with a thick Geordie accent, which is at odds with the cold, clinical surroundings. 'Do you have your own solicitor you'd like me to call? If not, one will be provided for you.'

I just about manage to shake my head.

'OK. In that case.' He nods to the skinny male officer standing to my right. 'PC Aziz will take you to your cell, and we'll come and get you as soon as we've sorted someone to come and talk to you.'

I don't know what to say to this.

Jones isn't finished. 'Do you need anything to eat or a cup of tea maybe?'

I shake my head again.

'What about a book? Would you like something to read to help you pass the time? It could be a couple of hours until we can sort your solicitor.'

'No, thank you.' My mind is going round like a washing machine. The last thing I feel capable of doing right now is reading a bloody book.

'All right, then.' Jones smiles. 'In that case, PC Aziz, she's all yours.'

PC Aziz places his hand lightly on my left shoulder. 'This way, Shelly.'

I turn to see him gesturing with his open palm towards a thick door just a few feet away.

He walks in front as I follow behind, and when he opens the thick door in question, the sight that greets me is utterly terrifying: a long corridor filled with more equally thick doors, some standing open and others locked shut. He leads me halfway along to the nearest open door and stops. 'This is yours,' he says, sounding more like a hotel bellhop than a custody officer.

As I step across the threshold into the dimly lit room, I'm

instantly struck by the sickly smell of industrial-strength disinfectant mixed with body odour.

'Sorry,' he says. 'The last guy we had in here was living on the streets. We've just finished cleaning it up.'

Again, I literally don't have the words.

'Like Jonesy said, as soon as your solicitor arrives, we'll come and get you. But if you need anything in the meantime, just press the buzzer on the wall.'

He begins to close the door now. 'Please. I didn't do anything wrong,' I plead.

He looks at me blankly before the door slams shut. The terrifying sound of the heavy lock clicking in place echoes around me.

It's all I can do to stand and take in the cramped, clinical space I'm now standing in. The floor appears to be made of polished, reddish concrete, and the walls look to have been painted cream. A low-level platform acting as a bed sits about a foot off the ground and is covered in a blue plastic mattress with a folded grey blanket sitting on top. The final thing I notice is the seatless metal toilet in the corner of the room.

'How can this be happening to me?' I whimper as I shuffle across the cell before dropping down onto the bed.

As I stare back at the locked cell door, I can almost feel the walls closing in on me. 'I'm not meant to be here,' I mumble, and shake my head as my panic begins to rise. I clench my toes and my fists as I try to stave it off. But it's no use. It's coming, and it's coming on fast. 'I'm not meant to be here,' I repeat, rocking back and forth on the edge of the bed now. 'I'm not meant to be here.' My voice is louder now as I rock faster and faster. 'I'm not meant to be here.' I hug myself to try to stop the rocking, but it's no use. I cannot stop. 'I'm not meant to be here!' I leap to my feet and run headlong towards the door. 'There's been a huge mistake. I'm not meant to be here!' I bang my fist against the metal, screaming now. 'Please. You have to let me out! You have to let me out. I'm not meant to be here!'

CHAPTER TWENTY-NINE

SHELLY

'Would you like me to arrange for you to see the doctor?' asks Helen Marsden, my newly appointed solicitor, from her position sitting across the wooden-top desk from me in the tiny, windowless meeting room. She has short platinum-blonde hair and a nose stud, oddly paired with a walking fleece jacket, black jeans and purple Dr. Martens boots. Certainly not what I was expecting my solicitor to wear.

'No, thank you.'

'Only, the custody sergeant said you were quite distressed when you were put in your cell.'

'Wouldn't you be?' I almost growl back.

Helen ignores me as she types furiously into her laptop. 'So the details of your case are as follows. You've been arrested under the Fraud Act, Section 4 – abuse of position, having allegedly stolen five thousand pounds from the charity you're a trustee of' – she checks the notepad resting to the left of her laptop – 'registered under the name Autumn Hearts.'

'Which is utterly insane. I've never stolen anything in my life.'

She looks me dead in the eye now. 'Before we get into the reeds of all this, I have one simple question for you, Shelly.'

I stare back at her. 'Which is?'

'Did you do it?'

I recoil. 'No, I bloody didn't.'

She's typing again as she shrugs. 'It doesn't matter to me if you did. I'll defend you either way.'

'I told you.' I genuinely can't believe she's asked me that, and in this moment I feel so much contempt for her, I'm almost snarling. 'I didn't do it. Right?'

Helen nods, then finishes typing. When she's done, she flashes a thin smile. 'So my advice is to reserve your right to silence in the interview and offer no comment to any questions.'

My face wrinkles. I cannot believe what I'm hearing. 'Why would I do that? I've done nothing wrong.'

'Then you have nothing to worry about, but until we know *exactly* what they have on you – because they wouldn't arrest you unless they had something worth pulling you in for – I'd suggest going no comment.'

I can't believe what I'm hearing. 'I am not going to sit in a police interview and answer no comment to every question.' I fold my arms across my chest. 'I may as well hang a sign around my neck saying guilty as charged.'

'At the end of the day, Shelly, you can do what you want—'

'I will!'

'—but you should know something very important before you make your final decision.'

'Which is what?'

'You may think you're doing the honourable thing by going in there and telling them everything. But remember this, if you inadvertently say something in interview that helps them create enough of an argument to convince a jury of your guilt – real or otherwise – then the maximum sentence that abuse of position in a charitable role carries is ten years. Ten years, Shelly, which means you'd serve at least five.'

Just as it did when DC Sherratt announced in my kitchen that I was being arrested, my whole world slows down around me, and I'm struck by an overwhelming urge to vomit.

Helen isn't finished. 'And whilst I'm sure you're desperate to get in there and protest your innocence, I would think very carefully before doing that. If I were in your position and wanted the best chance of staying out of prison, I'd definitely be saying no comment.'

I stare back at her, my eyes wide. I can't go to prison for a single day. Never mind five to ten years. This has to be a nightmare, and I pray to God I'm about to wake up.

CHAPTER THIRTY

SHELLY

The digital recorder beeps loudly on the table between us, and when the piercing sound finally stops, DC Sherratt, sitting opposite me in interview room 7, glances down at his notepad for a few seconds before looking up and staring me straight in the face. 'So, Shelly, can you explain how five thousand pounds of Autumn Hearts charity funds ended up in your personal current account on Thursday night?'

With my arms wrapped protectively around my middle, I open my mouth to speak, but once again I'm struggling to find the words.

DC Sherratt taps his notepad with his pen. 'Shelly, did you steal the five thousand pounds?'

It's almost impossible to comprehend how that question is being directed at me. As I glare back at him in silence for a moment, I let out a long silent breath before finally uttering the reply I really, really do not want to give. 'No comment.'

CHAPTER THIRTY-ONE

OLIVIA

Monday Night Group

Of the seven chairs that have been laid out in the usual circle, only six are filled tonight. Shelly's is empty, and as the clock on the mantelpiece ticks onto 6.05 p.m., I cannot keep my powder dry a moment longer.

'Are we not expecting Shelly tonight?' I say, trying to appear nonplussed about her absence, when inside I'm absolutely dying to know where she is and what's going on with her.

Dr Galanis crosses her right leg over her knee. 'I have not heard from her today to say she wouldn't be coming, so maybe she's running late.'

'That's not like her though, is it?' I say, all innocent. 'I mean, she's usually the first one in here on a Monday night.'

'That's true,' replies Dr Galanis in her usual ambivalent way. I swear, part of a therapist's training must be teaching them to say something whilst at the same time saying pretty much nothing. 'So who would like to start us off tonight?' she eventually adds.

It seems Vikram is keen to speak first tonight. Something about an argument he's had in the last week with his parents about him turning down an arranged marriage they want him to have. I can hear him speaking, but in reality I'm having a very hard time listening. Because all I can do is stare at Shelly's empty chair and wonder why there's no sign of her tonight. I fully expected her to be here given what's potentially going on. But then again, she really didn't sound very happy at all this lunchtime when we spoke on the phone. Has George looked into my accusations for real? Is she under investigation? Was that the police at the door when I was on the phone? My mind is filled with delicious fantasies of her unravelling at home this afternoon. One thing is certain though in all of this, there's absolutely no way I can sit through another eighty minutes of these losers whinging and whining about their so-called troubled lives. Not a chance. I need to know what the hell is going on.

'I'm sorry,' I say, cutting across Vikram's inane chatter. 'I'm really not feeling very well. I'm going to have to go.' I'm out of the chair before Dr Galanis can object, and out of the room fifteen seconds later.

Rushing out of the building, I pull out my phone and, as I reach the pavement, hit redial in my contacts list. Holding the handset to my ear, I rehearse what I'm going to say: Hi, Shelly, I'm not feeling well either. Maybe it's catching. I just wanted to call and see how you're doing, etc. But sadly, they are lines I won't get to deliver, as the call goes straight to voicemail. I try again and get the same result. 'What going on with you, Shelly?' I whisper under my breath as I walk along the street, feeling the nervous excitement in my stomach. I try calling her one last time, but again it goes straight to voicemail. Is this it? I wonder. Have I finally done it? Have I succeeded in sending Shelly over the edge? The suspense is killing me, and one way or the other, I'm going to have to find out.

CHAPTER THIRTY-TWO

OLIVIA

Two Days Later

Having tried to contact Shelly since Monday night without any luck, I make the decision to visit her at home. I'm literally bursting to find out what's going on with the stolen money and to know whether George Edwards has taken the bait. Thanks to my self-certified Covid isolation, I'm not due back at work until tomorrow, so I figure today is the day to go and see her, with the added bonus that, as it's a weekday, she's likely to be alone.

I reach her house just after 10.30 a.m. and park the car down the street out of sight of the house. This is a deliberate move on my part, as I really don't want Shelly to know what car I drive, because you never know when I might need to follow her without being spotted at some point in the future. After activating the central locking, I make my way up the street, carefully scanning the cars around as I go looking for any signs of Nick's giant 4x4 in the vicinity. Thankfully I can't see it anywhere, which I'm hoping means that Shelly is indeed home alone.

I feel unusually nervous as I take the last few steps up towards the grand entrance to the house before ringing the ancient metal bell, which is recessed into the brickwork to the side of the door. I step back and wait with bated breath, hoping that it's Shelly who answers as opposed to Nick. Glancing to the left, I can see that unlike the last time I was here, the blinds are fully closed in the lounge. Is that a coincidence? I wonder. Or further evidence that Shelly has gone to ground?

After a few minutes of waiting without an answer, I ring the bell again and frustratingly get the same result. So I try it for a third time, this time keeping the bell pressed for at least ten seconds. Again I wait without an answer, and I'm just about to give up and leave when I notice the blind in the window nearest to me twitch slightly – as if someone has just taken a sneak peek outside. It can't be more than ten seconds later that a figure appears on the other side of the mottled glass in front of me. It's hard to tell for sure, but it certainly looks like it's Shelly on the other side. 'Showtime,' I whisper to myself before whoever it is unlocks the door and pulls it open on the chain.

As I hoped, it's Shelly who peers out through the gap now, and I'm genuinely shocked at how different she looks. Her eyes are surrounded by dark shadows, and her face appears gaunt – her features far more angular than I remember. 'Jess? What are you doing here?' she asks in a strained voice.

'I hope you don't mind me turning up unannounced like this, Shelly,' I say in Jess's best concerned voice, 'but when you missed group on Monday and Dr Galanis hadn't heard from you, I started to get really worried.'

Her brow wrinkles. 'How do you know where I live?'

'I called into the shop to see if the ladies had heard from you,' I lie. 'They gave me your address. I hope that wasn't the wrong thing to do.'

She stares back in silence, and I'm struggling to get a read on how she feels about my impromptu visit. I make a point of looking left and right at the neighbouring houses. 'I don't suppose I can come in, can I?' I say in a low voice. 'I feel a bit like a door-to-door salesman out here.'

Shelly nods. 'Sorry. Where are my manners,' she says, closing the door for a second to release the chain before opening it again and gesturing for me to step inside.

I do as requested, and while she locks the door behind me, I take in the house around me. It's truly stunning. Every detail seems perfectly placed, from the expensive parquet flooring that covers the hall from the front door to the kitchen ahead of me, to the grand staircase that runs up the left-hand side of the hallway to the first floor above.

She wanders past me in silence, and I presume she wants me to follow, so I tuck in behind her as she guides us into what can only be described as a gargantuan kitchen. Gleaming white cabinets surround an enormous cooking island, which wouldn't look out of place in even the grandest lifestyle magazine. It's obviously a recent extension to the original building and comprises floor-to-ceiling glass that offers views out into the small, but expertly landscaped yard-cum-garden.

'There's coffee in the pot.' Shelly keeps her back to me as she points to the filter machine on the countertop. 'Would you like one?'

'That would be lovely. As long as it's no trouble.'

'No trouble at all.' Shelly's voice is much flatter than usual, and she appears slightly aloof.

I take a seat on one of the stools at the island. As she turns around and passes me my drink a minute later, I'm once again struck by the darkness of the shadows that surround her red, bloodshot eyes. It's obvious she's been crying recently. 'Are you OK?' I ask, doing my best to sound concerned when in actual fact I'm bursting with anticipation of what's really going on with her.

'No. I'm not,' she says, tears welling in her eyes.

I place my mug down on the countertop. 'Shelly? What is it? What's wrong?'

The tears come now.

'Oh my God. What's happened?'

She wipes her nose noisily with the back of her hand. 'I'm not staying away from the office because I'm ill.' Her lip trembles. 'I'm not allowed to go in because I've been suspended from my duties with the charity.'

'Suspended?' My God. This is better than I thought. And there's more.

'And I was arrested on Monday.'

'*Arrested?*' My double-take reaction is genuine, but not for the reasons she thinks. 'You're kidding me?'

'I wish I were.'

'But what for?' I'm struggling to keep the smile from my face and have to remind myself of the importance of staying in character. Olivia may be loving every second of this, but Jess has to express grave concern.

Shelly exhales sharply. 'Fraud by abuse of position.'

'Fraud?' I shake my head in mock disbelief. 'So what on earth are you supposed to have done?'

'The police think I stole five thousand pounds from the charity's fundraising account.'

'You stole five grand?' It takes all my strength not to succumb to the utter joy I'm feeling inside, and I allow myself to laugh out loud. 'I don't believe it.'

'I didn't do it, Jess,' she says weakly.

'Of course you didn't,' I reply, just about managing to keep a straight face.

'But somehow – God knows how – the money ended up in my personal account. Transferred directly from the Autumn Hearts fundraising account. I just don't get it.'

I tilt my head to the side. 'You're saying that the alleged stolen money was *actually* in your account?'

She nods as she wraps her arms protectively around her middle. 'It has to be a glitch in the system. I've never stolen anything in my life, ever. Not once.'

Apart from stealing my entire family from me, I'm tempted to say, but manage to control the urge to speak my truth, Dr Galanis style. 'But how did the police even know the money had been transferred?'

'You remember I told you about George, the other trustee on the board?'

'Your friend George? The detective?'

'That's him. Well, he received an anonymous tip-off.'

'What? On email? Like the sex tape?'

Shelly shakes her head. 'No. Whoever told him called him directly at the station on Friday morning.'

'Really? Why would anyone want to do that?'

'I have no idea. But like you say, after what happened with the sex tape, I'm starting to think that someone has it in for me.' She fixes me with a cold stare.

I get a shiver down my spine as a shot of adrenaline

surges round my body, and for a split second I'm convinced she can see straight through my act and is looking directly at Olivia. I swallow the lump that's suddenly stuck in my throat as subtly as I'm able to. 'Surely not.'

'Well, why else would all this be happening?'

For obvious reasons I'm keen to move as far away from this theory as quickly as possible. I'm also desperate to return her attention to the specifics of what happened with the police. 'So did George arrest you?'

'No. First up it was a couple of uniformed officers who came to the house on Saturday to ask me some questions and then two plain closed detectives turned up on Monday—'

'Wow. That was quick.' I'm genuinely surprised by the speed of events. 'I didn't think the police moved at that kind of speed these days with all the cutbacks.'

She lets out an ironic chuckle. 'That's down to George and the fact he was trying to do me a favour. Because he had to suspend me from the charity, he said he didn't want it hanging over me for months on end. I think he believed me when I said it was a glitch and was keen to get it all straightened out. That way I could get back to working with Autumn Hearts as quickly as possible. So he pulled a few favours from his opposite number in the Fraud Squad to get the case expedited.'

I offer a concerned nod, again trying my best to hide my inner glee. My plan could not have worked any better. 'So what actually happened? When they arrested you, I mean.'

She pauses before replying, and it's clear she's struggling to keep the tears at bay again. 'Like I said, they called here on Monday lunchtime and asked if they could come in. I was feeding Alfie at the time and a bit distracted, so I let them in without even asking what they wanted. I came back through here to finish up giving him his lunch, and as soon as they got into the kitchen, the lead detective came straight out with it. Telling me he was arresting me for fraud by abuse of position, under the Fraud Act.'

'I really can't believe that.' And I mean it.

'He put me in handcuffs and carted me off to the police station in the city.'

'Handcuffs? You're kidding.' Glorious.

A single tear trickles down her left cheek.

'And what happened to Alfie? You said he was here with you at the time.'

'My mum came round straight away. Thank God she was available otherwise they were threatening to take him into care.'

'I can't believe that.' Again, I mean it. 'And what about Nick? Where was he when all this was going on?'

'In a meeting at work. Mum called him and let him know what was happening while I was en route to the station. He came home as soon as he heard.'

'Wow. That must have been quite a shock for him.'

'Seriously.' She shakes her head. 'You can't imagine how horrific it's been for all of us.'

I take a sip of my coffee to help conceal the grin that threatens to break out across my face. It's cooled down a bit now, which allows me to take a few large mouthfuls while keeping the mug in front of my mouth. 'So what happened at the station?' I ask when I eventually regain some control.

'They locked me in a cell for two hours while they sorted me out with a solicitor. Honestly, Jess. It was terrifying.'

For the next five minutes, I sit in relative, yet gleeful silence as Shelly talks me through the gory details of the events that played out while she was under arrest. The heated conversations with her solicitor, her reluctance to offer a no-comment response to questions, and the absolute icing on the cake – the fact she could face up to ten years in prison if convicted. I still can't believe my plan has worked so well. I knew if George took my tip-off seriously, it would cause her major problems with the charity and damage her reputation – which I hoped in turn would be very detrimental to her state of mind – but I could never have imagined she could end up in prison for the next ten years. This whole thing is utterly brilliant.

'So have they charged you?' I ask when she's finally finished.

'Not yet. DC Sherratt said they need more time to investigate. So they bailed me.'

'My God,' I mutter. 'I'm so sorry you've had to go through all this.'

She closes her eyes for a few seconds and bites her bottom lip, while all the time her right leg bounces rapidly. Further evidence that she's struggling to regulate her emotions, something I'm keen to seize upon. 'And how has it affected your anxiety and your OCD?'

'It's off the scale,' she shoots back. 'I'm really struggling with all of it – and my intrusive thoughts have been horrendous.'

'In what way?'

'Horrific thoughts about harming Alfie.' She glances to the ceiling above her head. 'He's having a nap at the moment, thank God. Because whenever I'm around him, I can't stop myself thinking about horrific scenarios that involve him.'

'Oh no.' I make a point of allowing my shoulders to visibly sag to demonstrate Jess's disappointment on her behalf. 'And you were doing so well with that over the last few weeks.'

'Honestly, they're out of control, and I'm having them constantly. And not just about Alfie.' She glances at me coyly now. 'Please don't judge me, Jess, but I even thought about turning around and throwing the red-hot pot at you when I was pouring your coffee.'

'Wow.' I raise my eyebrows. 'Well, I'm glad you didn't do that.'

'Please believe me.' Shelly's voice is barely a whisper. 'It's the absolute last thing I would ever want to do. I just cannot control the thoughts.' She shakes her head. 'I'm not sure how much more of this I can take.'

'You poor thing. That must be awful.' I step off the stool and draw her into a hug as Jess while all the time Olivia wants to dance a jig.

As she hugs me back, the tears begin to flow again.

'There, there,' I say softly. 'Everything's going to be OK.'

A minute or so later she pulls away and grabs a tissue from a box sitting on the countertop before dabbing her eyes and wiping her snotty nose. 'If it weren't for Nick, I really think I'd have gone under, mentally. He's been amazing.'

I make a deliberate point of glancing around the big open-plan kitchen. 'I take it he's at work just now?'

'Yeah.'

'Would he not be better working from home at the moment? So you're not on your own quite so much?' The reality is I'm delighted he's left her to stew in her own shit, but once again, my role as Jess requires me to appear as concerned as possible.

'We did talk about it,' she replies. 'But his business is really under pressure at the moment, financially. If he can find some new investors it would relieve a lot of the financial pressure on us both. And that means being out on the road, drumming up potential leads.'

I nod as if I care when obviously I don't.

'In fact, he's away next week for a couple of days at a trade show in Edinburgh, which I'm absolutely dreading.'

'And does he really have to be there?' I ask as I slip back onto the stool.

'Yes. It's a huge property developer conference with people coming in from all over Europe. He has a stand there, which he's already paid for. It was a couple of grand, so as much as I don't want to be left on my own, I'd hate for him to waste the money or miss out on the opportunities it might bring.'

'Well, as long as it's not just a jolly in a posh hotel for him.'

Shelly shakes her head. 'He's there on his own, so it's definitely not a jolly. And the Regency Airport Hotel is decent, but not posh by any means. Plus, according to Nick, a lot of the networking gets done in the bar the night before. So if he wants to stand the best chance of landing some investment, he really needs to get as much face time with the dealmakers as possible.'

'I guess so.' I fold my arms across my chest. 'So what are you going to do? Are you going to be all right staying here on your own?'

'My mum's coming to stay.'

'Ah, well, that'll help, I'm sure.'

'Yeah. I'm hoping she can take up a lot of the slack with Alfie because I'm really struggling with him at the moment.'

As if on cue, the little man I've heard so much about but am still yet to meet starts crying in the room above us, and as he does, Shelly's chin drops to her chest. 'Oh God, that's all I need right now,' she mutters under her breath.

Without thinking, I'm up on my feet. 'I'll go,' I say cheerfully.

Shelly's face softens. 'Really? You don't mind?'

'Not at all. I'm only too happy to help. So where am I headed?'

'Top of the stairs, small room at the end of the landing.'

A minute later I march towards Alfie's bedroom door and the source of the continued crying with a growing sense of anticipation. I'm intrigued to know what this kid actually looks like in the flesh, having only ever seen photos of him on his mum's phone and Facebook account.

As I push open the door, his crying gets even louder, and he comes into view in his cot. I can see his beetroot-red face scrunched up into a knot, intently focused on sharing his considerable displeasure with the world. Moving next to his bed, I bend down and pick him up, holding him in front of me for a few seconds as I take him in. He's super cute with chubby cheeks and a chunky little body, dressed in blue joggers and a little yellow T-shirt. And he smells delicious – like how I remember my brother, Dan, smelling when he was about the same age.

Holding him in my left arm, I scoop up his dummy from the small mattress and place it into his mouth. 'Sh, sh, sh, sh, sh,' I whisper in a soothing voice, tapping his bum with my right hand – just like I saw my mum do with Dan when I was a kid. 'You're OK. You're not on your own anymore. I'm here. You're safe.'

Amazingly he begins to settle almost immediately, and I cannot stop the wide grin that lights up my face. 'Who's a gorgeous boy, hey? You are, aren't you? Yes you are, yes you are.'

A few minutes later, after more bum tapping and baby talk sees him settle completely, I make my way carefully back downstairs to the kitchen. As I walk into the large open space, Shelly's gaze locks on Alfie contently lying in my arms, the dummy bouncing lightly his mouth, his eyes half closed as he drifts off back to sleep.

'You're a natural,' she whispers with a smile. 'You can come again.'

I look down at the little man nestled in my arms and then back at Shelly, the smile on my face a match for hers. 'I'd like that,' I whisper back. 'Very much.'

CHAPTER THIRTY-THREE

OLIVIA

I eventually left Shelly's around 1 p.m. after helping to feed Alfie his lunch while she took a shower and, in her own words, attempted to 'stop looking like the wreck of the *Hesperus*'. The sun was high in the sky on another warm day as I headed out the door, and with nowhere to be this afternoon, I decided to take a walk around Tynemouth village, which was surprisingly busy given it was a Wednesday lunchtime. I grabbed a ham and cheese sandwich and a latte from the deli on the high street, which I ate overlooking the sea before wandering back to my car around three. 'What a place this must be to live,' I muttered as I opened the door to my battered old Honda and slipped into the driver's seat.

Soon after, I found myself gazing out the car window at Shelly's large, three-storey house as I drove past on my way back to my shitty little shared house in Fenham. The juxtaposition of how our two lives have played out since Dan's death was never more evident or in stark contrast.

With my initial excitement at hearing Shelly's significant woes now almost completely dissipated, my mood on the drive back grew progressively darker as I thought of everything that Shelly still has compared to all the things I've lost over the years. By the time I got home, I was in a foul state, angry and agitated with absolutely zero desire to bump into any of my so-called housemates. So instead I rushed straight up to my room, locked the door behind me and, after jumping on the bed, opened up my laptop.

And that's where I sit now, scrolling through Shelly's Facebook, clicking through her photos as I continue to compare her privileged and blessed life to my pitiful excuse for an existence.

In particular I cannot stop looking at the images in the album called Alfie. He made such an unexpected impression on me this afternoon. Not since Dan died have I felt anything remotely close to the connection we made today, and I'm struggling to understand how or why he impacted me so much.

Scanning through the vast array of photos of him – which seem to capture every moment of his life from the day he was born to the last photo posted just a few weeks ago and pictures of him sitting in the sand on the beach in Tynemouth – I feel a sense of warm-heartedness I'd almost forgotten was possible. His chubby cheeks, those big brown eyes and thick head of hair, and the chunky little legs all remind me of Dan as a baby – bringing back memories of helping Mum look after him when he was about the same age. Wonderful times that have so often been too painful to relive.

Tears well as I close my eyes and allow myself to remember my gorgeous little brother, as well as the fun times we shared together as a family while he was still alive. God, I miss that life so much.

I blow my cheeks as I open my eyes and decide it's probably best to stop torturing myself. Clicking back onto Shelly's profile page, I decide instead to take a closer look at Nick. Her so-called saviour and the man she claims is keeping her afloat while her world crashes down around her. I soon find him listed as one of her friends and click through to his profile page now.

Recent photos are limited to just a few of the family, but he does seem to have been quite a prolific poster in his younger years. Like Shelly, it seems he did quite a bit of travelling in the late 2000s. Looking at the pictures of him – primarily shirtless in various sunny locations around the world – it's fair to say he was a very handsome man back in the day. And even now, judging by the more recent photos on his profile – posted about a year ago – it's clear he still looks after himself. With his thick, salt-and-pepper hair and rugged jawline, he has the look of a young George Clooney, and in my opinion, he's far too good for Shelly.

I'm keen to know exactly what he looks like now, so I jump out of Facebook and into Google. It doesn't take me long to find an article featuring him, written by one of the North East business magazines about six months ago. Scanning through the article, I find various images of him captured outside a selection of revamped industrial properties that his firm, NE1 Developments Ltd., have renovated in the last five years. He stares out at the camera, looking every inch the handsome, high-flying property tycoon in his smart, fitted grey suit, matched with his chunky gold watch and movie-star smile.

Given that Shelly shared the fact Nick's business is under pressure at the moment, I'm intrigued to find out how successful it was in the first place. I wonder if perhaps the big house and the flash cars only exist in a world of keeping up with the Joneses and heavy borrowing. It's simple enough to find out, and a few minutes later, after locating his business accounts on the Companies House website, I read through last year's accounts filing. Looking at the numbers for NE1 Developments Ltd., it's evident that the business, until last year at least, was doing very well indeed. If what Shelly has told me rings true, it does seem that it's only because one of his investors went bust without paying what he owed that Nick's having any money issues at all. Ruggedly handsome and good at business? Nick Walker really is quite the catch. Which begs the question of how plain-Jane Shelly managed to snare the man she credits as being her rock, her best friend and, since the sex tape I created for her, her reinvigorated lover.

However it happened, after listening to her today, one thing is so obvious to me now: Nick's support is the only thing standing between Shelly and a total nervous breakdown. So if I'm going to make her complete unravelling a reality, then it's clear I need to take his support away from her. And thanks to our conversation at her house today, Shelly has gifted me the perfect way to do it.

CHAPTER THIRTY-FOUR

OLIVIA

This evening's performance will require a slightly different wardrobe to what I'm used to. Because I'm not customer-facing, I normally just wear jeans and a T-shirt or hoodie to work, but tonight I need something a little smarter, more woman-on-a-business-trip kind of vibe. Thankfully, half an hour in Primark was all it took to pick out an outfit that will help me blend right in with the crowd at the Regency Airport Hotel in Edinburgh.

As Shelly suggested, the place is a couple of minutes' drive from Edinburgh Airport and home to the European Property Developer Trade Convention for the next two days. The hotel itself is smart enough, and the ground floor comprises a large, light and airy lobby, with a connecting bar and restaurant to the right. The rooms themselves are spread across three storeys from the ground level up to the second floor.

After leaving the Honda in the far corner of the expansive car park, away from all the company BMWs, Audis and Jaguars, I make my way to the hotel reception, dragging my freshly purchased rolling suitcase-cum-briefcase behind me. It looks as good as any of the more expensive Swiss-made brands, but only cost £20. I'm wearing what I imagine to be a good likeness of a travelling business outfit, smart black boots, grey trousers, matched with a white shirt and finished off with a black blazer. All purchased for under a hundred and fifty quid on my trip to Primark this morning. My hair is tied back in a ponytail, and the whole ensemble is finished off with a pair of metal-framed, clear-glass spectacles.

As I stand in line waiting to check in, I catch a glimpse of myself in the floor-to-ceiling mirror fixed to the wall of reception to my left, and can't help but smile. Jess looks good in business clothes.

A few minutes later, it's my turn to check in. As I step forward, the pretty red-headed receptionist, whose name tag states she's called Olga, flashes me a wide smile filled with perfectly straight teeth. 'Good afternoon,' she says in a thick Eastern European accent. 'How are you today?'

'I'm good,' I say, and feel it.

'Are you checking in?'

'Yes, please. Jess Morton.' This is fun.

She taps into her keyboard for a few seconds before finding my booking. 'You are staying with us for one night. Is that correct?'

'Yes.'

'And the room has been prepaid.'

'That's right.'

'Would you like to add breakfast to your booking?'

'No, thank you.' I glance around the lobby. 'Just the room is fine.'

'And would you like to leave a credit card for any extras in the bar or restaurant?' she asks.

'No need. I'll pay cash,' I reply, and for good reason too. I want to leave as little digital footprint here as possible.

Olga turns her gaze to her computer screen.

'By the way,' I cut back in, 'would it be possible to get a room near my boss, Nick Walker? It's probably booked under NE1 Developments Ltd.'

She nods lightly as she goes in search of his booking, which she soon finds. 'He hasn't checked in yet, but I can put you both at the far end of the second floor. Is that OK?'

I smile widely. 'Sounds perfect.'

Olga spends the next few minutes tapping into the computer as she processes the details of my booking and eventually presents me with two key cards in a little hotel branded envelope. She circles my room number with her pen. 'So you're in room 247 on the second floor. Mr Walker is 246, opposite.' She points to my left. 'The lifts are through that arch, and the cards in the wallet activate the fob to get into your room.'

'Thank you,' I say as I grab my keys – then suddenly catch myself. 'Oh, and if you do speak to Mr Walker when he checks in, could you keep the fact I'm here to yourself? He's not expecting me, and I'm hoping to surprise him.'

'Of course.'

'Perfect,' I reply before grabbing my trolley case and striding confidently towards the elevator. It's time to get up to my room and transform Jess from travelling businesswoman to Jess the fully loaded weapon.

CHAPTER THIRTY-FIVE

OLIVIA

It's just after 5 p.m. when I get into my room. When we spoke the other day, Shelly told me Nick would be setting up his exhibition stand most of the afternoon. Based on that, I figure he's unlikely to make it down to dinner for at least a couple of hours, which gives me a decent amount of time to prepare.

After laying my outfit for the evening on the bed, which includes matching blue silk underwear, I have a long hot soak in the bath, where I make sure to shave my legs and under my arms, as well as trimming my pubic hair into a neat little strip. Grooming on this kind of level is not something I can be bothered to do ordinarily, but tonight I'm pulling out all the stops to give myself the best chance of success.

After slipping into my underwear, which includes a push-up bra, I pull on a pair of black stay-up pantyhose before pulling up my charcoal pencil skirt, which fits perfectly around my curves and makes my bum look incredible – even if I do say so myself. A cream silk camisole is next, and I finish off the outfit with a matching cotton shirt. Inspecting myself in the full-length mirror, I make a few adjustments to my bra – to really make my cleavage pop, and whilst I've not been blessed with massive breasts, my 34Cs look pretty impressive tonight.

The final touches involve a pair of black stiletto shoes and a flash of bright red lipstick that really accentuates my full-bodied lips – one of my favourite features that I inherited from my mother.

With one more lingering look at myself in the mirror, I feel stage-ready, and after slipping my phone into my purse, I leave my room and make my way to the bar.

As the lift doors open, I'm struck by the sudden increase in volume in the lobby area, and the previously quiet space of this afternoon has transformed into a bustling, vibrant area filled with hordes of people chatting, laughing and joking all around me. For a split second I begin to lose my nerve, and a sudden sense of panic washes over me; I don't belong here, and all these people will see right through me. I'm half tempted to run back up to my room, pack my bag and get the hell out of here, but I remind myself I'm here to do a job. And that job needs doing *tonight* because I may never get the opportunity again. Remembering my old drama teacher's advice about handling stage fright, I take a couple of deep breaths and recite my favourite quote from Samantha Morton in my head – *I'm an actor. That's what I'm gifted at. It's what makes me breathe.*

A minute later, I'm fully focused on the task in hand.

Wandering through the lobby, I make my way into the bar where as yet there's no sign of Nick. After ordering myself a small glass of rosé, I take a seat at a high table towards the back of the room, which gives me full sight of anyone coming in or out of the area.

Sitting on the stool, I cross my right leg over my left knee and settle down to wait for Nick.

After ten minutes and no sign of him, I pull my phone out and decide to take another look at the most recent article I found on Google, just to ensure I'm looking for the right person. Staring down at the screen, I'm once again struck by the rugged good looks of the man smiling back at me. In fact, I'd go so far as to say I think he's pretty damn gorgeous.

Draining my glass, I set it down on the table in front of me.

'Can I get you a refill?' says a man's voice to my left.

I break away from my phone and come face to face with what can only be described as your stereotypical, wide-boy salesman, complete with a poorly fitting shiny grey suit, slicked-back dark hair, and mahogany sun-bed tanned skin. To top it all off he smiles at me with tobacco-stained teeth as he holds out his hand. 'Jonny Swallow.'

I can just about bring myself to smile thinly at him before turning my attention back to my phone without saying a word. Sadly he doesn't take the hint.

'I'm with Maxfit Concrete. Who are you with?'

I exhale loudly as I turn to face him again. 'My boyfriend.'

'Really?' He makes a point of looking at the empty chair next to me. 'He must be very small.'

I open my mouth to speak, but before I can say anything, my heart jumps in my chest as I spot Nick walking into the bar on the other side of the room. 'You must be a comedian,' I say as I nod in the direction of the entrance. 'Actually, he's just walked in.' I slip off the high stool. 'Well, enjoy your night,' I add, and without waiting for a response, start walking in the direction of Nick, who looks very dashing in his crisp white shirt and blue suit pants.

By the time I reach him, he's standing alone at the bar with his back to the room, and up close, I can see for myself just how tall and broad he is. 'Excuse me,' I say softly.

He turns to face me. 'Sorry.' His raised brow gives him a slight look of confusion. 'Are you talking to me?'

I'm struck by just how good looking he is in the flesh, better than any photo I've seen of him so far. I make myself appear small – which is not difficult standing so close to his large frame – then tilt my head backwards slightly in the direction of where I've just come from. 'Is there a ridiculously tanned guy looking over at us?' I ask.

Nick glances over my shoulder for a second. 'Greasy-looking fella with black hair?'

'That's the one.'

'Yeah. He's staring right at us.'

I smile coyly. 'He's been pestering me all night. And well, I'm sorry to ask, but would you mind pretending to be my boyfriend for a few minutes?'

Nick recoils and frowns. 'You want me to pretend to be your boyfriend?'

I offer an anxious nod. 'Yes.'

The frown remains. 'And why would I want to do that?'

I bite my bottom lip and wince apologetically. 'Because I might have just told him you were.'

He flinches. 'Well, that's not something that usually happens to me at events like this.'

'Sorry. He wouldn't leave me alone, and when I saw you

walking in on your own, I just blurted it out. It was the quickest way I could think to get rid of him.'

Nick looks over in the direction of my supposed stalker again for a few seconds before turning his attention back to me. 'I'm not sure it's something my wife would approve of.'

'I know. And I'm sorry to put you on the spot, but you'll really be helping me out. He's a total sleaze.'

He glances at Jonny Swallow for a second time now before shaking his head softly. 'Why not. So, what would you like to drink, *darling*?' he says loudly for effect.

I let out a sigh of relief and smile widely. 'A small rosé, if that's OK?'

Nick turns to the barman. 'Can I get a rosé for the lady and a pint of Guinness for me?'

'Thank you,' I say, placing my hand on his arm. 'You've done me a massive favour.'

He nods nonchalantly. 'Happy to help.'

Silence descends as we wait for the drinks to be delivered.

He turns towards me again now. 'I'm Nick, by the way.'

'That's a strange surname,' I reply quick as a flash. 'Is it German?'

His brow furrows now, and he looks confused. 'I'm not following you?'

'"Nick By-the-way,"' I say, adding a deliberately nervous giggle. 'It's a strange name.'

It takes a second for the joke to land, and then he finally allows himself to smile – which is a relief, as I thought I'd lost him for a second there. 'Sorry.' I lean ever-so-gently into him with my shoulder. 'Ignore me. I have a strange sense of humour.'

He nods. 'No. No, it's funny. I was just being a bit slow on the uptake. It's been a long day.'

'I'm Jessica, by the way,' I say softly. 'But everyone calls me Jess.'

'Well, it's a pleasure to meet you, Jess,' he replies as he passes me my wine.

'Thank you.' I grab the glass. 'The pleasure's all mine.'

CHAPTER THIRTY-SIX

OLIVIA

'Has he gone?' I ask in an attempt to keep Nick talking.

Nick slips onto the barstool in front of him as he glances across. 'Looks like it.'

'In that case, I'll leave you alone.' I sigh before flashing my best sad smile.

Thankfully, he takes the bait. 'You don't have to leave on my account.'

'Are you not meeting someone?'

He shakes his head as he takes a mouthful of his Guinness. 'No. I'm here on my own this evening.'

'Me too.'

'Well then.' He shrugs. 'Even more reason for you to pull up a stool in that case.'

'Are you sure you don't mind?'

'No. You'll actually be doing me a favour. Gives me a legitimate excuse to avoid doing any proper networking this evening. I hate it at the best of times, and with a baby at home, I'm absolutely knackered tonight. Besides, I'm expecting a full day of client schmoozing tomorrow, so I have zero interest in doing any just now.'

'Are you here for the conference?' I ask as I slide onto the stool next to him.

'Yup. I have a stand at the expo. Just finished setting it up before I came in here.'

'Who are you here with?'

'My own firm, NE1 Developments Ltd.' He reaches into the top pocket of his shirt and passes me a business card. 'This is me, here.'

I glance down at the card and pretend the information I'm looking at is brand new to me. 'Nick Walker, CEO?' I raise my eyebrows for effect. 'A big cheese, huh?'

He chuckles. 'Hardly. I'm pretty much a one-man band these days, apart from my PA, Linda, that is. I subcontract everything else out. Much less hassle and far more tax efficient that way. What about you? Are you conferencing, too?'

I take a sip of my wine. 'No. I have a meeting at the airport tomorrow. I just happened to pick the busiest hotel in the area by mistake.'

'And what do you do?'

'I'm in finance. Well, banking, really. IT systems for finance in the main.'

'And do you like it?'

'No, not really,' I say before laughing loudly. 'It's pretty bloody boring, actually.'

He laughs along. 'Well, at least you're honest.'

'My passion is acting,' I add. 'But I think I might have missed my window on that one.'

'And what makes you say that?'

'I'm too old now.'

He waves me away. 'Nonsense. A smart-looking girl like you, I'm sure you'd look great on the big screen.'

I allow myself to blush and smile softly. 'Thank you.'

Silence descends again as we both savour our drinks.

As he's on his own, I'm not sure how long he intends to stay at the bar. I need to keep him engaged. 'I don't suppose you know if the food is any good here?' I ask.

He shrugs. 'If the chef is the same as last year, then it's certainly not going to make it into the Michelin guide, but it's not too bad, I guess.'

'I was just wondering whether or not to give the restaurant a go.'

Nick takes another mouthful of his Guinness but remains silent.

I continue, 'I hate eating on my own. I feel like such a loser.'

'Do enough of these conferences and you eventually get used to it,' he says.

'I don't suppose you fancy some food, do you?'

He turns his face to mine, his left eyebrow raised. 'With you?'

I offer a faint smile. 'Yeah. Why not? Beats eating alone.'

Nick appears to be considering the offer.

'I promise I'll behave,' I tease. 'Mrs Walker can sleep easy tonight. I'll have my dinner and go straight to my room afterwards.' I put three fingers to my temple. 'Scout's honour.'

He glances right towards the busy restaurant and then back at me a second later. 'Well, I am quite hungry.'

'That settles it, then,' I say firmly as I slip off the stool. 'I'll go and see if they have a table free.' Without waiting for a response, I march off towards the restaurant, returning a few minutes later with the good news. 'We're in luck. They have one walk-in table left.'

'Well, it looks as if it was meant to be,' he says through a slight grin before draining the remainder of his drink.

A few minutes later the hostess escorts us to our semicircular booth in a dark corner of the busy restaurant. The air is thick with chatter, and looking around the tables, it's clear a lot of alcohol has been flowing in the hotel this evening. As we take our seats, our waiter appears, a short man called Eric with an accent similar to the receptionist. He explains that we'll find the specials for this evening on a small chalkboard sitting in the middle of the table, before promising to come back in a few minutes to take our order. A moment later he's gone.

I'm keen to capitalise on Nick's earlier comment about me being smart looking and decide to turn up the heat. 'I think that waiter thought we were a couple, you know?' I pretend to be focused on the menu. 'Either that, or he thinks we're having an affair.'

'Pah,' Nick scoffs as he picks up his own menu. 'I doubt it. I'm old enough to be your dad.'

'Nonsense!' I shoot back. '*I'm* twenty-seven, and *you* can't be a day over forty. So unless you were thirteen when you had me...'

'Forty?' He raises his eyebrows. 'That's generous, but I'll take it.'

I drop my menu and flash him a quizzical look. 'You're not older than forty, are you?'

'Sadly I am.' He sighs whimsically. 'Closer to fifty, in fact.'

I recoil. 'No way. Seriously?'

'Forty-eight.'

I eye him up and down. 'Well, you look a lot younger. That's for sure.'

He chuckles. 'Like I said before, generous, but I'll take it.'

For the first time I really notice the dimples in his cheeks, and I don't know if it's the rosé wine – or just the fact I'm getting to know him a little better – but I'm really starting to find him intoxicatingly handsome.

Silence descends as we turn our attention back to the menus, and after a few minutes have passed, Eric returns as promised, pad and paper in hand. Nick orders the fillet steak blue – claiming it's the only way to get a rare steak in a restaurant like this – and I order the goat cheese risotto.

'Are we having wine this evening?' asks Eric as he collects the menus.

Nick glances across at me. 'I wouldn't mind some red if you're up for it? Or you can stick to your rosé if you'd prefer.'

'Red is good with me,' I say, confident that means he'll order by the bottle as opposed to the glass, which will play into my plans.

'Great. In that case, we'll have a bottle of the Châteauneuf-du-Pape. And a bottle of sparkling water for the table.'

Eric nods before spinning on his heel and heading off towards the kitchen.

'Châteauneuf-du-Pape?' I nod. 'I didn't think they'd serve premium French wine in an airport hotel.'

'You know your reds, then?' he asks.

I wrinkle my nose. 'Not especially. A guy I saw for a while bought a bottle of it to try to impress me on our first date.'

'And did it? Impress you?'

'Not really. The fact he felt the need to tell me it cost

forty quid a bottle throughout the entirety of the meal kind of ruined the effect for me.'

Nick smiles. 'Well, it's only thirty quid here, so I'm afraid my wine choice is even less impressive than his.'

'Yeah, but you're *much* better looking than he was.' I smile bashfully as my words land. Being so up front with him is a risky strategy this early on, but one I'm willing to take.

He laughs. 'I should come here more often.'

Eric returns now with the wine and pours two large glasses before leaving the bottle on the table and making himself scarce once again.

Nick takes a large mouthful and sighs loudly, his whole body appearing to visibly soften as he places his glass back down on the table. Next he rubs his face with his hands, causing his cheeks to redden.

I watch him for a moment as I take a small sip of my wine. 'Are you OK? You look a bit fed up, if you don't mind me saying.'

'I'm just tired, I guess,' he replies. 'A baby who never sleeps through will do that to you, though.'

I return my wine to the table. 'You look like you could do with a little pick-me-up.'

His eyes bulge slightly. 'Er, no, no.' He waves me away. 'I'm not into that stuff.'

I know exactly what he's getting at, but I feign innocence. 'What stuff are you talking about?'

Nick glances nervously left and right before leaning forward and speaking in a conspiratorial whisper. 'You know. *Cocaine.*'

I recoil for effect. 'Coke?' I whisper back before bursting out laughing. 'I'm not talking about drugs, you daft thing. No. I have something else in mind completely.'

He looks slightly confused as I slip out of the booth. 'I'll be back in a tick,' I say, and then make my way to the bar.

Five minutes later I return to the table, holding a cocktail in each hand. 'Here, try this.' I slide one of the glasses in front of him. 'Espresso martini.'

He eyes the glass with suspicion for a few seconds. 'What's in it?'

'You've never had an espresso martini?'

'No. Never. I don't really drink spirits. They make me do stupid things.'

Music to my ears, I want to say, but instead I take a sip of my own cocktail as if to prove it's safe to drink. 'It's just vodka, espresso and coffee liqueur. Try it, it's really good, and it'll give you a boost.'

Nick picks up the glass and takes a tentative mouthful before eventually nodding. 'That *is* good. Really good.'

I smile. He has no idea there's a triple measure of vodka hiding in all that coffee flavour. I sip mine for a moment, which contains no vodka at all. I need to keep my wits about me, after all.

Ten minutes later, with the cocktails despatched and Nick evidently much more relaxed, Eric appears with our meals, which look and smell delicious.

As we work our way through the food and the wine flows, we talk about a wide array of topics I really hadn't expected from this conversation tonight: music, travel, food, politics and eventually our favourite films and movie stars. It's a thoroughly absorbing exchange and really helps me see Nick less as Shelly's husband and more as the charming, funny and very intelligent man he actually is. I've said it before, but he really is one helluva catch, and one who's getting more alluring by the minute.

But the most interesting thing about the whole conversation is that as the wine flows and Nick appears to be getting more inebriated, all mention of his wife and son stops. And what's more, he makes no attempt to find out if I have a boyfriend either, which I find totally fascinating given the fact that Shelly paints a picture of them as a couple who are virtually bulletproof in their togetherness. Are they really as strong as she thinks? Well, with a bit of luck, we'll soon find out, I muse.

Sometime later, as Eric begins to gather up the empty plates around us, Nick pours the last few drops of wine into my glass. 'Looks like we're empty. That's a shame.'

'As it's *only* thirty quid,' I say with a wink, 'maybe you should order another one?'

He checks his watch. 'Well, it is only half ten, isn't it? Would you like some more?'

He's clearly had enough to drink already, but Nick in less control of his faculties is exactly what I want right now. 'Yeah,' I say with a playful shrug. 'Why not?'

He nods heavily, then turns to Eric, wiggling the bottle in front of him. 'Another one of these, please, buddy.' His words are already starting to show signs of slurring.

'Of course, sir,' replies Eric as he picks up the empty plates and heads back to the kitchen.

For the next hour, as the restaurant slowly begins to empty out, we remain locked in conversation, and the wine continues to flow – mainly and deliberately so on my part – into Nick's glass. And by the time Eric arrives with the bill in hand just as the restaurant staff are beginning to close up for the night, I decide now is the time to make my next move. 'What's the damage?' I ask before taking a sip of wine.

Nick's eyes narrow as he glances down at the cheque,

blinking hard as if trying to focus. 'Don't worry. This is my treat. On the business.'

I shake my head. 'No, come on. You don't have to do that.'

'Yes, I do. I was the one ordering the expensive plonk, after all.' He leans back in the booth and smiles. 'And besides, I've really enjoyed your company.'

I lock eyes with him as I hold my wine glass to my mouth for a long moment. 'Me too,' I say, before allowing my glass to slip so that the remaining red wine spills down onto my shirt. 'Oh shit!' I say, slamming the glass down on the table.

Nick appears to jump in his seat.

I stare down at my wine-stained chest. 'Look at the state of me. I'm such a klutz.'

He wets a napkin with the bottled water and passes it clumsily across the table. 'I know cream soda works on stains. Maybe sparkling water will do the same?'

I glance up at him and smile. He's fallen hook, line and sinker into my trap, and for the next couple of minutes I pretend to be focusing all my attention on my shirt as I rub the soaking napkin over my chest. By the time I'm finished, the wet material around my right breast is almost translucent, and *somehow* I've 'accidentally' managed to unhook a couple of buttons to leave even more of my cleavage exposed. I lift my eyes to find him staring at my breasts, and when he catches my eye, his face reddens, and he looks away.

Got him.

'Well, I think it's time I went to bed,' I say sheepishly.

'Yeah.' He clears his throat as he slips out of the booth. 'I should really go see the cashier about the bill.'

Whilst he's gone, I make a few more adjustments to my

shirt to maximise my assets even further and touch up my lipstick.

He returns to the booth a few minutes later and remains standing on slightly unsteady feet.

'Can I leave the tip?' I ask.

'No need. I sorted it.'

It's my turn to slide out of the seat now. 'Well, thank you once again for a lovely evening.'

'And you.'

'Walk me to my room?' I say, trying to sound as ambivalent as possible.

He nods and seems a little unsure of himself.

'I'm on the second floor,' I say.

'Me too.'

'Well, that's handy.'

He gestures towards the exit. 'After you.'

The short ride in the elevator passes in silence as we both look up at the illuminated floor numbers above the door. When we reach floor two and the doors open, he once again gestures for me to take the lead.

I'm happy to do so and make sure to walk far enough in front of him so that he gets a good look at my ass in the tight-fitting pencil skirt as I shimmy and shake my way down the long, dimly lit corridor.

A few minutes later, I eventually stop outside room 247. 'Well, this is me,' I whisper into the silent space as I reach into my purse for my room key.

'You're kidding me.' He thumbs to his left. 'I'm just here.'

'Well, what are the chances of that?'

He stares at me in silence now, his eyes glazed from the alcohol.

'Well, thank you again for dinner. I really enjoyed myself tonight.'

'Me too,' he replies.

I lean forward and peck him on the cheek, making sure to hold my face against his for longer than necessary, and to my delight, he doesn't pull away. I keep my cheek connected to his for a split second more before sliding back and locking my lips onto his. He doesn't resist and a moment later he's wrapping his arms around my waist and pulling me into him, kissing me passionately, his tongue interlocking with mine. I pull away just long enough to touch my key against the door with my right hand to unlock it before hooking my left hand into his waistband and dragging him with me as I shove the door open with my butt. 'It's time for dessert,' I whisper, as he follows me inside and begins ripping open my shirt.

CHAPTER THIRTY-SEVEN

OLIVIA

Through the slight gap in the door, I can hear Nick snoring softly in the bedroom as I stare at my naked reflection in the bathroom mirror. I cannot wipe the satisfied grin off my face. That was probably the best sex I've ever had, and every cell in my body is tingling. I've had orgasms before but nothing compared to what I experienced tonight. The intensity was off the scale, due in part to Nick's skills as a lover, but also the additional excitement of knowing I was tasting forbidden fruit – quite literally in this case.

My lipstick is long gone, replaced by a red hue around my mouth, and my hair looks like I've been standing in a wind tunnel, but I've never felt more sensual and sexy in my entire life. What another stellar performance as I executed the first part of tonight's plan to perfection. Now it's time to action part two.

Reaching down into the sink, I pick up Nick's used condom, which I retrieved from the waste bin in the bedroom just a few moments ago. It contains an impressive amount of his sperm, which suggests he found the whole experience as exciting as I did. Grabbing the nail scissors from my washbag, I snip a tiny tear in the end of the condom before carefully squeezing the contents out into the sink. A quick blast of water washes it away, and with the condom in hand, I carefully tiptoe back into the bedroom, where I put it back in the bin next to Nick's side of the bed. He doesn't stir, which allows me to sit down on the bed next to him. Taking in his handsome face and muscular torso as he sleeps, I'm unbelievably tempted to wake him up and go at it again, but I know that could potentially derail my plan, so I steel myself for the job in hand and shake him by the shoulder.

'Nick,' I say in an elevated whisper as I shake him again. 'Nick, I need you to wake up.'

He stirs now, his eyes blinking slowly open as he takes me in.

'Nick, I need to talk to you.'

His eyes lock on my naked breasts in front of his face, and he suddenly sits upright. 'Jess...'

I give him my best look of concern.

He glances around the room and then returns his attention to me. 'Erm... did we?'

'You don't remember?'

'It's a bit hazy.'

'That'll be the wine.' I must admit to feeling slightly offended he doesn't remember every detail in the same way I do.

He stares at me in silence.

'I think we've got a bit of a problem.'

His brow wrinkles. 'What is it?'

'I think the condom broke.'

His eyes widen like saucers as he sits to attention now. 'What?'

'I was just in the loo, and I felt something coming out of me.'

'What do you mean "you felt something"?'

I pause for effect before answering, 'Something from you.'

'As in cum?'

I nod.

'Are you sure?'

'I think so. It looked like it on the toilet paper.'

'Where's the condom?'

I look down at the bin next to the bed. 'I think you threw it in there.'

Yanking back the duvet, he jumps out of bed, naked, drops to his knees and begins rummaging through the small bin until he finds what he's looking for, pulling the condom out a moment later. Holding it up in front of his face, he inspects the end, which is clearly ruptured. 'Oh fuck. It's ripped,' he mumbles.

'Nick' – it's time to land the knockout punch – 'I'm not on the pill.'

As his gaze flips from the condom to me, his eyes look like they could literally pop out. 'You what?'

'I'm not on the pill.'

'I heard what you said,' he growls as he stands now. 'I just can't believe it. You're going to have to get the morning-after pill.'

'I'm not doing that. It's against my religion.'

He recoils, clearly perplexed. 'What are you talking about, it's against your religion?'

'I'm a Catholic,' I lie. Never was, never will be. 'And the morning-after pill is as good as having an abortion.'

'Don't be ridiculous. It just stops the sperm and egg from fertilising. It's got nothing to do with abortion.'

I shake my head sternly. 'No. I'm not doing it.'

'Well, what about sex before marriage?'

'What do you mean?' I feign innocence, but know exactly what he's getting at.

'If you're such a good Catholic, then how come you're OK with having sex before marriage? I thought it was forbidden.'

'That's different.'

'How?' The volume of his voice is bordering on shouting now.

'It just is.' I grab the bedsheet and wrap it around my chest and waist as I stand now.

'I don't fucking believe this is happening,' he grumbles.

'Will you tell your wife what happened?'

'I don't know what the fuck I'm going to do,' he growls as he pulls on his boxer shorts before bending down and gathering the rest of his clothes.

I watch on in silence as he picks up his shoes. 'I've gotta go,' he mumbles. 'I need time to think.'

As he heads for the door, I grab his business card from my purse, and just as his hand locks on the handle, I call after him. 'Hey, Nick.'

He turns to face me.

I hold the card up so he can see it clearly. 'At least I know how to find you if I *am* pregnant.'

His mouth falls open as he stares back at me.

'So I'll be seeing you,' I add with a smile.

He doesn't reply, and a second later the door closes behind him, and he's gone.

Stage two complete.

CHAPTER THIRTY-EIGHT

OLIVIA

Monday Morning

I've been at work for two hours now, and I have done absolutely nothing. I just can't seem to concentrate, and all I can think about is my night with Nick. Despite the fact it was part of my carefully orchestrated plan to take away the one thing keeping Shelly from going under completely, I have to admit to myself that from start to finish it was one of the best nights I've spent with any man for as long as I can remember. From the excitement of getting him to pretend to be my boyfriend to help fend off that goon Jonny Swallow, in the bar of the Regency, to the flirting over dinner that eventually led to the best sex of my life, everything about that night has left me feeling like a lovesick teenager, pining to see the gorgeous Nick Walker just one more time. I don't even mind that he didn't remember the sex in the same way that I did. I know he enjoyed it just as much as me. That was evident from his moans of passion at the time.

Unable to shake the image of him greedily grabbing at my breasts and backside as we went at it like a couple of honeymooners, I can't stop myself from picking up my phone and jumping onto Facebook, just like I have so many times over the weekend. As has been the case for the last few days, Nick's profile-picture album fills my screen, and I click back and forth through the photos, admiring his rugged features and muscular frame. He really is unbelievably gorgeous.

Imagine if the condom had broken, I wonder. What beautiful babies we would have made. I almost wish I'd figured out a way to stop him using protection on that night, but sadly he had insisted. He had some with him in his wallet, which I must say surprised me. I always thought condoms were the exclusive domain of single guys, not married men like Nick. Unless, of course, the image Shelly has been painting of their happy marriage is all a charade. That she and Nick are actually having issues, and he took condoms to a work conference on the off chance he might get lucky.

Is the truth that he's unhappily married and seeking out the excitement he cannot get from his plain-Jane wife maybe? I tingle excitedly at the thought of it. Because if their relationship *is* actually on the rocks, then if and when he tells her about us, I've no doubt it'll be the final nail in the coffin and will leave the door open for him and me to pick up where we left off. And despite his initial negative reaction when he found out I might be pregnant, deep down I know we had a real connection that night in Edinburgh. Something deeper than I think either of us truly appreciated in the heat of the moment.

Now I've had some time to think, what I want more than anything is to be with him again. And with some time to consider his options, maybe Nick will feel the same way too. Honestly, it's like being a teenager again, and thinking about him is all-consuming.

My mind replays the fantasy I've been having of Nick and me walking along the path that overlooks Tynemouth beach, pushing a stroller with our own little baby sitting proudly out in front. And that's when I suddenly remember something we were once told in sex education at school – that a man doesn't actually have to ejaculate to get a girl pregnant. Apparently, the liquid that comes out before the sperm, pre-cum I think they called it, can contain enough traces of sperm to fertilise a woman's eggs if you have unprotected sex, even for a short time. Which is what Nick and I did before he put on the condom at the end. What if his pre-cum had sperm in it? What if I was ovulating at the time?

I quickly click out of Facebook and go in search of an app that can track your ovulation cycle. It doesn't take long to find one, and there's a whole bunch of free options available to download. I choose the version with the highest star rating and, after registering as a user, follow the prompts to start tracking my cycle. It takes a couple of minutes to sort out, but it's worth the wait as I stare down at the results onscreen; I *was* ovulating around the time we were together in Edinburgh. Butterflies leap in my tummy. I can't believe it. What if I *am* actually pregnant?

I'm so giddy my fingers won't work properly as I type into my phone – googling the earliest stage you can check for pregnancy over the counter. According to a couple of sources online, some very sensitive tests can detect a pregnancy up to a week before your next period, which for me would be about a week away. Digging a little deeper, it turns out the early tests are only sold in the US, but are available to order online from a company called Pharma.Net. I click on the link, and it takes me straight to the page to buy the tests. Frustratingly, due to the export duty and shipping costs, they are very expensive, just under £40 for three tests, but the prize at the end of all this will be worth it. So I buy two boxes just to be on the safe side. And anyway, if I do turn out to be pregnant, I'm sure Nick will only be more than happy to pick up the tab.

After reviewing my basket, I proceed to check out and process the payment, selecting the fastest possible delivery time of '5 to 7 days'. One click later and my order is complete.

I lay my phone down and place both my hands on my belly. I'm so excited to find out if I have a baby growing inside me. Almost as much as I am to see Shelly tonight at group. I can't wait to see if her and Nick's marriage has come to an end, because hearing that news this evening would make this perfect day complete.

CHAPTER THIRTY-NINE

SHELLY

Monday Night Group

I wish I hadn't come tonight. As soon as the group members filed in around me at the start of the session, I realised I'd made a mistake. I'm struggling to stop myself from crying, and I feel sick to my stomach in a way I've never experienced before. A sickness that has overwhelmed me since Nick dropped the bombshell that he cheated on me while he was away in Edinburgh.

I had a feeling something was bothering him when he arrived home in a dark mood on Friday evening, but he just brushed me off when I asked if everything was OK. Said he was tired and wanted an early night, which I could totally understand. He's never liked networking and meeting new people, so it made sense that his head was probably a little fried.

But then on Saturday it was obvious there was something

seriously not right with him that I just couldn't put my finger on – a distance between us that I've never felt before and a level of irritation in him that I've rarely ever seen. So when he still hadn't snapped out of it come yesterday morning, I had it out with him and asked what the hell was going on. But by God, I wish I hadn't. I wish I'd never opened the door to this kind of pain.

He was remorseful, of course. Apologising profusely and saying he never meant for anything to happen. That he drank too much and lost control of himself. That it meant nothing, and he wished he could take it all back and make it all right.

All I could do was stare back at him in silence – utterly heartbroken and unable to comprehend what he had done. Fifteen years of total and unwavering trust destroyed in one night thanks to his dalliance with a tart he picked up in a bar.

Sitting here now as the session starts and the room falls silent around me, all I want to do is get up and walk out. To go home, close the blinds and lock out the world. But I can't do that because *he'll* be there, and right now I cannot stand to even look at him.

You'd have to be blind not to notice something is bothering me, so it's no surprise that Dr Galanis turns her attention to me first, especially given the fact I missed the last session and didn't explain why.

'So how are you doing, Shelly?' she asks now. 'Would you like to share anything with the group?'

I just about make eye contact as I shake my head. 'Not just now if that's OK?'

Dr Galanis offers her usual slow, deliberate nod before asking if anyone else has anything they want to talk about.

'I'd like to share something,' Jess says brightly.

'The space is yours,' replies the doctor.

I drop my gaze to the floor now, my mind numb and my heart aching.

'Is it OK to talk about positive stuff in here?' Jess's voice is brimming with excitement.

'Of course,' replies Dr Galanis. 'The group is an expression of all emotions, good and bad.'

Jess giggles as she clasps her hands together. 'Well, in that case, I've just had *the* best week.'

I glance up to see her beaming. At least someone is happy.

She continues, 'I've met a guy, and although it's really, really early days, I think he could be the one.'

'Well, that sounds positive,' says Dr Galanis in a low voice.

'Where did you meet him?' asks Polly.

'Online initially. But then we met up for dinner last week.'

The stark contrast between Jess's excitement at her newfound love versus my abject grief at the loss of mine hits me like a hammer blow. No offence to Jess, but this is the last thing I need to hear after Nick's heartbreaking confession yesterday.

'He's quite a bit older than me, which I'm sure some people might frown upon, but I don't care. I love him, and that's all that matters.'

'How old is he, if you don't mind me asking?' Claire cuts in.

'Almost fifty.'

Claire folds her arms defensively across her chest. 'So what's the age difference?'

'Twenty-two years, give or take. But it really doesn't bother me. Age is just a number, after all, and he makes me feel like I'm the only person in the world who matters. Plus' – she giggles like a lovesick schoolgirl again – 'he's absolutely gorgeous.'

Polly cuts back into the conversation now. 'Do you think part of your attraction to him might actually be *because* he's a lot older than you?'

'No.' Jess scowls slightly. 'Why would it be?'

'Because he provides a father figure for you. A replacement for your dad, maybe?'

'Not at all. He's nothing like my dad.'

'Polly makes a good point,' says Dr Galanis. 'And as exciting as new love can be, it might be prudent to consider any underlying connections that may be in play here before deciding that this man could be, as you put it, "the one".'

'There's no underlying connections in play. It's just me and him, and nothing else matters.'

'Are we going to get his name?' asks Pascal, resembling a protective father talking to his young daughter.

Jess shakes her head as she bites her bottom lip. 'I promised I wouldn't say. He's married, you see.'

Those two words are like a dagger to my heart as another wave of nausea crashes over me.

'I mean, it's over between him and his wife,' adds Jess. 'He's just waiting for the right time to leave her.'

There's no way Jess could know how much her words are hurting me tonight. Deep down, I'd love to be happy for her, but I can't. It's way too close to home, and I simply cannot stand to hear another word of it. 'I'm really sorry,' I say as I lean sideways over the arm of the chair and grab my bag. 'I'm not feeling very well, and I think I need to go home.'

Dr Galanis opens her mouth to speak, but I have no intention of engaging any further. 'Have a good night, everyone,' I say to no one in particular before heading for the door and away from Jess's nauseating love-life update.

CHAPTER FORTY

SHELLY

Who would have thought the small piece of plastic I'm holding in my hands right now could have such a significant bearing on my life at the moment. I've not been feeling myself for the last week – even before all the shit with the police and Nick's revelation, and the last time I felt this nauseous in the morning, I found out I was pregnant with Alfie.

It's been almost three minutes since I peed on the tip, and according to the instructions, the results will appear any second now.

I can't be pregnant. I simply *can't*. I just found out my husband cheated on me, I'm under investigation for fraud and facing a possible prison sentence, and mentally I'm struggling to stay afloat on a daily basis. Having another baby is just not an option.

There's movement now in the little window, and I instinctively close my eyes and pray for one single line to indicate a negative result. The alternative just doesn't bear thinking about.

Conjuring up all the courage I can muster, I open my eyes and glance down at the result. 'Oh my God,' I manage to mumble before bursting into tears.

CHAPTER FORTY-ONE

OLIVIA

Not for the first time in the last few weeks, I'm sitting at my desk and getting away with doing the absolute bare minimum at work. The main reason today being that, since that night in Edinburgh, I cannot stop thinking about Shelly and Nick and what is going on with them. Has he told her about us? Did he tell her the truth about the fact it was more than just sex – *because it clearly was* – and is he going to leave her and make room for me in his life? The questions have been going round on a loop in my head nonstop since I saw the state of Shelly in the session last night, but annoyingly, she left early, before I could find out any of the answers.

In most workplaces, I'm sure my recent lack of activity would have raised a few red flags, but thankfully at Go Finance, my boss, Sunny, is about as effective as a chocolate fire guard. He rarely checks in to see how I'm getting on with my workload. That said, however, I do have the added advantage that the job is so easy I can rattle through my task list in about half the time of my colleagues, which allows me to play catch-up as and when needed. And that's what I'll do later this week when the project I'm working on is finally due to be delivered. I reckon if I get a couple of solid hours in on Wednesday and Thursday, I can have it ready to present by close of business on Friday afternoon. And that means for the time being at least, I can indulge myself a little longer. Which I do, allowing my mind to fill with fantasies of what Shelly's tortured face might have looked like if she did actually find out the truth about her husband's infidelity.

As soon as the group finished last night, I tried calling her. I just couldn't help myself, but frustratingly, she didn't answer. I'm assuming she must have switched her phone off because it didn't even ring at the other end and instead went straight to voicemail. I tried her again a few hours later but got the same result. And when I called her this morning, it did at least ring, which would suggest her phone was back on, but much to my annoyance, it eventually went to voicemail. Honestly I could have screamed; the suspense of not knowing what's going on with her is absolutely killing me.

I decide to try her one last time on my lunch break. As soon as I hit the street outside the office, I hit redial on my phone. It connects and rings for some time before once again Shelly's recorded message kicks in, telling me she's not available right now and asking me to leave a message.

I let out a low growl as I stare down at the screen. 'Why won't you fucking answer?'

I'm tempted to tell Sunny I'm not feeling well so I can leave for the day and pay Shelly a visit at the house, but I can't risk bumping into Nick at the moment with everything up in the air between us. When I see him next, I want it to be with Shelly out of the picture or at least heading that way. And anyway, taking yet more time off for sickness probably isn't the smartest idea right now based on what happened to Janis in the digital team last year. Thanks to her appalling sickness record, HR started asking for proof from her doctor she was really sick, and I definitely don't need that kind of attention at work. Being a small, anonymous cog in the big machine suits me just fine, and I'd prefer to keep it that way.

With my phone in my hand, I wander over to the side of the river and lean against the railings, allowing my gaze to fall on the still water as it glistens in the midday sunshine.

With nothing left to lose, I decide to send Shelly a text. She probably won't answer, but it's worth a shot.

> Hi Shelly. I've been trying to get hold of you without any luck. I just wanted to check and see if you're OK. You seemed pretty upset last night, and I was worried something I said in the session may have caused it. Let me know you're all right, and if you need a chat, you know where I am. Take care. Jess. xxx

I read it aloud a couple of times just to double-check it reads the way I want it to – as her caring friend just looking out for her – as opposed to coming on too strong or acting like a stalker. When I'm satisfied it'll do the job I want it to, I press send and stare at the screen to ensure it's gone. When the little green tick icon appears next to the message in the conversation, I put the phone back in my pocket and set off along the quayside in search of some lunch.

What I want to eat, I really don't know because when my focus is totally locked on something such as this, my appetite completely disappears. But I should eat something, if only to give myself a break from thinking about Nick and Shelly for a few minutes.

As I reach the main road, I feel my phone vibrate in my pocket, and my adrenaline spikes as it does. I grab at it like a kid in a sweet shop, and my excitement grows when I see Shelly's name on-screen. Standing perfectly still, I click into the message and read aloud in a low voice.

> Hi Jess, Sorry. I can't talk right now. Things aren't good at home. I'm taking time out from everyone, so please don't be offended if I'm not answering calls or texts. Take care Shelly. X

I read the message three or four times, and all my attention is fixed on that little collection of words, 'I'm taking time out from everyone'. Does that include Nick? I'm desperate to text back and ask just that, fantasising that 'yes, because he's in love with someone else' would be her reply. As hard as it is to play it cool, that's exactly what needs to be done, and although it goes against every fibre in my being, I send the most considered response I can muster.

> Sorry to hear that. Here, as and when you're ready to talk. Jess xx.

I hit send and stay rooted to the spot for the next few minutes in case she replies. But when nothing comes back, I decide it's finally time to get that food sorted. As I continue along the footpath with a spring in my step now, I allow my thoughts to wander back to Nick and our night together. With the warm sun on my face, I smile at the thought of his thick strong hands greedily grabbing at my body as he bundled me onto the bed. I wonder what he's doing right now and whether or not he's thinking of me too.

Stopping for a moment, I click on the Safari browser on

my phone and into the tab that has remained permanently open since he left my room on Friday morning: the business news article where he looks so damn handsome. Staring down at his chiselled face, I feel a growing sense of excitement about how things could pan out between us, and not for the first time in the last few days, I feel like a lovesick teenager. He's so gorgeous. God, I really need to see him again, but in a place where I'm confident Shelly won't be. And luckily, thanks to the business card he gave me, I know exactly where that is.

CHAPTER FORTY-TWO

OLIVIA

Nick's office is located about a fifteen-minute drive from the Go Finance offices on the Quayside. So it made sense for me to take the car into work this morning. At lunchtime as soon as the clock on my computer displayed 12 p.m., I was out of my chair and on my way to the public car park just a few minutes' walk away. Not long after that, I was on the road and heading to Newcastle Business Park, which sits about three miles further along the River Tyne, east of the city centre.

Like a lot of business parks that were built in the nineties, the whole area is made up of almost identical red-brick buildings, with very little external signage. More often than not, the only way to locate a specific office is to check the large list of tenants posted on the boards at the entrance to each building's car park, and then match them with the numbers fixed above the entrance doors. After several unsuccessful attempts to find his office, I pull my car up in front of the penultimate block, and much to my relief, it suggests I'll find NE1 Developments Ltd. in unit 70, which by my reckoning is through the door in the far corner of the block.

After parking my car in one of the bays marked for visitors, I march across the car park and in through the communal entrance, where I find a set of locked double doors that are only accessible with a fob – or by buzzing through to the office you want access to. So I locate NE1 Developments on the list, key in the code and press the bell icon. It buzzes at the other end for a few seconds before a woman answers, who I assume is the PA he mentioned when we were chatting in the bar the other night. Linda, I think he said her name was.

'NE1 Developments,' she says.

I'm so excited to see him, my nerves are jangling, and it takes all my focus to keep my voice measured when I answer, 'Amazon. I have a delivery for Nick Walker.'

'We're on the second floor, just at the top of the stairs,' she says. 'I'll buzz you through.' Soon after, the double doors open to my left.

I walk through, and a minute later as I reach the top of the stairs, I can see the NE1 Developments Ltd. sign fixed to the door ahead of me. I knock once, and without waiting for a response, I step inside.

I'd place the woman sitting at the desk in front of me as being in her fifties. She's smartly dressed in a cream sleeveless shirt with close-cropped auburn hair and gold metal-framed glasses. She raises her eyebrows and looks surprised to see me. 'Sorry. I was expecting a delivery. Can I help you?' she asks.

I feign innocence and get straight to the point. 'Er, I need to speak to Nick.'

Her brow furrows as she glances at her computer screen. 'I'm sorry, do you have an appointment?'

'No. But it is urgent.'

'Can I ask what it's regarding?'

'It's personal.'

She offers a thin smile as she looks me up and down. 'Mr Walker is in a meeting at the moment. I'm afraid he can't be disturbed. Would you like me to give him a message?'

'No,' I reply sternly. 'I need to speak to Nick in person.'

Her fake smile slips a touch. 'Like I say, Mr Walker is in a meeting, so I'm afraid you've had a wasted journey. If you'd like to give me your name and number, I can see if he has any appointments later in the week.'

I look her square in the face now. 'Tell him his dinner guest from Edinburgh is here, and I'm not leaving until he comes out and speaks to me.'

She prickles, still sitting in her chair. 'Look, I really must insist—'

'Tell him I'm here right now!' I cut her off, my jaw clenching as I glare back at her.

Linda holds my gaze for a few seconds before finally relenting, and a moment later she steps up from the chair and disappears through a door to her left. As it closes behind her, the office falls silent around me, and I take in the space. It's very neat and tidy, but lacks any personal touches, which I'm sure could help clients feel more welcome. I make a mental note to suggest that to Nick, as and when the time is right.

A couple of minutes pass before the door opens, and she returns with Nick at her back – his eyes wide when he spots me. My heart flutters seeing him again in the same navy-blue suit he was wearing at the hotel in Edinburgh, and he appears to be carrying a few extra days' of stubble compared to the last time I saw him. It suits him too. So much so, in fact, he looks good enough to eat.

'I'll deal with this, Linda.' He moves quickly across the space, and before I can say anything, he bundles me back out of the office. 'What the hell are you doing here?' he says in a low whisper the moment we're alone on the landing outside.

'I needed to see you,' I reply, looking deep into his gorgeous big brown eyes.

'You can't be here,' he mutters as he grabs my elbow and begins walking me towards the stairs.

I stop and stand my ground. 'Have you told your wife about us?'

He glances towards his office door and then back at me. 'Yes.' He exhales sharply. 'Yes, I have.'

A rush of euphoria surges through my body. He *told* her. He didn't lie. What happened really *did* mean something to him. I'm over the moon, and I want to hear all the details. 'How did she take it?'

'Look, you really need to leave.'

I reach out to grab his hand, but he pulls it away, and I can see sadness in his eyes now. Clearly he feels trapped in his marriage to Shelly, which I can totally understand. She's an emotional cripple, and she relies on him for everything, but it shouldn't have to be like that. *He* needs to be happy too. It can't always be about her and what *she* wants all the time. 'You don't have to stay with her, you know. You can leave her. You can be free.'

He shakes his head. 'I don't want to leave her. She's my wife, and I love her.'

I let out an ironic chuckle. 'If you loved her that much, then how come you ended up in bed with me?'

'Sssh!' He leans in closer, his voice an agitated whisper. 'What happened between us was a mistake. I was drunk, and I let the wine get the better of me. Look, I'm sorry if you thought there was something more to it, but there wasn't. I'm married, and I have a family, and I'm going to do everything I can to try to put things right.'

I grab both his hands and stare into his eyes. 'We're meant to be together, Nick; we both know that.' Standing so close to him with his hands in mine, I can literally feel the electricity between us.

He yanks them free. 'You need to leave now, or I'm going to have to call the police.'

I can see the pain etched in his face. A desperate man trapped in a loveless marriage, wishing he could follow the same urges that led him to me in the first place. The person who truly understands him and can give him everything he desires in life. 'I'm not going to let you destroy your life like this, Nick. I won't stand by and watch you wither away and die when you can be truly happy with me.'

He straightens and runs both hands through his thick hair as he turns his back on me for a moment. Eventually he turns to face me once more. 'Just go, Jess, will you? Please just go.'

It breaks my heart to see him hurting like this, and all I want to do is pull him into a tight hug. As I take a step forward to do just that, the door opens behind him, and Linda stares out. 'Is everything OK, Nick?' she asks.

He glances to her, then focuses back on me, and I swear I can see tears welling in his eyes. 'Jess was just leaving, weren't you?'

I stare at him in silence for a few seconds, and once more I can feel his pain as if it were my own. It's clear he cannot risk showing his feelings in front of Linda, and if I'm going to help him find the freedom I believe he craves, we both need to box clever for the time being. No sense showing our hand too early when there's so much stuff still to sort out. I nod softly. 'Yeah. I'll go. For now,' I say, holding his gaze for a moment longer before turning and heading for the stairs.

Back outside a few minutes later, I walk slowly across the car park before stopping to look back at the office block behind me. And that's when I spot Nick standing at the window. He stares down at me for a few seconds before stepping away and out of sight. His standing there like that is all the proof I need. He didn't want me to leave at all, and deep down I knew that. He just had to make a good show of it in front of Linda. My butterflies return instantly, and my spine tingles with excitement. Despite what he said in there, he really does want to be with me. I'm sure of that. And the only thing standing in the way of us being together now is Shelly, which settles it. Getting rid of her once and for all is now my number one priority.

CHAPTER FORTY-THREE

OLIVIA

I know calling in sick again today will likely get flagged with the HR team at work, but the truth is I really couldn't care less about that job anymore. I messaged Sunny last night to tell him I was suffering with anxiety, and the good thing is that, these days, I don't need to prove that I am. Because asking someone to actually prove they have poor mental health is one of the quickest ways for any organisation to find themselves on the wrong end of constructive dismissal or harassment charges.

So I feel pretty content that I can get on with my plans for today without fear of interruptions from the HR team.

It's just after 7 a.m., and I'm sitting in my car, parked up along the street from Shelly's house in Tynemouth. It looks set to be another sunny day as the village around me begins waking up, preparing for the influx of day-trippers and tourists who will likely start pouring into the area later this morning.

I have clear sight of Shelly and Nick's front door from where I'm positioned. I daren't take my eyes off it for a second as I sip the steaming coffee I picked up from the garage on the way over here about an hour ago. And whilst I can see the house, the way my car is parked behind a large 4x4, I'm confident there's little chance they can see me.

My phone is plugged into the dash, and my current favourite playlist fills the car, a mix of songs that reflect the love Nick and I share together, including classics like 'I Want to Know What Love Is', 'Take My Breath Away', 'I Will Always Love You' and 'More Than a Feeling'. I've been playing it on loop pretty much all the time at the moment, and I can't wait to share it with him the next time we're alone. I know he is going to love it just as much as I do.

For the next half an hour I sing along with my eyes locked on the house, and then out of nowhere I see Nick stepping out the front door and making his way down the steps. My stomach flips seeing him again, dressed in a grey suit this time, and as ever, he looks a million dollars – despite the fact he carries himself like a man with the weight of the world on his shoulders. It can't be easy for him living a lie like he is now. Still, if things go according to plan, it won't be long before he's free to live a life that will make him truly happy, *with me*.

I can't take my eyes off him as he walks along the street towards his branded Ford Explorer, and I have to physically stop myself from jumping out of the car and rushing over to be with him, but that will come in time. He deactivates the central locking now before climbing up into the cab. A minute later he pulls away from the kerb and slips out into the early morning traffic before disappearing around the corner and out of sight.

I check my watch and note it's coming up for 8 a.m. Despite being incredibly impatient to get cracking with my plan, I'm aware that it's still a little bit too early to get started. Another hour should do it, I reason, and waiting that bit longer also gives me the chance to check that Nick isn't planning on returning any time soon. That's the last thing I want when I get into the house.

CHAPTER FORTY-FOUR

SHELLY

I'm not sure how much longer I can go on living like this. Nick and I are stepping around each other like total strangers at the moment because I simply can't stand to be in the same room as him. Every time I look at him, I can't stop the awful images that fill my mind, of him and that woman, naked, writhing around having sex in his hotel. While I was at home here playing the doting wife and mother – worrying about his business going under, and at the same time trying not to let my raging OCD and anxiety completely overwhelm me. I feel so bloody stupid. How could he do this to me? To *us*?

I place Alfie in his little activity jumper and leave him in front of the TV, which is switched to the babies' channel. It's about all the parenting I can cope with at the moment. I know I should be doing more, but I just don't have anything left. It takes all my strength just to get out of bed in the morning because, if truth be told, I'd rather not, and it's only because he needs looking after that I actually bother.

Anyway, he seems content enough to bounce up and

down along with *Charlie and the Numbers*, so I head into the kitchen to make myself a hot drink. I used to love nothing more than a freshly brewed filter coffee, but I really can't be bothered with all the faff just now. So instead I make a cup of instant and take a seat quietly on the nearest stool next to the island in the middle of the room.

When the doorbell rings a few minutes later, I jump out of my skin with fright, and my heart races. Ever since the visit from DC Sherratt when he came to arrest me, I've been terrified that any ring at the door is him coming back to do the same again. With my mouth suddenly bone-dry, I slide off the stool and make my way tentatively along the hallway to the front door.

Based on the height and shape of the person standing on the other side of the mottled glass, I'm pretty sure it's not DC Sherratt, as it looks to be a female, but I am still slightly worried that it could be his colleague, DC Allinson. As I reach the door, I take a deep breath and activate the chain before opening the door. 'Hello?' I say, peering out through the gap at the woman standing with her back to me.

She turns, and I breathe a huge sigh of relief when I realise it's Jess, holding a box of Krispy Kreme donuts. 'Sorry,' she says sheepishly. 'I know you said you wanted to be on your own, but I was worried about you.' She lifts the box. 'I brought donuts.'

As much as I told Jess I didn't want company, I'm actually relieved to see her smiling face, and I smile back, for what feels like the first time in weeks. 'Give me a sec,' I say as I close the door to release the chain before opening it again. 'You'd better come in.'

I wander back through to the kitchen with Jess at my back.

'How have you been?' she asks from behind me.

I sigh heavily as I walk over to the kettle. 'Not great, I'm afraid. Not great at all.' I turn back to see Jess staring at me, her forehead creased with worry.

'What's been going on?' she says as she places the donuts on the countertop.

I shake my head. 'Where do I start?'

She shrugs as she slides onto one of the stools at the island. 'Wherever you like.'

'Do you want a tea or coffee?'

'Only if you're making one.'

I nod. 'Why don't I do some filter coffee? I haven't had a reason to make one of those for a while.'

'Sounds good to me.'

For the next few minutes I work my way through the process of sorting the coffee and eventually leave it to filter slowly through to the pot. While that's happening, I return to my own stool, positioned opposite Jess. The box of donuts is now open on the countertop between us.

She offers a sympathetic smile as she pulls out a glazed ring donut and grabs a napkin. 'So what's up, Shelly? What's so bad that you don't want to talk to anyone?'

I drop my chin to my chest for a moment as I consider how best to answer. As much as the truth is horrifically painful, I'm really feeling the burden of keeping it locked up inside. I glance up and see her warm elfin face gazing at me. 'Nick cheated on me.' As the words come out, it's like a weight has suddenly lifted from my shoulders for a split second before the reality of what I've just said out loud for the first time sucker punches me in the gut.

Jess puts her fingers to her mouth as her eyes widen. 'Oh my God, Shelly. You poor thing. That's awful.'

I nod sombrely.

'When?'

'Last Thursday in Edinburgh.'

She recoils slightly as she places the donut down on the napkin. 'The business trip?'

'Yes.'

Her mouth falls open, and it seems as though she's struggling to find the right words. 'But who with?'

'I don't know. He said it was just some random girl he met in a bar.'

'He *said* that?'

'Yeah. Said he got drunk and didn't realise what he was doing until it was too late.'

'And you believe him?'

'I don't know what to believe,' I say as I get up from the stool and head over to the coffee machine. I grab the pot along with two mugs and return to my seat and pour our drinks.

Jess remains silent for a few seconds as she picks up her mug and takes a tentative sip of the steaming coffee. 'Could he be lying?'

'About what?'

'About his feelings for the girl.'

'What do you mean?'

'Well, you said it was just a one-night thing. Could there be more to it? Do you think he could have feelings for her?'

'I haven't really thought about that, to be honest,' I say before Jess quickly cuts back in.

'I mean, the only reason I'm asking that is because I'm trying to protect you. I'd hate to think of you being taken for a ride. Nick claiming it meant nothing when all the time he could be in love with this girl.'

I take a sip of my own coffee now. 'He certainly never said anything that would make me think that's the case. Like I say, he picked her up in the hotel bar, so I hardly think it's one of life's great love affairs.'

'Maybe not straight away, but that's how these things start, isn't it?'

I can feel my face wrinkling. 'If you're trying to cheer me up, Jess, it's not working.'

She holds her hands up in defence now. 'I'm sorry. It's just that the guy I've started dating was in a similar position when we met. Married with a kid, but deep down not at all happy. He wanted something else, and that's how he ended up with me. I'd hate for you to believe there's a chance that you guys can work things out if Nick's heart isn't in it.'

'That's just it.' I sigh deeply. 'I'm not sure we can work things out. Not after this. Not now the trust has gone.'

The room falls silent for a moment, and despite the fact I really don't want to talk about married men hooking up with younger women, I know I really should ask how things are going with Jess's fledgling relationship. 'So tell me about your new man.'

She suddenly beams now, and her neck flushes. 'I really don't know what to say other than he's absolutely gorgeous, and I'm head over heels in love with him.'

I take another drink, and I cannot help but feel the intense grief that comes with the loss of that feeling, because that's exactly how I used to think about Nick.

'I'm sorry,' adds Jess. 'I'm being insensitive. You don't want to hear about me being loved up when you've got all this going on with you and Nick.'

She's right, of course, and the pain I feel deep inside

threatens to overwhelm me. I bite my lip as I try to keep it at bay, but the tears flow a second later.

Jess reaches across the island and places her hands on mine. 'Oh, Shelly. I'm so sorry. I can't believe you're having to go through all this. Especially after what happened with you losing your job because of the sex tape – not to mention all that nonsense about you being investigated for fraud. I mean, how much can one person really take?'

I shake my head and close my eyes as I grip her hands tightly. 'There's something else too.'

Her eyes widen. 'What is it?'

I take a deep breath and then exhale slowly. 'I'm pregnant.'

Her mouth falls open, and she stares back at me in silence for a few seconds before responding, 'Does Nick know?'

'No. I haven't told him.'

'Was it planned?'

I shake my head vigorously. 'God no. The last thing I need right now is another baby. It's hard enough as it is looking after Alfie. Especially with my anxiety. The intrusive thoughts are worse than ever.'

'So what are you going to do?'

'I honestly don't know.'

'Will you keep it?'

'I don't know, Jess. I really don't. I hate the thought of having to terminate the pregnancy, but if Nick and I don't get past this, then do I really want to be a single mum with two kids under two? I mean, look at what having Alfie did for my mental health. Who's to say it won't happen again? And even worse the second time.'

Jess nods slowly and appears deep in thought. 'It's a

tough one for sure. That said, based on what we've talked about since we met – and I'm only thinking of your mental well-being when I say this – I think you'd be better off getting rid of it.'

Her words land hard, and for the first time since I saw the two lines in the window, it really dawns on me that I have another little human growing inside me. The thought of destroying that life cuts me to the quick, and at the same time, keeping it absolutely terrifies me.

'So will you tell Nick?' she asks.

'I guess I'm going to have to eventually, but right now I can't stand to even be in the same room as him. Just looking at him makes me so angry.'

'Would it be worth you guys taking a break from each other, maybe?'

'I have thought about that. In fact, I spoke to my mum last night, and she suggested the same. Said I could stay with her for as long as I wanted.'

'Might not be a bad idea.'

I offer a faint smile. 'She's always the first person I go to when things go bad. I don't know what I'd do without her.'

I notice Jess's face fall, and sadness fills her eyes.

I instinctively reach across and grab her hand again. 'Oh my God, that's so insensitive of me. Sorry, I wasn't thinking straight.'

She pulls her hand away and smiles thinly for a split second. 'Don't worry. I've got used to not having my mum around.'

I didn't think I could feel worse than I did when I woke up this morning, but now I do. I've managed to upset Jess, who only came round to cheer *me* up. God, I'm a shit person.

Jess sits to attention on the stool. 'I think a break would

do you good. Especially if it gets you out of this house and away from all the memories of you and Nick. It'll give you both time to think about what you want to do going forward.'

She's right, of course, but the thought of having to pack everything for Alfie into the car and move it to my mum's fills me with dread.

Jess eyes me up and down for a second. 'When was the last time you had a shower and got properly dressed?'

I shrug. 'I don't know. Probably not since Monday before I went to group. Why?' I let out an ironic chuckle. 'Do I smell or something?'

She smiles softly. 'No. But sitting in your PJs and wallowing in your own shit isn't going to do you any good, is it? Why don't you go and get washed and changed, and while you're at it, take some time to seriously think about going to your mum's.'

I glance over at Alfie, who is still watching TV in his activity jumper. 'But what about Alfie?'

'Don't worry,' she replies brightly. 'He'll be perfectly safe down here with me.'

CHAPTER FORTY-FIVE

OLIVIA

I can hear the shower running upstairs as I wander through to the lounge area, where Alfie is happily bouncing up and down in his little jumping-frame thing. It has jungle animals sticking out of it at various points, which wobble and jiggle in time with him. The TV is playing some sort of baby TV show that appears to involve talking numbers that are leaping around the screen. He doesn't notice me at first as I approach from his left-hand side, and continues bouncing, oblivious to me getting closer. But as I move further into his line of sight, his head jerks towards me, and he stares at me with the big brown eyes that I know he gets from his daddy.

I offer him a wide smile as I crouch down next to him. 'Hello, Alfie,' I say in a soft, sing-song voice. 'Remember me? *Auntie* Jess?'

He continues looking at me and appears uncertain.

'Who's a gorgeous boy, hey? Who's a gorgeous boy?'

His expression switches instantly from trepidation to abject joy as he smiles widely, exposing his two bottom teeth at the front of his mouth. The same deep feeling of connection hits me just like the last time I was here, and I'm filled with that luscious sense of warmth and fuzziness you can only get in the presence of happy little children. I feel joy and sadness all at the same time as Dan once again rushes to the front of my mind. Moving closer, I grab him under his arms and lift him out of the bouncer before standing up straight a second later. Holding him in my arms, I'm reminded how chunky he is, as well as how lovely and warm and snuggly he feels in my arms. He smells so good too, like only babies do.

Carrying him upright in my arms, I take a stroll back through the kitchen and along the hallway to the stairs, where I stop and listen. The bathroom is located at the top of the stairs, and even though the door is closed, I can still hear the water pounding on the wet-room floor as Shelly takes a shower above. Perfect. That's exactly where I need her right now.

My plan for this trip always needed to be fluid, as the outcome was based on how Shelly reacted to my visit – as well as what was going on with her and Nick. Now I know she's likely going to be staying with her mum for a few days – which is certainly what I'll be pushing her to do when she comes back down – I have a much clearer idea of how I'm going to move things forward at pace and get her out of our lives once and for all.

Still holding Alfie, I quickly return to the kitchen and head through to the back door to do a proper recce. 'Who's a good boy?' I whisper, jiggling him up and down as I go, much to his apparent delight.

Up close now, the back door looks to be an original feature – in fact, probably close to a hundred years old – and as such is made up of twelve small panes of glass fixed into a criss-cross-patterned wooden frame. I tap one of the panes with my finger, and it's clear that it's almost wafer thin, which is music to my ears. Peering out through the door, I can also see there's a gate at the end of the large yard that opens out onto the alleyway behind. And by the looks of it, it appears to be unlocked. There's certainly no sign of a padlock from what I can see. Perfect. I couldn't have asked for it to be any easier.

'Shall we go and watch TV again?' I ask Alfie as I start walking back towards the kitchen, rubbing his cheek as I go.

He smiles and giggles as he attempts to nibble at my fingers.

'You love your auntie Jess, don't you?'

His big brown eyes are bright and happy as he continues giggling.

I lower my voice to a whisper now as I sniff hard and take in the scent from the top of his head. 'I bet you'd like me to look after you instead of Mummy, wouldn't you?'

Alfie gurgles back as I squeeze him tightly, deepening our obvious connection.

'Yes you would,' I whisper. 'Yes you would.'

CHAPTER FORTY-SIX

SHELLY

'Am I doing the right thing, Jess?' I ask as I close the boot of my Range Rover. Alfie is in his car seat, and the rest of the car is filled with everything I need to look after him at Mum's for at least a week.

'Yes,' she replies emphatically. 'It's for the best, Shelly. You need some time to think. Both of you do.'

'You're right,' I say as I cast my gaze back to the house. 'I'm just worried that this could be the beginning of the end.'

She places her hands on my upper arms and locks eyes with me. 'In the end you've got to do what's right for you. It's not about Nick, it's about you, Alfie and the baby.'

Hearing those words sends a shiver down my spine. I still can't quite comprehend the fact I'm pregnant again. 'I'm still not sure that leaving a note was the right way to tell him,' I say.

'Like I said, it's not about Nick. This is about you. If you don't feel up to talking to him, then a note is fine.'

I can't escape the gnawing feeling clawing at my gut. 'Maybe calling him would be better?'

She shakes her head. 'What if he asks you not to go? What happens then?'

I stare back at her blankly.

'Will you have the courage to say no? The strength to walk away and get the space you need?'

'In all honesty, I don't think I would.'

Jess flashes a soft smile. 'Which is why leaving a note is the right way to tell him. You need to protect yourself in all this. That's the most important thing right now.'

Once again she's right, of course. And as much as it'll hurt him to read about why I've gone, it'd be absolutely horrific trying to explain things face to face or on the phone. 'Thanks, Jess, I really appreciate your help with this.'

'Don't thank me.' She pulls me into a warm hug. 'It's what friends are for.' It feels good to be held so tightly, so I hug her back for a little while longer before eventually pulling away. 'I couldn't have done this without you, you know.'

She waves me away. 'Don't be silly. Of course you could.'

'No.' I shake my head. 'You made a real difference to me today.'

'I'm just glad I could help.'

'In fact, I think it's fair to say that you've been nothing but a tower of strength since the moment we met.'

'Stop it,' she says coyly. 'You'll make me blush.'

'I'm serious, Jess. You've been such a big help to me when I needed it most, and I can't thank you enough.'

Jess nods. 'I knew when we met we'd come into each other's lives for a reason, Shelly. It was totally meant to be.'

CHAPTER FORTY-SEVEN

OLIVIA

I follow at a distance in my old Honda as Shelly makes the short trip to her mum's just ten minutes away in the neighbouring village of Whitley Bay. En route we pass by the recently restored and renovated Spanish City, which sits just fifty yards from the cliff edge. An imposing Renaissance-style, grade II–listed building famous across the northeast of England for its distinctive white dome. Personally, I've always thought it sticks out like a sore thumb and would look far more at home in Mumbai than its current spot, ten miles east of Newcastle city centre.

A few minutes later, Shelly indicates before pulling the car left into Glendale Road, which is typical of the suburban location, with semi-detached Victorian houses lining the street on both sides. She parks up soon after, which is my cue to get my own car out of sight. Thankfully, as it's early afternoon, there are plenty of parking spots available just now, because I can imagine that on an evening, with all the residents returning from work, this street could get pretty busy indeed.

From my position in the driver's seat, I can see Shelly as she exits her Range Rover – grabbing Alfie from the back seat a second later – before heading up the path to what appears to be a well-looked-after semi-detached house, which I assume belongs to her mum. My suspicions are confirmed soon after when the front door opens, and a woman who looks exactly like Shelly, but older, steps out. Sandra, I seem to recall Shelly saying her name was during one of our post-group drinking sessions.

With Alfie safely deposited inside the house along with his grandma, Shelly spends the next five minutes making several trips back and forth from the car to collect their belongings before the front door to the house finally shuts, and the street falls into a relative state of quiet.

I keep my gaze locked on Sandra's house for the next thirty minutes, and with no sign of any further movement during that time, I feel confident I can leave Shelly in the warm embrace of her mother. Funnily enough, I have the very same thing in mind for her husband.

Earlier, when we were discussing whether or not Shelly was actually going to stay with her mum, it came up in conversation that Nick normally gets home from work most days at around 7 p.m. – because if she was going to leave, she wanted to be out before he got back.

With the time now approaching 2 p.m., that means I still have plenty of time to run some errands and get everything sorted in readiness for another special night tonight. Imagining what lies ahead, I can't keep the smile from my face as I slip the car in gear and pull away from the kerb.

I spend the next couple of hours strolling casually around the Silverlink shopping park just a few miles west of Tynemouth, methodically working through my shopping list.

When I'm finally done, I can see from my phone that it's almost five o'clock, and I'm keen to get back on the road because I'd like at least an hour to get everything ready at the house, more if at all possible.

Twenty minutes later, after parking up further along the street from Shelly and Nick's, I grab the bags from the boot before walking up to the front door and ringing the bell. I can't see either Nick's or Shelly's cars, but I still need to double-check the house is empty; otherwise it'll completely ruin my plan. After ringing it several times with no answer, I feel happy enough to make my way round to the alleyway that runs adjacent to their backyard. Thankfully when I get there, the tiny street is as quiet as a mouse, and it's evident I'm the only person using it right now.

Whilst the row of connected houses all look very similar from the rear, it doesn't take long to figure out which is the back of theirs, and as I'd hoped, the gate is unlocked. Carrying my shopping bags, I head through into the yard and move quickly towards the back door. I stop for a second, attempting to look as casual as possible as I scan the surrounding houses, looking for any signs of life. As far as I can tell, the spot where I'm standing can't be seen by any of the neighbours, and from the looks of it, there's no CCTV I need to worry about either. So after setting the bags down, I reach into the orange carrier I got from the hardware store and pull out the small pin hammer I picked up this afternoon. After one more cursory glance around to ensure I'm all alone, I flick the hammer against the tiny pane of glass just above the door handle, and it smashes in on itself instantly. Reaching in through the gap, I release the latch, and a second later, after scooping up my bags, I move inside the house to the exact same spot where I stood holding Alfie just a few hours ago.

I wander through to the kitchen and set the bags down on the island before going in search of a dustpan and brush, which unsurprisingly I find under the sink. It takes a couple of minutes to sweep up the broken glass by the back door, and once the small shards are safely deposited in the bin, I head back to the kitchen to get ready for the next phase of tonight's action. I spy Shelly's note to Nick sitting next to the kettle. Opening it up, I can't help but laugh as I read it, 'I need some time... I'm not sure if we can ever be the same again... you broke our trust.' The pathetic ramblings of a broken woman. I rip it up and throw it in the bin where it belongs, along with the broken glass.

This house is deathly silent now, and I spend the next ten minutes wandering from room to room downstairs, taking it all in and once again marvelling at the sheer size of the place in comparison to my tiny digs on the wrong side of town. In the living room to the front of the property, I drop down on the gigantic sofa and allow myself to relax into the luxuriant cushions. With Shelly out of the way, I can begin to imagine how the place would feel as *our* family home; the perfect place for us all to live, blissfully happy together; me, Nick, Alfie and a little rug rat of our very own. I'm grinning from ear to ear as I head back to the kitchen to retrieve my shopping bags before making my way upstairs to the master bedroom.

Thankfully, Shelly's OCD means that the whole house looks military-standard tidy, and I marvel at the crisp edges on the bedding that has been neatly placed on the super-king bed. I place my bags on top of it and then move to the mirrored wardrobe, which glides open with ease, and I can really appreciate the quality of the craftsmanship. Inside, I find an array of Nick's clothes. I cannot help but wrap myself up in them, and as I revel in his masculine scent that clings to the fabrics, I'm transported back to the Regency Hotel in Edinburgh and our wonderful night of passion together. My body tingles all over, and my teenage butterflies return. It won't be long now until we can relive that passion again.

After stepping away, I make my way into the en suite, and my jaw drops when I see the sheer size of the bathtub that greets me. You could fit a small football team in it. A second later, I turn on the large taps and begin filling it, ready for a long, luxurious bath.

While I'm waiting for it to fill, I wander back into the bedroom, and out of pure curiosity I decide to take a look in the bedside drawers. The first set positioned nearest to the bathroom clearly belong to Nick and contain a couple of men's watches as well as a few books and a box of multivitamins. Nothing of interest to me.

The set on the opposite side, however, they're obviously Shelly's, and when I open the top drawer, what I discover stops me in my tracks. Her positive pregnancy test. Picking it up, I gaze down at the little window and the two thick blue lines contained within. A snarl forms on my lips, and I'm tempted to snap it in half, but I'm immediately distracted when I spot the open packet of tests underneath. Dropping Shelly's test onto the bed, I pull out the box and, when I take a peek inside, realise there's a couple of unused tests in there. Instinctively my left hand is drawn to my tummy, and I swear I can sense something moving inside me. I know these are the standard tests and not as sensitive as the ones I've ordered online, but as they're here, there's no harm in doing one.

Heading back to the bathroom, I unwrap one of the small kits, and after a minute or so looking at the instructions, sit down on the loo and get ready to take a pee. Thankfully, all the coffee I drank earlier with Shelly means I don't have to wait long for it to come, and with some relatively careful body positioning, I'm soon taking the test in earnest. When my wee finally stops, I hold the test window up in front of me and, after setting a countdown timer on my phone, get ready to see the results.

The next three minutes feel like hours as I wait to meet my baby.

As the countdown runs ever closer towards zero, I hold my breath and glare at the little window. I can see one blue line starting to form; now I just need to see the second one.

The phone chimes to indicate the countdown is complete, and I continue to watch the window, waiting for the second blue line. I know from the instructions that even the faintest of lines can indicate a positive result, so I just need to see any kind of second line to prove I'm pregnant. But after another minute passes, still nothing comes. No second line of any kind – not even in the faintest of forms.

Feeling utterly outraged, I throw the plastic stick into the open waste bin and take out the remaining test. I repeat the process and once again wait for the double blue lines to appear. But once more three minutes later, all I see is one solitary blue line. I always knew it could be too soon for these standard tests to pick it up, because I *have* to be pregnant. I can feel the baby growing inside me. I wish the early-stage testing kits I bought online would hurry up and arrive.

They'll soon prove that there's a little person in there, I have no doubt about that.

Jumping off the loo, I throw the useless plastic strips in the bin, then head back out to the bedroom. I connect my phone to the Bluetooth speaker system that runs throughout the house, and a moment later 'Let's Stay Together' booms out in every room. Dimming the lights in the bathroom, I strip off and slide into the foaming tub, allowing the sumptuously warm water to envelope my grateful body. Ahhhhh. Pure bliss.

For the next half an hour I lie in the deep water with my eyes closed, imagining my future life with Nick. Nights of passion, long walks on the beach, cosy Christmases in our beautifully renovated Victorian villa – because I'll need to make it my own, of course. Clear out all and any signs that Shelly ever lived here.

Finally, as the song 'Everything I Do' comes to an end, I realise that I'm half an hour into my lovers' playlist, and it's time to get out. I open my eyes and reluctantly stand up slowly and carefully to limit any chance of me passing out thanks to the heat of the water. A minute later, with one towel wrapped around my torso and a second tied up on my head, I walk through into the bedroom.

My skin's tingling as I rummage through my bags in search of my secret weapon for this evening, a mini satin open-back slip in black from Victoria's Secret. Holding it up against me in front of the mirrored wardrobe, a devilish grin forms on my lips as I imagine Nick's face when he sees me in this. He really doesn't stand a chance. He'll be putty in my hands and won't know what hit him.

CHAPTER FORTY-EIGHT

OLIVIA

As the playlist comes to an end, I press repeat, and it starts again from the beginning. With 'Let's Stay Together' playing out around the house for a second time, I grab the perfectly chilled bottle of Bollinger from the fridge along with two champagne flutes and head back upstairs to the bedroom.

I pour two glasses, keeping one for me and leaving the other on the bedside table for Nick, before relaxing on the bed as I wait for him to arrive.

Staring at my reflection in the mirrored wardrobes in front of me, I raise my glass and toast myself. Nick's gonna be so surprised. I really can't wait to see his face.

A couple more songs float out through the speakers over the next fifteen minutes or so, and as the champagne starts to kick in, I can feel my whole body relaxing. Glancing at the clock on the wall, I can see it's now 7.10 p.m. He should be home any minute now.

And sure enough, my heart skips when I hear the front door opening downstairs soon after.

'Hello?' Nick shouts up from the bottom of the stairs.

I resist the urge to shout back, 'I'm up here.' As I want the surprise to have the maximum impact, he'll find out for himself soon enough. I quickly assume my most alluring position, my left stockinged leg straight, the right bent with my toes pointed as I hold my champagne flute in front of my boosted cleavage. I can hear his footsteps on the stairs, and as he gets even closer, my heart threatens to explode in my chest.

He's on the landing now.

My stomach is churning with excitement.

His hand grips the door, and then he steps through.

'Hello, darling,' I say as sexily as I know how.

Nick stands rooted to the spot, his eyes wide and his mouth open.

'Surprise,' I add.

His eyes dart between me and out towards the stairs. 'What the fuck are you doing here? And how the hell did you get in?'

I can feel myself recoil slightly as I sit up straight on the bed. This wasn't exactly the response I was expecting. 'I let myself in through the back door, babe.'

As the bedroom door closes softly behind him, he clasps his hands together on the top of his head. 'Where the fuck's my wife?'

I grab his glass of Bollinger from the bedside table and jump up. 'Never mind her. Here. Have some champers.'

He steps back from me. 'I don't want any champagne. I wanna know what you've done with my wife.'

'Forget about Shelly,' I shoot back. 'I'm all the woman you need now.'

His brow furrows. 'How do you know her name?'

I move closer to him now. 'I know everything about you,

Nick. Because that's what people in love do. They do whatever it takes to be together.'

'And where's Alfie?' he snaps.

I wave him away. 'Don't worry about the little one; we can see him together soon enough.'

'You're fucking crazy.' He steps back further again. 'You need to leave.'

'But, Nick.' I laugh nervously, not understanding why he's being so standoffish. 'I've gone to a lot of trouble to make tonight special for us again. Just like it was in Edinburgh.'

'I told you. Edinburgh was a stupid mistake. I should never have gone anywhere near you that night. I was drunk and feeling sorry for myself. It should never have happened.'

'You don't mean that.'

'Yes, I fucking do.'

'Nick, why are you being like this?'

'Get the hell out. Now.' He starts aggressively gathering up my bags in his left hand.

'Nick, please!' I plead.

He's not listening as he turns his back on me and yanks the bedroom door open with his right hand.

I put the glasses back on the side before grabbing Shelly's positive test, gripping it between my fingers so the results window is facing towards him. 'I'm pregnant, Nick.'

He stops in his tracks and spins round to look at me. 'You're lying.'

I shake my head. 'See for yourself,' I say as I toss the plastic stick onto the bed.

He slowly places my bags back on the bed before carefully picking up the test, which he holds in his hands for a long moment. 'But...' He's shaking his head. 'We only had sex a week ago.'

'It's a specialist piece of kit I got online,' I lie. 'Used to detect early pregnancies. I've done two more tests this evening, and they both say the same thing.'

He locks eyes with me now. 'You need to get rid of it,' he mumbles.

'What? No way,' I spit back. 'I told you, I'm a Catholic. I can't do that.'

'Well, *we* can't have a child together.'

'Why not? We love each other.'

'Love?' He scoffs. 'Don't be ridiculous; there's no love here. It would be a child born out of one stupid night of lust.'

'Don't say things like that, Nick. I know you don't mean them.'

'I do. We got drunk. We had sex. We made a mistake. That's it. End of story. I have a wife and a family of my own already. This cannot happen.'

'It can and it will.' I rush towards him now and place my hands on his chest. 'We can be a family together, Nick. You, me, Alfie and *our* baby.'

He pushes my hands away. 'You're off your bloody rocker,' he growls before once again gathering up my bags, turning and marching out of the room.

'Why are you doing this?' I call after him as he heads down the stairs. 'Nick, stop. We need to talk about our baby.'

He doesn't respond or look back as he continues down the stairs at a pace.

I set off after him. 'Nick. Nick! Listen to me, Nick. Please.'

As he reaches the front door, he yanks it open.

I catch up with him and lock my hands onto his right arm. 'Stop it! What the hell do you think you're doing?'

He turns to face me now, his eyes wild and almost black.

'What I should have done in Edinburgh. Getting rid of you,' he says before launching my stuff out the front door.

I watch in horror as my bags and clothes cascade down the front steps and onto the pavement below. 'Please don't do this, Nick. I love you!'

His thick right hand grips my upper left arm as I dig my stockinged feet into the parquet flooring, attempting in vain to stand my ground. But he's too strong, and the soft fabric causes me to slide along the surface. 'Get the fuck out of my house!' he yells as he shoves me out onto the top step a split second later.

As soon as my feet hit the stone outside, I turn and attempt to get back in, but it's no use.

'And don't you even think about coming back, or I'll call the police!' he rages just before the door slams shut in my face.

CHAPTER FORTY-NINE

SHELLY

My heart sinks when I see my phone vibrating on the arm of the sofa and it's Nick's name and picture that fills the screen. I wondered how long it would take him to call. I'm tempted to let it ring out, but I know he'll just keep calling, so I figure I may as well get it over with. Picking up the phone, I hit the green answer icon. 'Hi,' I say in a low voice.

'Where the hell are you?' His tone is incredibly aggressive.

'Exactly where I said I would be.'

'You what?' he snaps back. 'What are you talking about?'

'I'm staying at Mum's for a few days with Alfie, like I said in the note.'

'What note?'

'The one I left by the kettle. Have you not seen it?'

'No. I haven't,' he says. 'But then I haven't been in the kitchen yet.'

'Well, why don't you try reading it before you start getting arsey with me.'

'Hang on,' he says, and I can hear the sound of his

shoes clicking over the tiles in the kitchen soon after. 'There's nothing by the kettle,' he says gruffly a few seconds later.

'Well, that's where I left it.'

'Whether you did or you didn't doesn't really matter now, does it? What's more important is what you're doing staying at your mum's in the first place.'

'I just need some time to think, Nick. That's all.'

'About what?'

'About us. And what happens next.'

'What does that mean?'

'Nick, please. I don't want to get into this over the phone. Not tonight.'

'Well, in that case, I'll come round. You can explain what's going on face to face.'

I close my eyes and exhale slowly. This is exactly why I left the note. It explained everything, including the fact I didn't want to talk about any of this stuff at all. Not for a few days at least. 'No, Nick. Please don't come round. Like I said, I just need space.'

He falls silent on the other end for a moment before he replies, 'Seriously, Shell. I know what I did was wrong, but hiding away from me is not going to make it any better. We need to work through it so we can get things back on track.'

'But that's just it, Nick. I'm not sure I want to get things back on track.'

'You what? What are you saying? That you want to split up?'

I lean forward on the sofa and run my hands through my hair as I stare down at the floor. 'I really don't know. And that's the problem. That's why I need some time to think things through.'

'Please, Shelly.' I can hear the desperation in his voice. 'Don't do this.'

At that moment I can hear Alfie start to cry in his cot upstairs.

'Like I said, I just need time.'

Alfie continues to cry.

'Please let me come round, babe. I'll go mad here on my own without you both.'

'No. Not tonight. I can't cope with that right now.'

Alfie's crying reaches fever pitch now, and my mum appears at the door a second later, a pensive look on her face. This is all my nerves need right now, a bloody screaming kid.

'Hang on, Nick,' I say, holding the phone against my chest. 'What's up with him?'

Mum shrugs. 'I don't know, darling. But whatever it is, I'm not having much luck fixing it. I think he might need a cuddle from his mum.'

I hold up my index finger and silently mouth the words *one minute*.

Mum nods and heads back upstairs.

I put the phone back to my ear. 'Look, I'm gonna have to go. Alfie's upset about something.'

'Maybe he's missing his dad,' Nick shoots back.

'Maybe,' I say, and my heart aches for my old life that Nick destroyed when he slept with that woman. 'We'll talk soon, OK,' I say, then end the call before bursting into tears a split second later.

CHAPTER FIFTY

OLIVIA

I've never been so humiliated in my life. Having to gather up my belongings and run down the street to my car in my underwear and stockings. I could kill Nick for what he's just done to me, if I didn't love him so much. I just don't understand his reaction at all. I know he's feeling guilty that Shelly is upset about what happened between me and him, but there's no need to take it out on me like that.

My eyes sting with tears as I pull the driver's door closed and take a moment to pull myself together. I hate the fact he made me cry. I promised no man would ever do that to me again after my dad walked out. But here I am again, tears streaming down my cheeks as I try to figure out what the hell has got into Nick. It makes no sense.

Glancing down at my phone, I can see on the screen I've had a few missed calls from Nan's care home. God. That's all I need right now. Just once I'd like to be able to sort out my own life without being constantly dragged into her problems. I think about potentially calling them back to find out what's going on, but I really don't have the bandwidth for it all at the moment. I'm absolutely sick of watching the dementia eat her up day by day, and not for the first time I'm starting to think my life would be a lot easier if she just died. I feel guilty for even thinking it, but the reality is she has no life these days, and neither do I. Well, whatever is going on with Nan just now, I can't let myself get drawn into that rabbit hole when I have this mess with Nick to sort out.

I grab the pack of wet wipes I keep in the glove box and use a couple to clean my face, trying to clear off some of the mascara, which has run down my cheeks. It takes me a good few minutes to get myself looking a bit more presentable and a little less Alice Cooper.

Finally, when I'm feeling a touch more human again, I decide to give myself a pep talk in the rear-view mirror. 'He was a bit shocked to see you, that's all, Liv,' I say to myself. 'That's why he overreacted. He'll be fine in an hour or so when he's had time to think about what he's done. You'll see. So let's just get home, get changed, and you can give him a call and talk it all through. Figure out how you move things forward after all this.' I flash myself a reassuring smile and then fire up the ignition. A few seconds later, I indicate and pull the car away as I set off back to Fenham.

I arrive home about half an hour later, and once again, intent on avoiding all contact with my housemates, I rush upstairs to my room without being seen. With the door locked now, I replace my underwear and stockings with a pair of sweatpants and a hoodie, and tie my hair back in a short ponytail.

Dropping onto the bed, I open up my laptop, clicking onto Facebook and through to Nick's profile. As soon as I see his handsome face on-screen, my heart melts, and all the hurtful things he did and said tonight seem a lifetime away. I kiss my index and middle fingers, then touch his face on the screen. 'I forgive you, my love,' I say, and stare at the photo in silence for a couple of minutes.

I can see from the clock in the top corner of my laptop that it's approaching 10 p.m., which means it's coming up to two hours since we had our first fight. I'm convinced he'll have calmed down by now, so I grab his business card and key his mobile into my iPhone before hitting the green call button.

It rings at the other end, but eventually goes to voicemail. So I try again. And again, and again. In fact, I spend the next hour ringing incessantly without reply, and I eventually come to the conclusion there must be something wrong with his phone. And if that's the case – and if we're going to sort this all out – there's only one thing for it. I'm going to have to go and see him at work again in the morning.

CHAPTER FIFTY-ONE

OLIVIA

The next morning I'm up with the larks and in the car by 6.45 a.m. I'm feeling really excited to see Nick, and I want to get to his office before he does. That way, I can talk to him outside without having to speak to his PA, Linda. This has nothing to do with anyone but us.

Traffic is light due to the early hour, and with my love-songs playlist booming out through the speakers, I make good time as I zoom along Scotswood Road before turning left into the business park, arriving at Nick's building just after 7 a.m. The car park is empty, which I'm pleased about, as it means he's not arrived yet.

I park in one of two bays marked for NE1 Developments, then switch off the engine and close my eyes for a moment as one of my favourite songs plays, 'Every Breath You Take'. Listening to the lyrics, I can really sense the pain in the vocals and the haunting darkness that comes with unrequited love. I'm grateful that Nick and I will have an opportunity to work things out. I'd certainly hate to feel like the person in the song for any length of time, watching the one they love, forever at a distance.

The sound of my phone ringing yanks me from my thoughts, and as I look down at the screen, I can see it's Nan's care home calling. I'm half tempted to let it ring out, but based on all of yesterday's missed calls and the early hour now, they obviously need to speak to me about something. Plus if I don't answer, they'll only keep on ringing. So I hit the green answer icon. 'Hello?'

'Is that Olivia?'

'It is, yes.'

'My name's Clara, and I'm calling from Beach House care home. Have you got a minute to talk?'

I have an overwhelming urge to say no but stop myself. 'Sure,' I reply. 'But I am expecting a visit from someone any time now, so I may have to cut you off if that happens.'

'Not a problem. This won't take a mo.'

'OK.'

'It's about your grandma.'

'And?'

'Well, it seems she's becoming increasingly more confused and, to be honest, quite volatile.'

'I see.'

'And, well, one of the specialist nurses thinks it would be a good idea if you or someone else from the family could pop in and see her soon. You know, a familiar face and all that.'

'I do visit. Regularly,' I say, trying hard to keep my agitation in check.

'Er, yes. Well...' Clara sounds suddenly unsure of herself. 'I can see from the visitor logs that she's not had a visitor for over a week now. Which, from a well-being point of view, is not ideal for your grandmother.'

'I've just had a hectic few days, that's all,' I snap back. And I mean it. There's been an awful lot going on in my life.

'I'm sure you have. We know life can get very busy,' says Clara. 'And if that's the case, is there someone else who could step in from the family or her circle of friends perhaps?'

'No. There's just me,' I reply flatly. 'It'll have to be me.'

'Right.' Clara pauses on the line for a second. 'Well, if you *could* pay her a visit in the next couple of days, the specialist team think it really would help her.'

Just then the deep growl of a diesel engine drawing closer catches my attention, and I turn to my right to see Nick's truck pulling into the space next to me. 'Look, I'm sorry, I've got to go. The person I'm meeting has just turned up. I'll call in and see Nan soon. OK?'

'Oh, right. Great,' she says before I end the call.

Jumping quickly out of the car, I lock eyes with Nick as he stands, staring back at me across the flatbed of his truck. A shot of adrenaline surges through me, and my schoolgirl butterflies return in earnest. God, he has such a visceral effect on my body. 'Can we talk?' I say softly.

'There's nothing to talk about,' he snaps back.

He's doing it again – being deliberately cold with me – and I have no idea why. 'We need to talk, Nick,' I say. 'About the baby. About *us*.'

He shakes his head. 'I have absolutely nothing to say to you.' Spinning on his heel, he begins walking quickly away towards the entrance to the offices.

I race after him and grab him by the arm, pulling him back. 'Please, Nick. Why are you being like this?'

He yanks his arm away. 'Don't touch me.'

His words are like a dagger to my heart. How can he be so cruel? 'Nick, stop this.'

'No. *You* stop it.'

'Stop what?'

'Stop stalking me, for God's sake.'

I recoil. 'I'm not stalking you. How can you say that?'

He touches both his hands against his temples. 'Are you fucking mad? You broke into my house through the back door when my wife was out. Helped yourself to a fucking bath using all her toiletries, and then lay on our bed, waiting for me to come home with a bottle of champagne you nicked out of *my* fridge. If that's not stalking, then I don't know what is.'

I'm shaking my head in disbelief. How can he say those things? 'I didn't break in. I just let myself in without a key. And I had a bath because I wanted to look my best for you.' I step closer and place my hands on his muscular chest. 'So we could pick up where we left off in Edinburgh.'

He brushes them away. 'I told you. Edinburgh was a mistake. We got drunk, and we had sex. It was nothing more than that.'

'It was much more than that, Nick. It was the coming together of two lost souls—'

'Two bottles of wine, more like.' He cuts across me. 'It meant nothing.'

'It meant *everything*, Nick!'

He shakes his head. 'I wish I'd never gone to the bloody hotel bar that night. If I hadn't, none of this would have happened. I'd still be happily married instead of going out of my mind figuring out how I could have been so stupid to throw it all away on a one-night stand.'

'You don't mean that, Nick.'

'Oh yes, I do.'

'But we love each other,' I plead.

'No,' he growls. 'I love my wife and son, and I'm going to do whatever it takes to try to salvage what's left of my marriage. That's all that matters now.'

'But what about the baby?' I say, stepping closer to him again.

Nick retreats. 'I told you. Get rid of it.'

'But, Nick... it's *our* baby.'

'Is this about money? Is that what you want?' he snaps, before marching back towards the truck, where he opens his briefcase on the covered flatbed at the rear.

My mouth is open, but I'm struggling to find the words. I can't believe he's being like this.

Just then a small Audi turns into the car park.

Nick glances towards it. 'Shit. It's Linda,' he says before scribbling on something on top of his briefcase.

The Audi pulls into one of the visitor bays about twenty feet away.

'Here,' says Nick as he shoves a piece of paper into my hand. 'That's a cheque for a thousand pounds. Use it for the termination, or don't. I don't care either way. But just know, there's no more, all right? I want nothing more to do with you or whatever is growing inside you, OK?'

I can't stop the tears streaming down my cheeks now. 'But, Nick, I need you.' I touch my stomach with my left hand. '*We* need you.'

'You *need* to leave me alone. Because if I ever see you anywhere near my office or my house again, I'll call the police. You got that?'

Linda gets out of her car now. 'Is everything all right?' she asks.

'She was just leaving,' says Nick curtly.

The sense of rejection and humiliation I feel is all consuming, and I want the ground to open up and swallow me whole. 'Please, Nick! Don't leave me like this,' I beg.

But it's no use. He turns away and marches off at speed towards his office, with Linda following at a pace behind him.

CHAPTER FIFTY-TWO

SHELLY

Mum still uses one of those old-school kettles that whistles as it comes to the boil on the gas stove, and right on cue, just as I walk into the kitchen, it begins to blow loudly. Alfie is in his highchair; his little cheeks and the plastic bib under his chin are covered in what appears to be soggy Weetabix. Mum is sitting just in front of him, holding a small plastic Peppa Pig bowl in one hand and a yellow matching spoon in the other.

Having someone to help with Alfie over the last couple of days has been a godsend, and I'm starting to realise how much pressure I was feeling having to be responsible for him all the time since I quit my job. And as much as I love my boy, spending all day every day with can be challenging at times.

'Do you want a tea or coffee?' I ask as I wander over to the countertop.

'Tea, please,' says Mum before spooning another mouthful of cereal into Alfie's grubby mouth.

I make two teas and then take a seat next to them both at the kitchen table.

'So what are your plans today?' Mum asks, pulling her mug across the table.

'Same as when we talked last night. I have an appointment with the divorce lawyer at eleven.'

Mum frowns. 'I didn't say anything last night, but I can't help thinking it might be a little soon to be getting involved in all that, darling.'

I take a sip of my tea. 'Not for me.'

'But I thought you were here because you were taking some time to think – to see if you can work things out between you and Nick.'

'I am. But part of that is knowing what my options are.'

'And is divorce *really* an option for you?'

'Maybe.' I shrug. 'I mean, we always said that cheating was not something either of us would ever tolerate. Whether it was just a kiss or sleeping with someone, it didn't matter. If the trust was gone, then the relationship was done. End of story.'

Mum feeds Alfie the last mouthful from the bowl before placing it down on the table next to her. 'Shelly, I know what Nick did was unforgivable, but it shouldn't mean that you both give up on your marriage. Not without a fight at least.'

'But the trust is gone, Mum, and I don't think we'll ever be able to get it back.'

She shakes her head slowly and offers me a sage look. 'I promised your dad I'd never tell you this, even after he died, but given what's happened I think you need to hear it.'

I can feel my brow wrinkle. 'Hear what?'

She exhales sharply. 'There's no easy way to say this, but your dad had an affair once.'

I do a double take. 'He did what?'

Mum takes a sip from her drink. 'He cheated on me.'

'Dad?'

She nods.

'When was this?'

'When you were little. Still at primary school, if I remember rightly.'

I'm absolutely gobsmacked. 'What happened?'

'He ended up in bed with his secretary, Trisha.' She lets out an ironic chuckle. 'Clichéd, I know, but it hurt like hell at the time.'

'And did he say why it happened?'

She shrugs. 'We married young, and apparently he felt trapped when we started a family. Like his life was slipping away and he needed to experience sex with someone else besides me. I don't think he ever had feelings for Trisha. It just happened one night when they were away on a business trip.'

'I can't believe this. Dad was a cheater?'

'Yes. But only the once. I think he realised pretty quickly that the grass wasn't quite as green as he had been expecting.'

'And how did you get over it?'

'I just did.' She taps her nails against the mug now. 'It took time, but he swore it was a mistake and said he was very, very sorry. And of course he promised he'd never do it again. And he never did.'

'But the trust, Mum. How did you ever trust him again?'

'I guess over time the pain and the memory started to fade. And with you to look after, I just had to get on with it. Looking back, I guess the trust returned eventually. And it could with you and Nick too. If you're willing to work at it, love.'

'But that's just it. I don't know if I am. He's hurt me so much.'

Silence descends as she takes another mouthful of tea before placing her mug back on the table. 'Do you still love him?'

'Yeah, but—'

'Then there are no buts,' she says, cutting me off. 'If you love him, you need to give him a chance to make it up to you. To prove, just like your dad with me, that he's sorry and will never do it again.'

My eyes are locked on hers as I try to process what I've just heard.

Mum rubs the top of Alfie's head. 'Because this little fella needs his dad around all the time, not just on weekends and school holidays.'

I cast my gaze to my little boy giggling happily in his highchair, wiggling his arms and swinging his feet back and forth as he does.

'All I'm saying is think about what you're doing, Shelly. Don't go diving in head first.'

I say nothing for a few moments, my focus still on Alfie. 'It's because of Alfie I want to speak to a lawyer.'

Mum tilts her head slightly and appears confused. 'How do you mean?'

'I want to know what will happen to him if Nick and I do split up and I end up in prison.'

'What?' Mum's face is incredulous. 'Don't be daft. *You're not going to prison.*'

'We don't know that for sure, Mum. Fraud by abuse of position comes with a sentence of up to ten years.'

'But only if you're convicted and you didn't do anything wrong.'

'*We* both know that. But what if they do charge me and it ends up in court? If the jury think I did it...' My words tail off.

She waves me away. 'Then we'll deal with that *if* it happens. But you can't spend the next however long making decisions based on ifs, buts and maybes.'

I blow my cheeks. 'Perhaps not, but I'd feel better knowing my options. And I'm also hoping that by speaking to a lawyer, I might start to feel like I have a little bit more control, too.'

'I understand,' says Mum. 'And you need to do what you feel is right. You know I'll support you whatever you decide.'

I smile softly. 'Thanks, Mum.'

She smiles back before draining her mug.

'So what are your plans while I'm out?'

Mum turns to Alfie now. 'We're going for a lovely walk in the park, aren't we?' she says in a sing-song voice. 'Going to get an ice cream at the new café that's opened, hey?'

Alfie giggles as he continues to wiggle in his highchair.

'Well, I shouldn't be long.' I stand. 'The offices are in Sandyford, so I should only be out a couple of hours tops.'

Mum's eyes remain fixed on my gorgeous little boy as he continues to gurgle at his grandma. 'You take your time. It's a lovely day, and we're going to be fine on our own, aren't we, little guy?' She wipes away a small blob of Weetabix from his cheek. 'Just the two of us. In our own little Grannie and Alfie world.'

CHAPTER FIFTY-THREE

OLIVIA

As I watch Shelly crossing the street, heading for her car, I can't quite believe Nick would choose her over me. I mean, look at her. Her hair pulled back tightly against her head and her baggy clothes, plus not a stitch of make-up on. She looks a total mess. And that's just from the outside. Inside, I know better than most how much of a basket case she is – fantasising about harming her husband and baby most days. It doesn't make sense, and it's certainly not fair either. Why should someone like Shelly, with everything that's wrong with her, get to be with a man like Nick after everything she's put *me* through? She took my brother, my parents, and now she's taken my man. But after the way he treated me in front of Linda this morning, she's welcome to him. Nobody treats me like that and gets away with it. I grip the steering wheel tightly to help stem the rage brewing inside me. A second later she fires up the ignition of the Range Rover.

Staring at her as she sits in the driver's seat, adjusting her ponytail in the mirror, my mind is fizzing with ways to finally get even with her and get my own justice for Dan and for my mum. The first thought that springs to mind is how easy it would be to ram her off the road. To push her into oncoming traffic when she stops at the traffic lights. That could work, but I'd need to be careful about where I do it. After all, a lot of the busier junctions are fitted with CCTV and police cameras.

My attention is suddenly drawn to Sandra now as she steps backwards out of her front door, pulling a pushchair behind her. She spins round a second later, and I can see Alfie is strapped into the seat in front of her. And that's when the inspiration hits me. *Alfie*. That's it. *He's* the key to getting back at both her *and* Nick for what they've done to me. He's at the centre of their world, and he's the lever I've yet to pull. I honestly don't know how I didn't think of it sooner.

At that moment, Sandra bends down by the side of the pram and says something to the little boy before waving at Shelly in the car opposite. She toots back just as she pulls the car away from the kerb and drives off up the road.

I watch with bated breath for a few seconds, waiting to see what Sandra will do next, and when she reaches her garden gate and turns right with the pram, it seems obvious she's taking him for a walk.

Slipping on my sunglasses, I jump out of the car and make my way across the road. I can hear Sandra chatting happily to Alfie as they walk at a casual pace, fifty yards further along the path. After glancing round to ensure no one is watching me, I tuck in behind and follow them down the street.

Sandra continues to amble along, stopping every now and again to point at the seagulls in the sky or squirrels in the trees, and when they do, I have to think quick so as not to look suspicious for stopping in my tracks at the same time. I bend down to tie my shoelaces at one point, pretend to be reading a message on my phone the next, and another time I act as if I'm admiring the view out to sea to my left, which, as ever, looks pretty spectacular on another sunny day like today.

After about fifteen minutes they eventually head into Northumberland Park and follow the path round to the duck pond, where Sandra takes a seat on a bench, with Alfie parked up next to her.

My heart is pounding as I draw ever closer to them. I actually have no real idea of what I'm going to do until I'm virtually upon them and suddenly hear myself blurting out the words, 'Is that little Alfie?'

Sandra turns to me with a quizzical look on her face. 'Hello,' she says with a smile. 'Do we know you?'

I smile back. 'I'm Jess. A friend of Shelly's. You must be Sandra.'

She nods.

'Wow. You guys are so alike,' I say before dropping to my haunches next to Alfie. 'And I'd recognise this little munchkin anywhere.' I rub his cheek with the back of my finger, and he giggles back at me before I turn my focus back to Sandra. 'How's Shelly doing? I was so sorry to hear about her and Nick.'

Sandra raises her eyebrows. 'You *know* about that?'

'Yeah, I was over at her house yesterday, and she told me all about Edinburgh.' I straighten before dropping softly down on the bench next to her. 'In fact, I must apologise, Sandra. I was adamant she needed some space, and I think that was one of the reasons why she moved in with you. I'm sorry if I've caused a problem for you.'

'Not at all,' she replies. 'I'm enjoying having them stay. Especially this one.'

I offer a faint nod. 'She's really been through the wringer lately, hasn't she? What with losing her job and then the potential court case.'

'She told you about that as well?'

'I help out at the charity from time to time.' I fold my arms across my chest. 'I couldn't believe it when she told me what had happened. I mean, of all the people you could accuse of stealing money, it'd never be Shelly.'

Sandra nods sagely. 'It's hard to see her so upset and so worried. It doesn't matter how old she gets, she's still my little girl.'

I can see the genuine sadness in Sandra's eyes now, and in that instant the agony of not having my own mum to care for me cuts deep into my core. 'I can only imagine,' I manage to mumble.

We both fall silent for a minute or so, and Alfie continues to chatter in the pram next to us as a couple of ducks waddle past.

It's Sandra who eventually speaks first. 'Well, I don't mean to be rude, but I really need to get to the café. These tablets I'm taking for my heart make me pee like I don't know what. And if I don't go soon, I'm worried I might have an accident.'

'There's a café? I thought it shut years ago.'

She stands. 'It did, but they reopened it about a month ago. I haven't tried it yet, but I've heard it's quite nice.'

I stand too. 'I'll walk with you if you don't mind. I could do with a coffee myself.'

'Sure,' she replies. 'It's just round the corner.'

With Alfie happily gurgling away in the stroller, Sandra

pushes him along, and we chat about nothing in particular, making inane small talk, mainly about the weather and the unusually hot summer we're having for a change. The staple shared conversation of British people who don't really know each other.

When we reach the café a few minutes later, it looks absolutely rammed, filled to the brim with customers both inside and out.

'Looks like a lot of people had the same idea,' says Sandra as we approach. 'We might have to make do with a takeaway.'

'Yeah. It certainly looks that way, doesn't it?'

She stops in her tracks and stares in through the window of the small building, a grave expression forming on her face. 'God, I really need the loo. But I'm not sure the pushchair will fit between the tables in there.'

'I can watch Alfie for you,' I say brightly. 'Save you the bother of having to take him in with you.'

'You don't mind?'

'Not at all. You get yourself sorted, and we'll be out here waiting when you're done.'

Sandra blows her cheeks. 'You're a lifesaver, Jess. Thank you.'

'Not a problem,' I say with a wide grin.

She hurries away now, and I watch as she opens the door to the café a second later before rushing inside. Through the window I can see her making her way across the room, then disappearing through a door on the far side of the café. As soon as it closes behind her, I grab the pushchair and march away with Alfie as fast as I can.

CHAPTER FIFTY-FOUR

SHELLY

The meeting with the solicitor was pretty quick, mainly because it was an initial intro as opposed to a full consultation. Which meant I was in and out within half an hour. So I'm more than a little surprised to see I have ten missed calls from my mum as I head back to the car. And then just as I'm about to call her back, she rings again.

'Mum? Is everything OK?'

'They're gone, Shelly. I can't find them!' Her voice is laced with panic, and it's evident from the background noise that she's calling me from somewhere outdoors.

'Who's gone?'

'Alfie. Alfie's gone.'

An ice-cold shiver runs down the length of my spine as a shot of adrenaline causes my heart to pound. 'What do you mean he's gone?' I can hardly get the words out.

'Your friend was watching him while I went to the toilet, and when I came out, they'd gone. I've looked all over the park, but I can't find them.'

'Which friend?'

'Jess.'

'*Jess* was watching him?'

'Yes. We got chatting in the park, and when I needed the toilet, she said she'd watch him because the café was rammed, and I couldn't take his pushchair in.'

'You left him with her while you went to the toilet?'

'I'm so sorry, Shelly. You know what my bladder's like on these water tablets. I was worried I would wet myself.'

I'm struggling to process what I'm hearing, and a rundown of how my mum's heart medication affects her toilet habits is not something I need to hear right now. I have so many questions swirling through my brain about how and why Jess was in the park and what she was doing talking to Mum, but my priority in this moment is figuring out where she's gone with Alfie. There has to be a perfectly logical explanation to all this. 'Where are you now?'

'Standing outside the café in Northumberland Park, near the duck pond.'

'Stay there. I'm on my way,' I say, before ending the call and racing to my car, which is parked a hundred yards along the street.

The journey from Sandyford back to Tynemouth will take just under fifteen minutes. As soon as I'm on the road, I pull up Jess's mobile on the car's infotainment system and call her. Frustratingly it rings out, so I try it again. And again, and again with the same end result. 'Where are you?' I mumble as I speed along the Coast Road.

After five minutes of constant calling and no response, I can feel the panic beginning to take a firm hold. Where has Jess taken my gorgeous little boy? I call Mum again to see if there's any updates, but there isn't, and like me, she's now seriously starting to panic.

Despite how angry I am at him for the damage he's caused our marriage, the only person I can think of who can calm me down in a situation like this is Nick, so I ring his mobile.

He answers within just a few rings. 'Hi, Shelly,' he says softly. 'You all right?'

'Alfie's gone missing,' I blurt out on the verge of tears now.

'Alfie's what?' His tone is incredulous.

'He's gone missing. He was out with Mum in the park, and my friend Jess was watching him when Mum went to the loo, and now she can't find either of them.'

'*Who* did you say was watching him in the park?'

'My friend Jess.'

'Jess?'

'Yeah. Why?'

He pauses before replying, 'It doesn't matter. Which park were they in?'

'Northumberland. I'm heading there now to help Mum look for them both.'

'I've just finished my meeting in Blyth. I can be there in fifteen minutes.'

'OK. We'll meet you at the café by the duck pond.'

'I'll be as quick as I can,' he replies.

The only thought that is consuming my mind right now is getting to the park as fast as I can. I end the call without responding before accelerating into the fast lane.

AFTER DITCHING the car at the side of the road, I run flat-out into the heart of the park and a few minutes later turn the corner to see my mum standing outside the main entrance to the café. When I lock eyes with her, I can see the fear etched on her face, and she bursts into floods of tears as I approach.

'I'm so sorry, love,' she says as I wrap my arms around her. 'I never thought for a second something like this would happen.'

I pull away and clamp my hands on her upper arms as I stare into her eyes. 'Are you sure the woman was called Jess?'

She nods. 'Yes. Said she'd been at your house yesterday and knew all about you and Nick and the fact you'd moved in with me.'

I still cannot understand why Jess would be wandering around a park in Tynemouth on a weekday. She works on the Quayside and lives in Fenham, after all. The only thing I can think of is that maybe she's been over to see Edna and Nancy in the shop. I know that she really enjoyed working for Autumn Hearts and maybe she could have popped in today to say hello.

'Have you tried calling her?' asks Mum.

'Yeah,' I say, scanning the area around me in the vain hope I might see her and Alfie strolling back to the café – ready to explain that this has all been one massive misunderstanding. But there's no sign of her anywhere. I press redial on my phone and try calling her again, but like the last time, it rings out. *Damn it.*

I figure it's worth calling the Autumn Hearts shop next to check she's not there, and it's Nancy who answers after a few rings.

'Yes?' she says in the uniquely abrupt tones that are ubiquitous to pensioners.

'Nancy, it's Shelly.'

'Oh, hello, dear.' She softens as soon as she realises she's speaking to someone she knows. 'Long time no speak. Are you feeling any better?'

Her question catches me off guard for a second, and then I remember that George told them I was taking a break due to ill health rather than explaining I'd been suspended. 'Er, yes,' I say, attempting to keep the panic out of my voice. 'I don't suppose Jess has been in to the shop today, has she?'

'Jess? Oh, no, dear. We've not seen her for a couple of weeks now. Not since you were both in the office together, in fact.'

'Really? I thought she called in to see you last week to ask for my address?'

'Jess. No. She's not been in at all.'

I can feel my forehead wrinkling. 'Are you sure?'

'Oh yes, dear. Quite sure. We've definitely not seen her, have we, Edna?'

I can hear Edna saying no in the background, and in that moment I feel a sense of total dread consume me. Why would Jess lie to me about getting my address from the shop? And if she didn't get it from Edna or Nancy, how the hell did she know where I live?'

Just then I see Nick marching towards me. 'Look, I'd better go, Nancy,' I say.

Nancy ignores my comment in the way that elderly ladies do. 'Will you be coming back soon?' she asks. 'Only a lot of people have been asking after you, and I have no idea what to tell them. I mean, we had Mrs Wilkinson in last week, and she was saying—'

'Sorry, Nancy.' I cut her off mid-flow. 'I really do have to go,' I add, then kill the call.

Nick arrives now, his face grave. 'So why was this woman looking after Alfie?'

Mum begins crying again. 'I'm so sorry, Nick. I never should have left him with her. I should have taken him into the café with me.'

I glare at Nick. 'None of this is Mum's fault,' I say before turning to face her again. 'Don't blame yourself, Mum. She told you she was my friend and had been to our house. Of course you'd think she was safe to watch him for a minute.'

'I'm sorry, Sandra,' says Nick sheepishly. 'I didn't mean to upset you. I'm just panicking.' He focuses his attention on me now. 'You said this woman is called Jess.'

I nod.

'And she's a friend of yours?'

'Yes.'

'You never mentioned her before.'

'I met her in group therapy.'

'She's in *therapy*?' He looks aghast.

'Yeah. Why? What's that got to do with anything?'

'Well, what if she's crazy?'

I shake my head in disbelief. 'Is that what you think? That because she's in therapy she has a screw loose? Is that what you think of *me* for going?'

'No. No.' He raises his arms in defence. 'It's just that...'

'It's just what?'

He runs both his hands through his hair. 'It's just too much of a coincidence.'

'What's too much of a coincidence?' I feel my brow wrinkle. 'What are you talking about, Nick?'

'Have you got a picture of her?'

'Why?'

'Do you or don't you?'

Feeling like we're wasting precious time, I reluctantly dive into Facebook on my phone and key her name into the search box. A moment later her profile picture appears on-screen, and I thrust it angrily in front of his face so he can see it. 'Happy now?'

His eyes widen as he stares at the image, his skin suddenly ashen. 'Oh fuck,' he mutters as he cradles the back of his head in his hands.

I flinch. 'What do you mean, "oh fuck"? Oh fuck, what?'

Nick glances awkwardly at Mum and then back to me.

'What is it?'

'I don't think we should be having this conversation in front of your mum.'

'We haven't got time to mess about, so whatever it is, just spit it out, will you?'

He exhales sharply as he nods at the screen in my hand. 'She's the girl I slept with in Edinburgh.'

His words hit me like a hammer to the head, and for a split second I question whether I heard him right or I just imagined it. I push the phone closer to his face. 'You slept with *this* woman?'

He nods sombrely.

I hold the phone closer still. 'You slept with *Jess* from my *group* therapy sessions?'

'Yes.'

My mouth is open, but no words will form for a long moment. 'Why would Jess, who works in banking, be in a hotel in Edinburgh?' I say eventually.

'She said she was there for work.'

'For work? At the airport hotel?'

'Yeah. Said she booked it by mistake.'

My mind is spinning as I try to make sense of all this.

'We need to call the police now,' says Nick firmly. 'She's fucking batshit crazy. I'm telling you. She broke into the house last night and was waiting for me when I got home.'

I feel like the world is closing in on me. What the hell is he saying? 'Jess broke into *our* house?'

'Yeah. I walked into the bedroom when I got home from work last night, and she was lying there half naked on the bed.'

I can't believe what I'm hearing. 'She did that last night?'

'Yeah.'

'But she came to see me yesterday morning. In fact, she was the one who persuaded me to go to Mum's in the first place.'

'Probably so she could get you out of the way. She opened a bottle of champagne and told me she loved me. That we were meant to be together. That we're soulmates.'

'But she's supposed to be my friend.'

'She's a bloody lunatic, and she's got Alfie. We really need to call the police.' Nick quickly keys 999 into his phone.

Mum and I both watch in silence as he waits for them to answer.

Just then my phone beeps, indicating I have a new message. As I glance down at the screen, my heart races when I see it's from Jess.

Nick answers the operator's initial question. 'Police, please.'

I click open the message, and my blood runs cold as I stare at a photo of Jess holding my little boy in her arms, standing on what looks like a cliff edge somewhere. The message underneath is terrifyingly to the point, and my legs feel like they could give way under me.

> If you want to see him again, meet me at the Tynemouth Priory cliffs. Come alone. No one else and no police. It's very slippery underfoot. I'd hate to drop him.

Acting on autopilot, I step forward and pull the phone from Nick's hand. He gawks at me, confusion filling his face.

'No police,' I manage to whisper. 'No police.'

CHAPTER FIFTY-FIVE

SHELLY

I'm running so fast over the rough terrain that I've come close to falling flat on my face several times since ditching the car in the car park at the priory a few minutes ago. The ancient ruins of the old monastery tower over the sea-filled horizon about two hundred yards ahead as I race towards the cliff edge, praying with every step I take to anyone who will listen that my boy is safe by the time I get to him. The last time I came anywhere near these cliffs was almost two decades ago, and thanks to the horrific events of that day, even just looking at the remains of the priory has filled me with abject terror ever since. But right now I have to block out my own fears and anxieties because the only thing that matters is reaching those cliffs as fast as I can and getting Alfie back safely.

Nick wanted to come with me, but based on Jess's state of mind, we simply couldn't risk it. So here I am, running as quickly as my legs will carry me, trying to block out the terrifying images of what might await me when I eventually get to the cliffs. 'Please, God, let him be OK,' I mutter in between taking in gulps of air. 'Please, God, let my baby be OK.'

I run flat-out for another couple of minutes. Then suddenly I hear Alfie crying somewhere nearby. I race past the warning sign telling me to keep clear of the cliffs because of the imminent danger of death, and my panic mounts as I round the six-foot-high wall that was once part of the ancient monastery. And that's when I see her standing perilously close to the edge with her back to me. 'Jess!' I scream at the top of my voice as I come to a stop, about twenty feet further back from her position.

She spins round to face me, and my heart almost stops when I see Alfie locked in her arms, his little face puce as he wails with all his might. She flashes a sinister grin, and I'm not sure if my mind is playing tricks on me, but her eyes appear almost jet black.

I can hear the sea pounding on the rocks some hundred feet below as I hold my hands up in surrender. 'Please, Jess. Please don't hurt him.'

She drops her gaze to Alfie for a second, then turns her attention back to me. 'Are you alone?'

'Yes. Yes, I am.'

She nods slowly before glancing around the space she now occupies. 'Do you know the last time I was here?'

I have zero interest in playing twenty questions with her, but I need to get my baby back, so I play along. 'No, I don't.'

'Fifteen years ago next month.'

She's staring at me as if this is supposed to mean something to me, but exactly what, I have no idea.

'It was a brutally hot day in August when it happened.'

I can hear her talking, but I'm struggling to process

anything, as my eyes are fixed on Alfie. 'When what happened?' I say, shuffling slightly closer.

'When my brother was killed.'

I'm nodding, but I still don't know what she's talking about.

'Murdered at this very spot.'

With my hands still in their defensive position, I move a few steps closer still. 'You're saying your *brother* was murdered?'

'Yeah. He was.'

I'm reminded now of the group sessions when Jess talked in detail about her sister dying of cancer when she was a kid. There was never any mention of her having any other siblings. 'But I didn't think you had a brother, Jess.'

'You're absolutely right.' She stands to attention now, still gripping Alfie tightly in her arms. '*Jess* doesn't have a brother. But Olivia does.'

Olivia? What on earth is she talking about? 'Who is Olivia?' I ask.

'She's me,' she replies flatly. '*I'm* Olivia.'

Her reply stops me in my tracks and confirms my suspicions that Jess is having some kind of delusional episode, verging on a total mental collapse. I have to get Alfie away from her immediately. I consider rushing her and yanking him out of her arms, but she's so close to the edge that I daren't risk it. So instead, I slowly take a couple more steps closer.

Her demeanour changes again as she tilts her head to one side and stares at me with a quizzical look. 'Tell me, Shelly. Why did you never admit to what you did that day?'

I have absolutely no idea what she's talking about, but with Alfie still wailing, locked in her grip, I'm desperate to keep her onside, so I continue to humour her. 'What is it that you think I did, Jess?'

'I told you,' she growls, 'I'm not Jess, I'm Olivia.'

I raise my hands in defence again. 'I'm sorry, *Olivia*. What is it that you think I did?'

'You killed him.'

I can't help but flinch at her reply. She's definitely lost the plot. 'Who? Who did I kill.'

'My brother. Dan.' She points to the ground. 'Here at this very spot.'

I shake my head slowly. 'I'm sorry to tell you, Olivia, but I've never killed anyone, and I didn't know you even had a brother, so I'm pretty sure I've never met him.'

'Oh yes, you have.'

'No,' I say flatly. 'I haven't.'

'We all called him Dan at home, but you'll remember him as Daniel Kingston. He died at this very spot when you pushed him over the edge.'

I can feel my eyes widen as her words land, and everything slows down. In that instant I suddenly recognise the face staring back at me. I can't believe I didn't see it before. She's older now, and she's blonde as opposed to brunette, but there's no denying it's her. '*You're* little Liv Kingston.'

A wide grin spreads across her face as she nods. 'Finally she's sees it. I must say, you took your time.'

My mind is blown. *Jess is Liv Kingston.* I really can't believe this is happening, and if it weren't for the fact I need to get my terrified son out of her grip, I'd have a thousand questions for her. Like why she's been pretending to be Jess since we met? How she managed to get into my closely guarded therapy group? What possessed her to seduce my husband? And why she decided to kidnap my son? But all that can wait. The only thing I'm focused on right now is getting Alfie away from this lunatic.

'Do you have any idea what you took from me that day?' she shouts across at me just as more waves crash onto the rocks below. Terrifyingly, her eyes seem even blacker now, as if her soul has long since left.

'I didn't take anything, Liv. Daniel's death was an accident.'

'Just stop, will you?' she snaps back. 'Stop with the lies. *You* killed him, and you got away with murder.'

'What are you talking about? It was a tragic accident. Dan fell, Liv. I didn't kill him. In fact, *I* was the one who tried to save him.'

'No. That's not true.' She's shaking her head vigorously now. 'I saw it with my own eyes. You pushed him; you pushed him onto the rocks.'

I take another step closer. 'I'm telling you the truth, Liv. Please believe me, that moment has haunted me my entire life, and sadly I still remember it as if it were yesterday.' I point to the path that runs along the edge of the cliffs. 'I saw a bunch of kids messing around there just as I was jogging past. They were larking about, pushing and shoving each other. I thought they were playing dangerously close, so I stopped to warn them, but one of the girls – I didn't see which one it was – slipped and knocked into Dan. And that's when he lost his footing and went over the edge. I rushed to help and found him hanging on to a rock a few feet below. I tried to grab him, but I couldn't reach. So I started climbing down, but before I could get to him, he lost his grip and...' My words tail off.

'You forget I was there Shelly, and that's not what happened. It wasn't one of us who knocked into him. It was you. *You* pushed him over the cliff. *You* murdered him.'

'No, Liv. I didn't. It was an accident.' I pull my phone from my pocket and hold it up in front of her. 'You can google the inquest report. It's all in there. The coroner's verdict was accidental death. I know because I was in court when he read out the verdict. And so were you!'

Olivia begins edging back towards the top of the cliff.

I follow her and hold my hands out in front of me with my palms facing upwards. 'Please, Liv. Please give Alfie to me.'

She shakes her head again. 'No. You can't have him. You need to suffer like *I* have. You need to know what it's like to lose everything that matters to you. Because that's what happened to me when Dan died. Everything that was good in my life was taken from me. My little brother, my mum, then my dad, and now... now I'm even losing my nan.'

'I'm genuinely sorry you've had to suffer so much,' I say as tenderly as I can given the abject terror that's consuming me in this moment.

'And yet *you* get the perfect life, don't you? The dream house, the handsome husband, the babies, you get it all. And I get nothing.'

'I know you think I have everything, Liv, and I'm sure that seems unfair after what happened to you, but I really don't. Nobody ever does. We're all struggling in our own way. All of us. No matter how perfect things might appear on the outside.' I'm shouting now as I attempt to be heard over Alfie and the sound of the waves, which continue to batter the rocks below. 'Come on, Liv. Alfie hasn't got anything to do with this. Hurting him isn't going to make it better or take away your pain. But if you let *me*, maybe I can help with that. We can talk to Dr Galanis – go back to the group together, the two of us.'

She laughs loudly. 'Fuck Dr Galanis and fuck that group. The only reason I conned my way in there was so I could hear you finally confess to what you did and figure out how to get back at you for it. I don't need therapy. I just wanted to get my revenge for everything you did to me. For everything you took.'

'Please, Liv. I didn't take anything.'

'Yes, you did!' she screams. 'I lost everything. And now it's time for you to know how that feels.' She shifts her grip on Alfie and a split second later holds him kicking and screaming aloft above her head. 'Welcome to my hell, Shelly.'

'No!' As she turns her back to me, I throw myself at her, grabbing Alfie's little body with all my might.

Olivia spins back, desperately trying to yank him from my grip and, as she does, drags us all closer to the edge. I'm staring into her dark soulless eyes now as I attempt to pull Alfie out of her grasp, but she won't let go. 'Give him to me!' I growl.

'No. You can't have him!' she yells back.

In that instant, pure survival instinct kicks in, and without thinking, I thrust my head back with all my might before smashing my forehead down onto the bridge of her nose with a sickening crack.

She screams in agony and instantly releases her grip as she staggers backwards, blood streaming from her nostrils. With Alfie now locked in my arms, I watch as she loses her footing just a few feet in front of me before toppling backwards over the edge. She screams in terror as she disappears out of sight, but her cries are silenced a moment later.

Pulling my little boy into a tight hug now, the relief I feel having him back in my arms is like nothing I've ever known. His warm, chunky little body locked tightly against my chest feels like manna from heaven. 'It's OK, darling. Mummy's got you. You're safe now,' I say, attempting to stop him crying, but he's inconsolable in this moment.

He continues to wail as I quickly survey the scene, looking to see if anyone has witnessed what has just happened, but from what I can tell, there's no one around.

As much as I can't stand heights – and as terrified as I am of what I might find – I force myself to shuffle slowly forwards towards the edge, still cradling Alfie.

And that's when I hear her crying out. 'Help me. Help me!'

Peering over the top of the cliff, I can see Olivia hanging on to a rock about three feet below, and my mind flashes back to the exact same situation that I experienced with Daniel all those years ago. After everything this woman has done to me and my family, I'm tempted to walk away and never look back, but I know deep down I cannot leave her to die. I might not have been able to save Daniel, but if there's a chance I can save his sister, I need to at least try.

Stepping a good distance back from the edge and with no one in sight, I carefully lay Alfie down on the grass. He's still crying, but I can't risk having him anywhere near the edge. Leaving him here is the lesser of two evils. Kissing him on the forehead, I promise I'll be right back before quickly making my way over to her position. Looking down at her, I can see her knuckles are white from gripping the rock about three feet below me, as the rest of her body hangs over the hundred-foot drop to the rocks below.

'Help me!' she screams hysterically. 'Please help me!'

I carefully slide down the rough terrain until I'm level with her hands, balancing on a ledge next to the rock she's clinging to. Taking a few seconds to wedge myself in, I reach down and wrap my left hand around her right wrist.

'Don't let me die!' she wails.

'I've got you,' I say as I grab her left wrist with my right hand and begin pulling. She feels like a dead weight and doesn't budge at first, but I try again, leaning back with all I've got, and she eventually begins to shift. I dig my feet into the ground and pull as hard as I can once more, gritting my teeth as I do. Finally she moves close enough for me to reach down and grab her around the shoulders. 'Pull yourself up,' I shout as I yank a little more of her towards me.

She follows my instruction, and a few seconds later she's able to haul herself up closer to my position. With more of her now over the top of the rock than hanging below it, I reach down and lock my hand around the belt of her jeans. With one last heave, I pull her up and over and finally down on top of me. Thank God. We made it.

My relief is replaced with shock a split second later. The first punch takes me completely by surprise as she hits me square on the nose, and I instantly see stars. The second is a left hook to my right cheek. My head is spinning as I try to fight her off, but she's like a raging bull and continues to rain blows down onto my head and face. And then, quick as a flash, she leaves me in the dirt. 'I'm gonna finish what I started,' she rages as she scrambles up the rocks back towards the priory.

Despite feeling dazed and confused, I'm acutely aware of Alfie's cries ringing out from above me. 'My baby!' I yell as I get to my feet and scramble after her.

I draw level with the top of the cliff just as she's getting to her feet on the grass above me. She cannot be allowed to get to Alfie. Instinctively and with a strength I never knew I possessed, I reach out and grab her ankle, then yank her backwards. Her momentum forces her forward, and she falls flat down in front of me. Even before she hits the ground, I'm up and over the crest of the cliff, grabbing a loose rock as I go. Running on pure adrenaline, I hoist the sharp stone high into the air, and before she can get back up, I bring it down on the back of her head with a heavy thud.

I straddle her back now as my chest heaves, and grab her bloodied blonde hair in my left hand before lifting the rock into the air again in my right. The rage I feel is like a wild animal fighting to get out from within. All thoughts of saving her are long gone. Now all I want to do is make sure she's dead.

'Shelly, no!' bellows Nick as he appears from behind the ruined wall before racing towards Alfie just a few feet away. 'She's not worth it.'

Nick's booming voice brings everything into sharp focus, and I'm suddenly aware of the police sirens in the distance, drawing closer with every second, as well as the bloodstained rock in my hand.

Staring down at the motionless Liv lying underneath me, I drop the stone on the grass and climb off her before staggering over to Nick, who's now holding a still crying Alfie in his left arm. As soon as I get close enough to him, he wraps his free arm around my shoulder and squeezes tightly. 'It's over, babe,' he whispers, resting his chin on top of my head. 'She can't hurt us anymore. The police are on their way.'

CHAPTER FIFTY-SIX

SHELLY

One-to-One Therapy Session – Two Months Later

'It feels like an important decision,' says Dr Galanis.

'I think it's the right one, though,' I reply.

She offers her usual silent nod, and I have to stifle a smile. I'm sure like most therapists, she really has no idea how irritating clients find that kind of passive reaction. Still, I must admit – that small annoyance aside – I have found real value in the handful of talking therapy sessions I've done since what happened at the priory a few months back. One-to-one sessions, of course. I really couldn't face going back to the group.

'So when are you looking to move?' she asks.

'As soon as the house is sold, which the estate agent thinks won't be long. Three-storey townhouses in Tynemouth don't come up all that often, so we're expecting a quick sale.'

'And Nick is fully on board with it all?'

'Yeah,' I say. 'After everything that's happened with the sex tape, the police investigation and then the affair, we both realise we need a fresh start away from Newcastle.' I instinctively place my hands on my bump. 'Especially with baby number two on the way. Plus he's reached a point where he's really had enough of the property game, and I have no desire to go back into finance.'

'So what will you do for money?'

'The house in Tynemouth is worth close to a million. We don't need anything quite as grand in the Lake District, so we'll get something smaller, which will give us some spare cash to play with. We've even talked about maybe buying an old barn and turning it into an Airbnb.'

She nods *again* before crossing her right leg over her left knee. 'And have you had any thoughts about therapy once you get there? Will you continue with the work?'

'We both think couples counselling could help. I mean, as much as Nick and I want to make a go of it, we still have to work through the fact Nick cheated on me. Not surprisingly, I still have real issues around trusting him again. But at the same time I do realise he was a victim of Olivia's delusions too.'

She shifts in her seat and looks uncharacteristically unsure of herself. 'I must admit, she had us all fooled.'

'Speaking of Olivia,' I say, 'I talked to my friend George, who's the detective inspector, the other day. He was talking to the team who are handling Olivia's case, and it seems her legal team are claiming diminished responsibility. Based on the fact she was likely suffering with PTSD and CPTSD at the time.'

'I can see that,' Dr Galanis replies. 'The death of her brother, as well as her mother's suicide – coupled with her father's alcoholism – will have had a profound effect on her. Not to mention the slow deterioration of her grandmother's faculties. Just one of those events would be tough enough for most people to cope with.'

'And Olivia had to deal with all of them,' I cut in.

'Indeed she did. Sounds like she had a complete breakdown, which might go some way to explaining the false memories she projected onto you.'

'Yeah. That occurred to me too,' I say. 'That and her guilt at being next to Dan when he fell. In fact, looking back, even though it was never proven at the inquest, I think she might have actually been the one who caused him to lose his footing up there.'

'A terrible burden for her to carry,' says the doctor.

'I know.' I fold my arms protectively across my chest. 'If it weren't for all the terrible things she did to me, I could almost feel sorry for her.'

'And how are you coping with that now the dust has settled? The fact she tricked her way into your life and was behind the sex tape and the bank fraud, etc.?'

I shrug. 'I honestly don't know how to feel about it. I mean, part of me marvels at how committed she was to her plan to get her so-called revenge – not to mention creative. I mean, the sex tape and the bank fraud were really clever scams. And the reality is that if she hadn't lost the plot like she did at the end when she snatched Alfie and alerted us to who she really was, I'd probably never have known she was behind any of it.'

'Does your friend George know what she's ended up being charged with?' she asks.

'Kidnap and attempted murder.'

'And what about the other things she did to you?'

'He reckons they have a good case against her on the bank fraud because of the digital footprint she left behind, but the sex tape is looking unlikely, as it's so hard to prove. But it doesn't really matter in the end. With the two main charges, there's little chance she'll be getting out of prison any time soon.'

'No. I think you're probably right.'

The room falls silent, and not for the first time in this space, the only sound I can hear is the rhythmic ticking of the clock on the mantelpiece, which Dr Galanis glances at now.

'Well, we're almost at the end of our last session together,' she says finally. 'Is there anything else you'd like to share before we finish up?'

Ironically, it's *me* who finds myself nodding softly now. 'It's probably quite a big thing to bring up with no time left to discuss it properly, but I guess it's struck me over the last couple of months just how much better my OCD has been after what happened with Olivia on that cliff. I don't think I realised how much Dan's death has been affecting me all these years, and because I buried it so deep for so long, it had begun to eat away at my sanity. Thankfully I've realised it was actually witnessing him fall that caused me to develop PTSD, and that that has been the cause of my anxiety and intrusive thoughts all this time. Not Alfie coming into the world. His only crime was giving me the sleepless nights which brought it all to a head.'

She nods. 'Astute observations, Shelly.'

'But the real thing that I can't stop thinking about is that I'm actually quite *grateful* for what happened between us while she was in the group.'

'Really? And why is that?'

'Because in her own weird way, despite everything she put me through, and what she tried to take from me, Olivia, Liv, Jess – whatever we want to call her – forced me to finally face my demons after so many years of being tortured by them. And in doing that, she inadvertently saved me from myself.'

EPILOGUE

OLIVIA

Rampton Secure Hospital – One Year Later

Having sat through countless hours of mind-numbing therapy in Dr Galanis's group sessions, I vowed I would never again put myself through the pain of listening to other people whinging about how hard their lives are. But that was *before* I was transferred to this loony bin a month ago. If I'm going to be stuck in here for the next however many years of my sentence, I need to find some way of saving my sanity and keeping myself entertained. Not to mention the fact the sessions get me out of my cell for an extra two hours each week.

And so, here I sit on my plastic chair, my knees drawn into my chest in my prison-issue grey tracksuit, surrounded by the biggest collection of clowns you'll find outside of the circus – each of them sitting in the same circle as me and in various states of confusion. I thought the gang in Dr G's group were two cans short of a six-pack, but this lot take crazy to a whole new level.

The facilitator of the sessions is called Dr Elizabeth Tempest, a short, round woman who wears unnecessarily bright-coloured clothes every day, as if they'll somehow combat the clinical surroundings of the hospital. She's also the only therapist I've met who smiles at *every* single possible opportunity, and she has an incredibly annoying 'down with the kids' habit of insisting everyone call her Lizzie. She gets right on my tits, if I'm being completely honest.

'Good morning, everyone.' Lizzie looks at each of us in turn. 'And welcome to the first session of the week.'

There she is again. Smiling like a bloody Cheshire cat. I can't stand to look at her because her goonish expression irritates me so much. I drop my chin to my chest and hide my face behind my knees.

'Olivia,' says Lizzie a second later, 'As we've discussed many times before, these sessions are about being fully engaged and committed to the group. So seeing as you look to be doing your best to avoid any involvement, why don't we start with you?'

I can feel my jaw clenching as I lift my face and look her straight in the eye. 'How many times do I have to tell you, *Lizzie*.' I spit the next words out slowly and through gritted teeth. 'My name is not Olivia – my name is Jess!'

ACKNOWLEDGMENTS

This book was a long time in the making. Having already written thirteen crime fiction novels, turning my hand to psychological thrillers was not only daunting, but also felt like a big risk. Thankfully, I had a brilliant team of people helping me every step of the way. Special mention goes to Connal and Brian at Inkubator books, who patiently guided me into the right head space to bring this story to life. And a big thank you goes to the rest of the Inkubator team for all their support, including Alice, Lizzie, Claire, Garret and Stephen.

As ever, I cannot thank my wife Kim enough for her unwavering belief in me, and this book is dedicated to my gorgeous kids, Vaughan and Beau. I'm so proud to be your daddy.

To my coaches, Donna and Cheryl from 'Now Is Your Time' – I wouldn't be writing my fourteenth novel without you both in my corner.

And finally, thank you to my readers for reading The Therapy Room. If you could spend a moment to write an honest review, no matter how short, I would be extremely grateful. They really do help readers discover my books.

ALSO BY OMJ RYAN

Psychological Thriller

THE THERAPY ROOM

The DCI Jane Phillips Crime Thriller Series

DEADLY SECRETS (a series prequel)

DEADLY SILENCE

DEADLY WATERS

DEADLY VENGEANCE

DEADLY BETRAYAL

DEADLY OBSESSION

DEADLY CALLER

DEADLY NIGHT

DEADLY CRAVING

DEADLY JUSTICE

DEADLY VEIL

DEADLY INFERNO

DEADLY FURY

DCI JANE PHILLIPS BOX SET

(Books 1-4 in the series)

Printed in Dunstable, United Kingdom

71531430R00180